BURDENS

SERAYA

Published by SeRaya

Editor & Proofreader: Emily A. Lawrence (Lawrence Editing)

Cover Designer: Cat Imb (TRC Designs)

Interior Formatting: SeRaya

Map Illustration: Frederick Kroner (Whiskey & Ink)

*To anyone who's ever wondered their worth, you are and **always** will be worth it.*

I love you.

Author's Note

Readers discretion advised. *Burdens* is a dark, contemporary romance and contains strong language, explicit sexual content, and topics that may be sensitive to some readers.

It is my hope that I've handled these with the care they deserve.

For a detailed list, click here or scan the code below.

Disclaimer: The Vendetta Series is a series of interconnected standalones with an overarching plot. Nemesis, Book 1 in the series, must be read first.

Playlist

_____

⏮ ▶ ⏭

"Tallac" by Booba
"River" by Bishop Briggs
"listen up (radio edit)" by SOLOMON
"LET THE WORLD BURN" by Chris Grey
"First Time" by Teeks
"Constellations" by Jade LeMac
"Nothing Left to Say" by Katie Garfield
"the grudge" by Olivia Rodrigo
"Falta Amor" by Leroy Sanchez
"Fallin' All In You" by Shawn Mendes
"Cedar" by Gracie Abrams
"Let Me In" by Tanerélle
"hostage" by Billie Eilish
"Doctor, My Eyes" by Khamari
"Rescue" by Lauren Daigle
"Menak Wla Meni" by Inez
"Por Siempre Jamás" by Leroy Sanchez
"Stuck On You" by GIVEON
"Empire Now" by Hozier

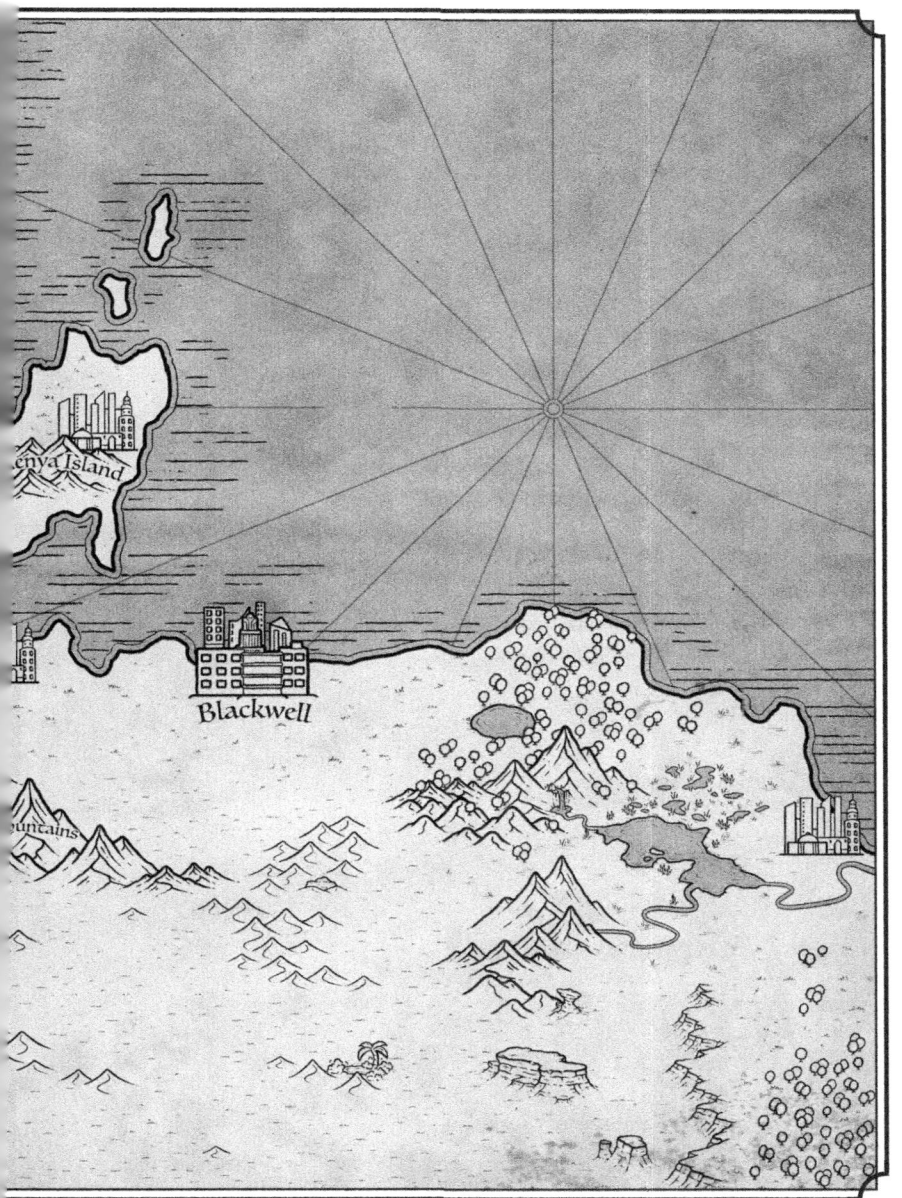

enya Island

Blackwell

untains

PROLOGUE

FUCK.

I gripped my steering wheel tighter and tighter until the strained skin of my knuckles turned white and the leather on the sides burned my palms. I tried to take a deep breath and release the tension building in my chest, but it was in vain.

"Fuck, fuck, *fuck*," I groaned, the echo of my frustration bouncing within the confines of my car as I slammed a fist on top of my dashboard.

My entire life was a lie.

I'd spent years putting on a facade, building up walls constructed on well-thought-out and fabricated lies. I'd spent my whole life hiding who I truly was, where I came from, and everything that tied me to my past.

And for nearly thirty years, I'd succeeded.

Until today, when my past came crashing back like a

tidal wave, erasing all my lies and leaving me with only one truth.

I had to rid myself of my father permanently.

I'd stopped wanting him dead a long time ago, but he'd left me with no other choice. In the aftermath of what had just happened to Jamal's wife, things would stop adding up and someone would find out the truth about who I really was.

And I couldn't do that to Jamal. I couldn't have him find out that the person responsible for all his pain and suffering was none other than my own father.

I always thought I'd have more time, that there would be a perfect moment for me to tell him. I kept promising myself I'd wait until he was older, until he was more mature to understand why I'd kept the truth from him.

But the next thing I knew, my lies had become a habit and had erased all of my previous promises. And now, I couldn't bring myself to deceive him. He'd already lost so much. I didn't want to be another person on that list.

I'd never felt more ashamed of where I'd come from than that day and that was already hard to beat. So it hadn't been long before every word that came out of my mouth was false whenever he asked about what had happened to his parents, or asked me where *my* family was.

But that part of my fabricated life had always been easy to explain because the truth always worked in my favor. The only family I ever had was forever gone.

Selfishly, I'd always hoped that one of my father's

countless enemies would just put a bullet between his eyes and rid me of the weight I'd carried with me over the last two decades.

To my dismay, no one had.

Now the truth had to come out, but I wouldn't let it happen until the source of all my burdens was six feet underground.

The only thing my father had failed to do to me.

I brought my hand up, my fingers brushing against the small raised scar at the base of my neck, a reminder that he'd almost succeeded.

Images of my father teaching me one of his lessons assaulted me at every turn. His hand was raised high and on its way to strike me when I felt my bed shift. My eyes squeezed shut at the sore pain radiating across my cheek. The cool tip of his knife was pressed against the base of my jugular, but this time...

I could feel it. Feel the skin there break under the pressure of his blade.

Wait, that never happens.

My father was an abusive asshole, but he'd never actually cut me.

Tomorrow was my twelfth birthday and I was to be initiated into the cartel. He wouldn't jeopardize that since I was his only heir, to his dismay, of course.

My confusion was short-lived when the tip pressed harder against my skin before I felt it pierce the flesh and a sharp pain radiated throughout my body.

The tendrils of my nightmare dissipated and my eyes shot open, snapping to the ones of the person looming on top of me.

The person trying to kill me.

The basic fight training I'd gone through kicked in and I brought my palms up, hitting him in the face. My sudden attack caught him off guard and his serrated knife cut across my skin, drawing blood before it fell on my pillow, next to my head.

"Stop fucking fighting," he grunted. "We both know you're dying tonight, so there's no point in trying." One of his large hands slammed against my trachea, crushing it, while his other one reached for the knife again.

With what little nails I had, I clawed at his hands to get him off. But it seemed that the more I fought him, the more my air supply was cut off. I kept trying to fight him off, but any strength I had left slowly bled out of me.

I hadn't noticed I'd shut my eyes, but maybe it was because I'd realized what was imminent. Acceptance of my fate sank into my veins because something inside of me knew I wouldn't survive what he was about to do to me.

My brain should have focused on how long I had before I'd bleed to death. How my mother would feel when she found me like this. But I could only think of one thing.

How this death might be a sign of mercy, giving me what I'd always dreamed of.

Freedom.

I was a prisoner to my father and I would finally be set free.

The knife pressed against the fresh wound once more. I peeled my eyes open with the last ounce of strength I had. If one of my father's enemies was about to kill me, then he would have to do it while looking me in the eyes.

The blade moved against my skin as the intruder opened his mouth to say something, but no words came out. A deafening silence hovered in the air as blood gushed from his mouth. It splattered all across my face and I barely registered what had just happened as his large body collapsed on me.

I struggled under him, lifting my weak arms to push him off, but he was too heavy. I shut my eyes to muster any strength I had left and moved to lift him off again, this time succeeding—too easily.

My eyes slowly peeled open, only to find my mother standing next to my bed. A dark expression painting her features replaced her usual radiating smile. Even the way she was dressed was different.

Her light brown hair was pulled tightly into a ponytail when she usually wore it down. She was wearing a black outfit when she always wore a different version of a kaftan or a dress if she was accompanying my father to one of his numerous functions.

She swiftly tore a piece from the bottom of her shirt and used the fabric to put pressure on the cut on my neck. "We need to go, baby," she said as she helped me sit up at the edge of my bed. Her gaze trailed to the door behind her before she looked at me again. "Hold this tightly to your neck and don't let go until I tell you to, okay?"

I briefly nodded as she used her fingers to wipe off the blood on my face.

The urgency and panic in her voice sent goose bumps skittering across my skin, but despite her hurried tone, her fingers were surprisingly gentle. I was still trying to understand what had just happened when I saw that her other hand held my father's emergency gun with a suppressor at the end.

Wait, she did this?

My eyes traveled farther down and locked on the dead body now lying on the floor of my childhood bedroom. Blood pooled onto the dark wooden floor and a wide circle, oiled and dark, began to form around his body.

I'd seen men murdered countless times over the last two years to prepare for my initiation, but seeing this man lifeless on my childhood bedroom floor changed something inside me.

Something I'd never get back.

"Vamos, Noah. No tenemos mucho tiempo[1]," my mother said, pulling me from my thoughts.

I turned my attention to her to find her hand extended toward me. I looked down at it, pausing while a million thoughts assaulted my mind.

---

1. Come on, Noah. We don't have a lot of time.

If I took my mother's hand, I would finally leave the life I'd never wanted to be a part of.

But was it really what I wanted?

I was born into a dark palace, created for the sole purpose of becoming the heir to one of the most notorious cartels in the world. I might not have wanted to take over my father's empire, but leaving what I'd known my whole life for the unknown felt jarring even at my young age.

My eyes roamed over the stranger's dead body until they landed on the object that had almost taken my life. Moonlight reflected off it and my gaze locked on the familiar insignia engraved on the heel of the knife.

Realization dawned on me in an instant when I made out what the crest was.

My father was behind this.

No one was given that knife to execute someone unless the command came directly from him.

In that singular moment, my entire life found itself rewritten, paving the beginning of what my future looked like. Something inside of me fractured and who I once was, was snapped clean in half.

Before and after.

Taking my mother's hand would solidify that my father had sent someone to kill me, his own flesh and blood. The truth would leave scars lingering on my soul, a brutal stain I'd never be able to rid myself of.

But that pain seemed like the lesser evil at the moment, so I finally grabbed my mom's hand with my free one.

She breathed out a sigh of relief and pulled me toward her, briefly wrapping her arms around my back. Then she helped me down my bed and headed for my bedroom door, grabbing one of my light jackets from behind my room's door.

She draped it over my shoulders and turned around to step out of my bedroom. That's when I noticed she had a backpack strapped on her back.

"Where are we going?" I asked her as I hurriedly slid on my slippers before following her down the corridor, where a large oil painting of my father was hanging on display near the end of the hall.

"Tan lejos de este agujero infernal como podamos[2]," she replied, and I couldn't help but let out a small laugh. My mother never cursed in front of me.

"That's a bad word, Mama."

She turned around and gave me a small, sympathetic smile. "It's not if I'm telling the truth."

Only my mother could find a way to make me smile after I'd nearly been murdered.

We finally made it to the painting, and I looked up at my father's replica. He and I never had a good relationship to begin with, but he was still my father. And I'd thought I was still his son despite my shortcomings he always loved to remind me of.

---

2. As far away from this hell hole as we can.

Guess being his own flesh and blood wasn't enough to avoid being executed.

My mother pushed on the painting and ushered me in the secret corridor that lay behind. She glanced around, most likely making sure my father's henchmen weren't around, but no one was in sight. Which didn't surprise me since he probably ordered them to be on the other side of the property because he was planning to have me killed.

He wouldn't want them to know he was behind the murder of his own heir.

After making sure no one was following us, she finally stepped into the dimly lit space and closed the concealed door behind her. She guided me through a winding maze of halls and tunnels until we reached a dead end.

My brows furrowed. How are we getting out?

Although I knew about the hidden passages in our house, I wasn't allowed to venture into them. As per my father, my incompetence would get me lost and he didn't want to waste his resources on finding me.

I got the answer to my unspoken question when my mother moved her hand above my head and pushed against the concrete wall.

A gust of wind washed over us, rattling my bones as we stepped outside. It was usually extremely hot here in the summer, but the temperature drastically dropped at night. I shivered despite the coat I was wearing, so I grabbed one side with my free hand, tucking it closer to my chest.

My eyes roamed to determine where we'd landed and realized we were toward the far left end of our courtyard.

My mother peeked over the central fountain and over to the closed glass door that joined the living room inside and the outside. When satisfied with whatever she was looking for, she said, "Come on, baby. This way."

She then fastened her hand tightly in mine and walked us slowly, our backs pressed against the vine-covered high walls, the lush plants and trees decorating the majority of the yard concealing us.

She paused in her steps and crouched down, reaching for leaves and pushing them aside to reveal a hole big enough to fit a person in the wall. She swiftly climbed through it and gestured for me to do the same.

I tightened my hold on my neck and grabbed the edge with my free hand to help me through the concrete wall. My body was halfway through the hole when the sound of a thud echoed in the air.

My mother placed a finger on her lips and mouthed, "Stay still."

After a few moments of silence, she helped me get through the rest of the way. Once we were both on the other side, her eyes flitted to where my hand was still holding the piece of her shirt over my neck before locking her gaze with mine. Her hand that wasn't holding mine came to cradle my right cheek, her thumb brushing over my cheekbone.

"I know this is a lot, but I just need you to trust me. Can you do that?"

I nodded because I did trust her unconditionally. My mother had always tried to protect me against my father's temper and even though she wasn't always successful despite her hardest efforts, I would follow her anywhere.

"We don't have much time, so we'll need to walk faster," she softly commanded, letting go of my hand.

She reached for the side pocket of her cargo pants and pulled out a phone. She pressed a few keys before putting it to her ear. As she waited for whoever was on the other end to answer, she grabbed my hand again and walked us down the sandy pathway behind the mansion.

She breathed a sigh of relief when the person on the other end finally answered. "We're two minutes out and Noah's injured. The cameras are playing on a loop, but it won't be long before someone catches on." She glanced behind us as we made our way down the path before her gaze swiftly roamed over me from head to toe as if she were looking for any other injury. "So you better fucking hurry."

She didn't wait for a response and hung up on whoever was on the other end of the call before shoving her phone in her back pocket.

"Are we almost there?" I asked faintly, my arm getting numb from holding the soaked fabric against my neck.

She paused in her steps. "Yes, baby. We'll be there very soon and everything will be fine," she said, but her voice wavered at the end as if she wasn't sure.

She started walking again and I followed closely behind her, hoping that wherever we were going, we were almost there. Despite everything that happened tonight, this was the first time I started to wonder if we'd make it.

My father wasn't a good man and if he knew she was leaving him and taking me with her, he would never let her or me live. His wounded pride wouldn't let him find reprieve and he wouldn't stop hunting us until we were either back with him or dead.

And I didn't know which was more terrifying.

The screech of tires suddenly filled the quiet night and dust kicked up in the air. Once it settled, a rusty navy car came into view at the end of the alleyway. My mother grabbed my hand and picked up speed.

The passenger door flung open and my eyes widened when I realized who was behind the wheel. Reda, my father's right-hand and most trusted man, yelled at us to get in as we closed the distance.

Too shocked to think of what him being here meant, I climbed in when the sound of two men laughing echoed in the dead air. My mother whipped her head around as two of my father's night guards spilled into the back alley of our house.

We all watched with bated breath as they looked up. The glare of the street lamp illuminated their faces as their eyes widened when they realized who we were and what we were doing.

"Lalla³ Camila, stop," one of them yelled at my mother

---

3. Lady (used as a title of respect).

as they both drew their weapons and broke out in a run toward us.

My uncle cursed under his breath as my mother jumped inside and slammed the door closed just in time before the first bullet hit the door. I flinched into her arms and she hunched herself over my body to cover me.

"Hold on," my uncle Reda said before flooring the gas pedal, going from zero to a hundred. We were lurched forward from the sudden speed and my mother lay her hand on top of the glove box to hold us steady as Reda skidded across the dirt track.

The sounds of bullets erupted in the air as they ricocheted off the back of the SUV we were in. I squeezed my eyes shut, praying for this to be over. Eventually, one bullet fired at us made contact with the back window and blew it out, debris flying behind us. More bullets riddled the SUV with holes until the car surged to the left as we seemed to slide onto a road.

The dirt track shifted into concrete and my uncle Reda accelerated down the street, driving even faster until we were in the clear. I didn't know how long we drove for, but I was just grateful for the short reprieve from having bullets targeted at us.

The car eventually slowed to a stop and the engine shut off. My mother lifted herself off me and exited the car. I finally opened my eyes and looked up to see her hand stretched out to help me out. I grabbed it and hopped off.

She closed the door behind me and squeezed my hand in reassurance.

Uncle Reda had already exited and was at the back of the car, rummaging in his trunk. I glanced around and finally registered that we were on a landing strip. A small aircraft was ready and a tall man I'd never seen before stood at the bottom of the boarding stairs.

My uncle closed the trunk and walked toward the stranger, holding two duffel bags in his right hand. As they embraced, I glanced up at my mother and asked, "Mama, who is that?"

She kept her gaze on the small airplane and said, "Our ticket to freedom."

I dragged myself out of the memory and turned the engine of my rental on. After exiting the hospital's parking lot, I headed straight for the airport.

There was no more hiding from the truth.

We might have succeeded in escaping him all these years ago, but it was time for me to face my father one last time.

Amalia

CHAPTER 1

PRESENT

"LALLA INES, I SWEAR IT WASN'T ME," MEHDI SPUTTERED, his voice rising an octave. My silence weighed heavily on him—it always made them squirm—so he added, "Please, I didn't tell anyone where the drop would be." The panic in his voice grated my nerves and I played around with the idea of killing him to save myself another fifteen minutes of interrogation.

The only reason I hadn't yet was because I needed him alive for answers.

I released the bridge of my nose and flicked my gaze up to where he was hanging, blood pooling under him from the latest cut I inflicted him with.

His oily hair stuck to his damp forehead, his skin was pale from the blood loss and he was in his signature tracksuit. Chains encircled his wrists which were tethered to the hook that extended from the ceiling.

My eyebrow quirked up at his plea. "Spare me your lies, Mehdi," I said, cleaning my nail beds with the bloodied curved dagger. "I only told a few people. You happened to be one of them and all the others are dead."

Whatever color he had left drained from his face at my statement, the reality of his fate sinking in.

Metal scraped against concrete as I stood up from the chair I'd been sitting in. Cold indifference settled over me like a second skin as I walked over to the wall of his cell and pressed the button that controlled the hook from which he was hanging. The loud, clanging sound rattled against the walls and Mehdi's pleas rose.

"Please, Lalla Ines. I promise it wasn't me!"

"Beg all you want. I like it," I taunted. "You'll tell me what I need in a few seconds so I can go back to enjoying my breakfast before it was rudely interrupted."

I had barely taken a sip of my coffee when Hamza, Omar's underboss, came over to tell me they'd finally caught Mehdi, who had been on the run for the last five days.

I usually dealt directly with Barrera, but since his son Mateo had died recently, he'd been a little unstable, to say the least. He kept making rash decisions and snapped—or shot, depending on his mood—at anyone who disagreed with him.

Even, or should I say *especially*, when they were right.

We'd been having issues with our cargo over the last few months and this man right here was our leak. Every time we'd struck a deal with the Dutch and scheduled a drop to acquire the guns they provided us with, Alaoui's soldiers, Barrera's biggest rival, had magically shown up, stolen our cargo, and killed our men in the process.

The Alaoui cartel usually dealt in trafficking, but for some reason, over the last few months, they'd been stealing the guns the Dutch provided for us in exchange for access to our ports.

After a few failed drops, I'd decided to leak the information about our next *fictional* exchange to the few men I suspected were stupid enough to spill the information to any rival cartels that were interested for a couple hundred dollars.

"Please, Ines."

I snapped my attention back to him. "What did you just call me?" I asked as I strode closer, stepping into the blood-stained concrete, and pointed my knife at him.

"I… I'm sorry, Lalla Ines," he blabbered when I slid the bloodied tip down to between his fourth and fifth rib, right where the apex of his heart was. He closed his eyes as I pressed lightly. "I… I didn't mean… *Wallah*[1] I didn't say anything. I… I can help you…"

He kept going on and on, but I tuned the rest of his words out.

---

1. I swear.

God, were men exasperating when their lives were on the line. The lies, the pathetic pleas to save their skin. But the more they begged for their lives, the guiltier they were.

And the more I enjoyed terminating them.

An irritated sigh left my lips. "Stop making false promises. I already know it's you. I just need you to tell me who from the Alaoui cartel you've been leaking the information to." I pressed a little harder and blood bloomed on his already soiled white shirt from the force. "You can either be a good boy and tell me, or I can *make* you tell me." I twisted the knife slightly to help with penetrating his skin. "And trust me, you don't want that."

He recoiled when I made eye contact and fear emanated off his skin.

I reveled in it.

Being undercover for this long changed you, whether you wanted it to or not. After killing the amount of people I'd killed for Barrera, the darkness had skewed my sense of morality and blurred the lines of why I was actually here.

In my time here, the information I'd collected had ranged from how much it cost to pay off corrupt officials to how to efficiently slit someone's throat, something the Bureau definitely hadn't taught me before sending me here.

Over the years, I'd kept convincing myself that despite the innocence that had perished at my hands, I was serving justice.

By all means necessary, right?

I'd been undercover working for Barrera as his sicario

for almost three years now and spent the last five before that making a name for myself as one of the most feared hitmen in Morocco.

I knew Barrera wouldn't hire a woman to work for him, so I had to do everything I could to convince him I was the best person for the job after his previous hitman was killed in an accident.

And that bastard had been a tough one to kill.

Killing a cartel man was already not the easiest task, but killing a sicario was a bitch. They didn't have a routine and were suspicious of everyone. Although getting him alone and vulnerable wasn't an effortless mission, I'd finally done it because men always had a weakness.

I'd found his just in time to strike and finally get my in with Barrera.

After coming for many key players in his territories, I'd finally been able to put myself on Barrera's radar and he'd requested a meeting. He didn't meet with anyone unless they made themselves valuable and hard to kill.

And that's what I'd been across every region in the country.

Feared and respected.

Even if that came with a price.

My morality.

After that, the only thing I had to do was charm him off his feet and make sure no one else would take the position I'd worked years for. That ended up being easy because who would expect a woman to be behind all those murders?

Bringing Barrera down would cement my career and I needed to prove myself. Especially after rumors of me sleeping with a superior started roaming around the Academy while I trained there.

Cries grated against my ears and I snapped my attention back to my latest prey. Tears stained his bloodied face—a result of the previous session he'd had with Hamza—and snot dripped down his nose and over his mouth, landing on his soiled clothes.

My mouth twisted in disgust at the sight and annoyance pricked under my skin.

"Stop fucking crying. You know you're dying, so just tell me what I need to know."

"*Allah y hafdek Lalla Ines*[2], please… I'm sure we can come to an agreement," he sniffled, desperation coating his voice.

My ears perked up because desperation always led to bargaining and he was about to finally reveal what I'd been looking for.

"I can even get you information from Zak—" He slammed his mouth shut and my lips twitched.

There he goes.

"Did you mean to say Zakaria? As in Alaoui's underboss?"

Thinking he finally had bargaining power, Mehdi said,

---

2. God I'm begging you Ms. Ines.

"J-just let me down. I'm sure you can be reasonable and we can discuss this."

I didn't answer right away. I pretended to think about his offer, even though there was no way I was trusting him. The audacity he had to think him snitching to rivals then turning on them would make me consider keeping him alive and giving him a second chance.

There was no such thing when it came to the cartel, *especially* Barrera's.

Besides, if you couldn't be loyal to the hand that fed you, you could never be trusted again.

He must have taken my silence as his saving grace because when we locked eyes, hope swarmed in his brown irises.

But I gave him a cold smile and that same hope instantly faded. His eyes widened as blood pooled out of his lips.

Mehdi was lucky Barrera wasn't here today and I was hungry because his death would've been a much lengthier process otherwise.

I left my knife inside his chest cavity until his head slumped forward and the stench of urine filtered through my nose.

Thank fuck I don't have to deal with cleanup.

When the room quieted down and Mehdi took his final breath, I pulled my knife out of his body. A warm gush sprayed across my front and I looked down at my once white tank top, now painted in red.

I rolled my eyes and scoffed in annoyance—I'd just changed.

I reached for the pocket of Mehdi's tracksuit pants and retrieved his phone with the tips of my fingers, avoiding the large stain soiling the front. Using the tip of my dagger, I lifted his face and let the device scan it.

Once it unlocked, I let go and his head bobbed down. Zakaria didn't need to know Mehdi died yet, so might as well use it to my advantage.

I wiped my dagger onto the fabric of his pants before sliding it back into its sheath strapped to my thigh. After I stepped out of the cell, I ordered the two soldiers guarding it to call the cleanup crew.

Once I was back in the courtyard, I plopped back into my seat and reached for my untouched tea glass. The now cold liquid had barely touched my lips when Hamza's voice chimed behind me.

"Did you get what we needed?"

I let out a sigh when he plopped in the seat on the other side of the round tiled table. He grabbed a handful of qrishlat[3] and popped them in his mouth.

"It wasn't him, so we're back to square one," I lied, dumping the tea back into the teapot and pouring myself another glass.

Hamza grunted his discontentment. "Fuck. I was so sure he was the one."

---

3. Miniature Moroccan shortbread cookies.

I sipped on the hot tea and tore a piece of *msemen*[4]. "Yeah," was my only reply before dipping the flatbread into melted butter then honey and bringing it to my mouth.

"Well," he said, standing from his seat and making his way toward my seat. "I'll relay the information to *Ra'is*[5] and with all of them dead, hopefully the Alaouis stop stealing from us."

He placed a hand on my shoulder. "And take a shower before our meeting. You smell like death."

"Noted," I replied and returned to eating.

---

4. Moroccan flatbread.
5. Means "leader" or "chief" in Arabic and is the title Barrera's men call him.

Noah

CHAPTER 2

PRESENT - ONE MONTH LATER

WHAT THE FUCK WAS I THINKING?

As I sat in the passenger seat of the beat-up 1982 Mercedes they gave us for cover, flying down the deserted highway, I kept coming back to the only answer to my question.

I hadn't been thinking.

When I was training at the Academy, my only goal had been to keep my head down, graduate, and do my job. Going after my father hadn't been anywhere near what I aimed to achieve.

Until my mother died, and all the repressed anger I felt toward him resurfaced.

When she passed, my grief grew a life of its own and I could barely control it. So when I was tasked to join

Jamal's father's task force to do the one thing I'd told myself I wouldn't, I hadn't hesitated.

I'd spent countless days and sleepless nights finding anything that could rid me of my father once and for all. We were so close to doing just that until my dear father killed my partner and the only remote father figure I'd had in my life.

The hours spent at Jamal's side seeing him agonize through his recovery from the burns he'd suffered and the loss of the only family he had fueled the resentment I harbored toward my father even further.

I'd tried everything. And each failure in bringing him and his rotten empire down twisted deeper into the wound he'd created the moment I became the heir to his throne.

Guilt had gnawed at me day and night. I'd barely ate or slept and had focused all of my energy wrapping my head around my new and unexpected guardian role and seeking justice for what my own blood did to his.

After three months of dead ends, the bureau had forced me off the case because I'd neglected every other aspect of my job and they'd deemed me too close to the case to be objective over my partner's killer.

Not because of my lineage since they didn't know that the man I'd been after was my father.

I had objected and fought to be kept on the case until I'd gotten a call from Jamal's doctors announcing that he was finally ready to be discharged.

When I'd heard the news, it had been like a switch had

been turned off. The urge to bring down Barrera had evaporated and protecting Jamal had become the only thing I focused my mind on.

I'd quit my position, called the Academy to see if their offer to be a training officer was still standing, and accepted the position the same day. I'd then packed my life in Sardenya and moved back to Blackwell with Jamal.

I hadn't given a single thought to my previous life until my assistant, Sami, told me that Omar Barrera had been seen fleeing the docks with a building in ruins and a body in his wake.

I'd brushed it off like I'd always done until he'd mentioned Jamal's and his wife's names. I'd never felt fear so gripping as the one I felt when I thought Barrera had taken him away from me as well.

I'd never driven so fast to the hospital to make sure Jamal wasn't another body added to my father's long list of victims.

Seeing the look on Jamal's face when he confessed that he'd known Barrera was the man behind his parents' deaths had been a rude awakening. It might have been too late to confess to the burden I'd been carrying over the last twenty years, but I'd promised myself at that moment that I'd make sure the expression of defeat on my nephew's face would never see the light of day again.

After my visit at the hospital, I'd rushed back to work and locked myself in my office to look into the manila folder Sami had put on my desk before I'd left in a hurry.

To say I hadn't expected what I'd found inside would be an understatement.

My eyes had flicked over the victim's features. Features eerily similar to those of the man who had tried to kill me all those years ago—or should I say, had *someone* try to.

The victim left in the rubble of the building was none other than Mateo Barrera, Omar Barrera's only son (that he claimed) and my stepbrother.

I'd spent years detaching myself from the person I was born to become. I'd spent months making sure I would never become the person *he* wanted me to be.

I'd fooled myself into thinking I could move on and make a life for myself with no ties to him. But the reality was that my future had always been tied to him and I hated it.

There was only one thing I could do to end this.

Become the person I swore I'd never be.

"Will I get the silent treatment for the whole time we work together?"

I side-eyed Dale, watching as he reached for the A/C to crank it up. "We haven't started the job yet, so there's nothing to talk about."

"We could get to know each other since we'll be spending however long this undercover job takes us together," he proposed, giving me a tentative smile.

This wasn't my first time going undercover, but the Bureau had insisted that Dale, my point of contact—the one I was assigned to check in with every week—traveled with me instead of staying back at the Bureau. That had been their only condition before accepting that I take over the case since I had previous knowledge of the Barrera cartel.

"We're not dating," I grunted. This was exactly why I worked alone. No unnecessary chatting. "Just remember what your new identity is and don't fuck up."

Dale was a good agent, but he was too talkative for my liking. I preferred quiet, hence why I always kept to myself. I did my job and people respected me for it.

That's all I needed.

Relationships weren't made for me. The more distance I put between myself and people, the better. That way, no one could get hurt.

That's a little too late, my mind added, but I ignored it.

Besides, they were better off without me in their lives.

Dale sighed, resigning himself from trying. "Got it. You're not my type anyway. I prefer warmer people."

I groaned and kept my eyes on the road. A bead of sweat trickled down my forehead and I grabbed the hem of my white shirt to wipe my drenched face. Despite the A/C's best effort, it wasn't enough to battle the scorching weather outside.

It was late in the afternoon and I looked at the navigation system to see that we were about an hour away from Bab Al Mansour. I rolled my window down, hoping the highway speeds would help, and took in the air outside.

It was hot and extremely dry, but the smell of the mountains felt oddly familiar. I hadn't been back here since the day I left. I never had a desire to and still didn't.

I took a deep breath and tried to settle my nerves. Doing my job was easy. Facing my father after years, on the other hand, was setting my anxiety on fire. Coming face to face with the man who was supposed to love me but instead wanted me dead was turning out to be harder than I thought it would be.

I felt a multitude of emotions whenever I thought of him. I always believed I'd never cared. My mother had been so loving and caring that I'd buried all the horrible memories of my childhood involving him in the deepest parts of my mind until they'd vanished from my history.

But for some reason, every suffocated emotion was resurfacing even when, right now, I was pretending to be someone else.

Wringing my knuckles, I gazed out my window and worked to shut down the tumult inside my gut.

"I'm hungry. Can we stop?" Dale whined.

Why did they pair me with this guy?

"Can't you wait until we get there?" I said, glancing at him, only to find him giving me a pleading smile. If I didn't agree, he would keep talking and I'd rather delay our arrival than listen to him complain.

I shook my head and scoffed. "Fine, the next exit has a —" Before I could finish my sentence, I heard the skidding of tires and snapped my attention back to the road.

"Watch out," I shouted at Dale as I grabbed the wheel

to get out of the way of the two black SUVs now halted in front of us on the previously deserted road.

Dale stomped on the brakes and we swerved to the right in a haste. I whipped the steering wheel back straight in hopes of redirecting the car so we could flee away from whoever was ambushing us, but it was too late.

Everything happened so fast. Our vehicle veered off the road, hitting the roadside ditch with such force that it lifted us in the air and landed on its rooftop.

The moment stretched into what felt like an eternity before everything stopped. The front shield shattered into a million pieces and broken glass and gravelly dust flew all around us.

Sharp pieces pierced my skin and my head throbbed from the impact. Everything was such a blur when I opened my eyes. I shook my head and ignored the searing pain on my right shoulder because if we were to make it out alive, I had to act fast.

The engine was still running and smoke poured inside. The smell of gasoline overpowered my senses and I could hear Dale coughing in the distance, but I forced myself to tune him and everything else out to focus on how I could get out and get us out of here before we ended up gunned down.

Groaning, I reached for my seat belt to unfasten it. "*Tfou*[1]," I cursed through gritted teeth when it didn't give

---

1. Fuck.

way. "Unlock, you son of a bitch." I struggled for a few more seconds until I heard it click.

Then gravity pulled me with such a strong force that my breath caught in my throat as I fell down with a loud thud. I briefly glanced to my left and noticed Dale was barely moving. Gravel and glass grated my skin as I reached over and shook his arm to make sure he was still conscious.

"Dale, you good, man?" I whispered, praying I wouldn't have to drag his ass out on top of fighting my way out against whatever was waiting for us outside.

"Yeah," he coughed up. "Should be better once we get out of this mess."

Couldn't agree more.

I shifted my body under the crumpled metal and moved to scoot toward the glove compartment to grab a firearm. I was pulling my arm that was closest to it from under my body when I heard doors opening outside and footsteps approaching—five pairs of them.

Fuck.

I hurriedly popped the glove box open and grabbed my gun, then clicked the safety off. But before I could manage to get out and rid myself of whoever fucked with us, the sound of a bullet perforating skin pierced the air around us.

I looked up at Dale to see if he was injured, only to find a stunned expression on his face. His eyes widened and I spotted a familiar realization in them. And when he opened his mouth to say his final words, only blood poured out of it and ran down his face.

Fuck. Fuck. Fuck. I have to get out of here before I'm next.

I crawled out of the passenger window, the broken glass scraping against my body as I did. I stayed crouched behind the car, my back against the indented passenger door.

"No need to hide from us," a voice mocked. "You're outnumbered and outgunned, so why don't you take the easy way out?"

I wasn't here to die. I was here for someone else's last breath and I wouldn't give up that easily. I closed my eyes and counted to three before I whipped around and started shooting while keeping cover.

Bullets rained in my direction from different angles and by some miracle, I managed to dodge all of them except one that grazed my already injured shoulder. Fire sprouted across my skin and blood trickled down my arm.

I pushed the pain aside and kept shooting until my chambers were empty. I managed to hit two of them in the head and watched them collapse to the ground before I ducked down again to reload.

I took a quick glance from beneath the car to determine their positions. I was about to come out and fire again when the one who seemed to be their leader spoke again.

"Throw your gun out, Noah." The sound of my name out of his lips sent a shiver down my spine. *How the fuck does he know who I am?*

There was only one person in this region who knew who I was.

My father.

That motherfucker. I should have known better. I should have known he would find out I was back.

I mentally went through the options I was faced with. Either I surrendered and subjected myself to whatever he had planned for me or fought my way through and risked getting shot.

Either way ended with me dying, but one seemed like a much more appealing death.

I stood and aimed my gun to take the last few men out when the muzzle of a weapon caressed the back of my head.

"We're gonna tell you one last time, asshole. Drop. Your. Gun," the person behind me hissed.

I prepared myself to disarm him, but the moment I turned around to grab his weapon, something crashed against the side of my head. My vision blurred and my limbs weakened from the forceful impact against my skull.

I was teetering on the edge of blinding pain. Disoriented, I blinked repeatedly and tried to recover from the blow. But before I could regain consciousness and inflict damage to my assailant, I was hit again and the darkness at the edge of my vision became all-consuming, dragging me into its depth.

The sound of water dripping from a distance stirred me out of unconsciousness.

My head felt heavy as I lifted it and peeled my eyes open. But instead of discerning where I was kept captive, darkness greeted me.

I blinked a few times, thinking it might be a residual from the throbbing pain at the back of my skull, but the pitch-black darkness remained. My mouth was dry and I felt groggy, most likely a side effect from whatever drug they gave me after I collapsed.

Fighting nausea, I tried to take several deep breaths, only to realize something was covering my head. I moved my head around despite the pain to lift it off, but it was useless. The fabric barely moved enough for me to see the dark floor beneath me.

I didn't know how long I'd been in this position, but it was long enough that my shoulders were painfully sore from the tension exerted on them.

I winced and rolled them back to alleviate whatever was causing the tension, but that only sent more pain sweeping across my entire skull. I tried to reach to soothe it by bringing my hands forward, only to realize I'd been restrained.

My arms seemed to be suspended above my head and my wrists were bound so tight, the slightest movement sent the abrasiveness of whatever was restraining me burning across my skin. I tugged on what seemed like rope and rocked my body sideways to figure a way out, but I barely moved an inch.

The agony I felt with every movement combined with the stench weighing over wherever I was locked up sent my stomach churning and scorching bile rising up my esophagus. My breathing thickened beneath the black hood as I tried to breathe through the rising nausea.

I swallowed harshly against it and continued swaying, hoping they would eventually give out. I kept going, the sound of chains clinking from the ceiling, until I heard faint voices arguing in the distance.

I abruptly stopped.

If they thought I was still unconscious, they'd speak more freely and I might survive another day without a bullet to the head.

The chime of their voices grew louder as something creaked from afar before it seemed to be slammed shut. Dim lighting filtered inside my cell and their footsteps getting closer followed it.

Their chatter was barely perceptible, but I recognized one of the voices. It was the same one from the ambush. He most likely was my father's right hand since he was the only one who spoke directly to me. The others seemed to only be following his orders.

As they got closer, another voice in the mix sounded familiar—more than the others. But since I still couldn't quite pinpoint what they were saying or who was speaking, I simply brushed it off.

My mind must be playing tricks on me.

Instead, since I could barely see through the fabric, I zeroed in on all my other senses. One of them was bound to slip and say or do something I could use to escape.

"How long has he been out?" That same familiar voice asked again in Arabic.

A woman's.

My mind must be in such a fog because I was sure I was imagining it. My dad didn't hire women. He despised them.

"Three days now," someone answered.

I've been out for three days? Fuck.

I shut my eyes and forced myself to steady my breathing, staying as still as I could manage. The rattling of metal was followed by a *clunk* sound in the space before some sort of gate screeched on its hinges.

Their steps faltered to a stop a few feet in front of me. I couldn't see well through the fabric, but I did see their shadows dancing through the small slit between my chin and neck.

There were three of them—two men and a woman.

One of the men approached me and nudged my chest with a piece of wood, probably a staff. One of my dad's favorite tools for his men to use during interrogation. He'd always said that it was the perfect object to inflict pain with precision.

He ran the tip over my front before pressing the end of

his rod into my solar plexus as he eagerly asked, "Can I wake him up?"

If I could see him, I bet his eyes were lit up with malicious excitement.

My mouth pinched shut as he continued pressing further into my diaphragm, making it hard to breathe. It was becoming harder and harder to stay put and not kick him.

Instead of waiting for a response from whoever was in charge, I watched his shadow bringing the staff upward and swinging it like a baseball bat straight into my already bruised and probably broken ribs.

It took every ounce of willpower to stifle my reaction to the force of his hit. I'd been tortured in the past, more than most agents with how often my father beat me black and blue, but fuck if his strike didn't hurt.

He repeated the same motion a few times until *she* spoke up.

"Enough," she said sternly. "Remember *Rai's* wants him alive."

"But we could still toy with him a little," he replied, bringing his staff up once again. I prepared for his next hit when the sound of a gun cocking filled the room.

"I said no," she ordered.

"All good, Lalla Ines," he said with a nervous chuckle. She was probably pointing her gun straight at him. "I was just messing around."

After several moments, the man from the ambush let

out a loud sigh and declared, "We should get going. He's clearly not waking up anytime soon if he didn't after the roughing Zouhair just gave him."

The door screeched as they closed it and their footsteps were now going in the opposite direction. I didn't dare swallow or breathe until their steps were now a muffled sound.

Thank fuck.

The pained groan I'd been keeping in finally escaped my lips.

"Look who finally decided to join us," the woman, Ines, said.

I remained silent, hoping I'd just imagined her voice and that she wasn't actually here.

But I could feel her *watching* me.

I cursed myself under my breath. I should have known someone stayed behind. I was so focused on not giving myself up that I didn't pay attention to how many of them had left.

She spoke again. "Ready to tell me what an Agent is doing on Barrera's territory?"

I didn't respond.

"All right, I guess you're choosing the hard way," she said, turning a light on. I could feel her coming closer until she stopped right in front of me, the tip of her shoes brushing against mine. Then her hand tapped my covered cheek before she grabbed the fabric over my head and slid it off.

The hood landed on the ground next to us.

I peeled my eyes open and my vision slowly adjusted until my gaze met my captor's. Piercing dark green eyes clashed against my dark brown ones—eyes that had haunted my dreams since I last saw them.

I opened my mouth to say her name, but no words came out as my mind debated whether she was a mirage or not, something my mind manufactured to torture me.

Awareness of who was in front of me filtered through my haze and acted as an earthquake to my senses. My body jerked back to life after being asleep for three days. Everything around us faded into oblivion and all the memories we shared together swept through my veins until they invaded my brain.

That's when her furrowed features smoothed into the same conclusion I'd come to.

Standing in front of me was the woman I hadn't stopped thinking about since the first time I saw her.

The one who got away.

And now my father's sicario.

Amalia fucking Abara.

CHAPTER 3

PAST

I KNEW I WAS IN TROUBLE THE MOMENT I LAID EYES ON HER as she walked into the bar.

That she'd obliterate the first rule I'd given myself when I moved to Blackwell ten years ago the moment she sat a few seats down from me.

But in my defense, how could you look at this woman and *not* want to know more about her?

I'd tried my best to ignore her over the last thirty minutes, but it was impossible. Her presence alone sent my skin buzzing like it'd been electrocuted and revived all my senses back to life.

The bar was crowded for a Sunday night, but all I could focus on was her.

She was on her own and nursed whatever was in her

glass quietly, occasionally chatting with the bartender, Andrea. She was wearing a high-waisted long green skirt and a black vest that revealed a sliver of her tanned midriff every time she shifted on her barstool.

Her dark brown hair cascaded down her back in waves and some pieces framed her face. I'd only caught a glimpse of her face, but it was enough to make my breathing stutter.

High cheekbones, pert nose with a tiny diamond stud piercing, and plump lips that begged to be devoured.

My mind wandered to thoughts of slowly peeling back her layers and exploring her with my lips, but I kept reminding myself I was here for one drink only before I turned in for the night like I always did.

When Jamal and I had moved here after the Bureau had dismissed me from his parents' case, Theo had forced me to go out before my first day back at the academy, saying I needed to relax if I wanted the new recruits not to think I was an asshole with a stick up my ass.

I'd brushed him off and ignored his request until he'd shown up at my door saying he would watch over him while I went out.

I'd spent the entirety of that night staring blankly at an empty tumbler, thinking about how much my life had completely changed in a matter of weeks, how much more it was about to change.

I was becoming a guardian at the age of twenty-three. To a kid I'd barely known at the time aside from the occasional get-together his father had thrown every once in a while and forced me to attend because he'd thought it would be a good idea for me to socialize with the team instead of staying in my own corner.

At that point, all I'd known about Jamal was that I liked him, but I didn't know the first thing about parenting. I wasn't even sure I *wanted* kids, especially with the type of father I grew up with.

I had millions of unanswered questions spinning in the back of my brain. What if I ended up being like my father? What if I became a bad figure to Jamal and fucked him up? Most importantly, what would happen to him if I didn't accept guardianship?

The answer to my last question alone had overtaken my worries over the others. If I hadn't, Jamal would have ended up in foster care and after everything his dad did for me, I couldn't let that happen. Jamal was a good kid and he deserved as good of a childhood as he could get despite becoming an orphan so young.

Although I'd hated to admit it, Theo had been right. I'd needed that night away from everything to sift through my thoughts. There had been no time for that when I had to take care of a whole other human being. Jamal's needs had immediately overtaken mine the moment Ayoub and Nina's lawyers had called me to announce that I was now the sole responsible adult tasked to take care of their son.

So every year like clockwork, I showed up at Faro, nursed a single drink, and went home. I'd convinced myself that coming here the night before my first day was necessary. Besides, it was cheaper than therapy.

Faro wasn't exactly my scene, but I was a man of routine. I liked predictable.

And *she* was anything but.

I mentally cursed myself. Why was I so intrigued about her? Nothing ever really captured my attention easily, but something about her just... I didn't even know how to describe it.

The right thing to do would be to stay away from her and go to my place. Because if her presence alone was making me feel like there wasn't enough oxygen in my lungs, getting closer, even just for one night, would be life-altering and the last thing I needed.

I forced myself to focus on finishing my drink and getting the hell out of here before I gave away to temptation. Except...

One last look wouldn't hurt, right?

I chanced a sideways glance and expected her to be in the same position, hopefully oblivious to my admiration, but her seat was now empty.

"Are you going to keep staring all night, or will you do something about it?" a sultry voice murmured from my left.

I turned my head to the side, only to find *her* standing right next to me. One of her hands was propped against the counter, while her other swayed behind her back. She was so close, her front brushed against my shoulder as she looked down at me.

I slowly brought my gaze up, letting my eyes wander over her body and relishing the opportunity to really take her in. I knew I should be a better man, but my eyes lingered on her luscious breasts before I finally met her gaze.

Every thought I ever had seemed to fade away when her dark green eyes locked on my brown ones. For a moment, I lost myself in them and let myself drown in the lust swarming in her pupils. I thought she was beautiful from the little I'd seen, but she was even more stunning up close.

And when she gave me one of the sexiest smiles I'd ever seen, my heart skipped a beat.

I suddenly felt nervous and I *never* got nervous. I prided myself in being confident and good at everything I put my mind to. I never failed or gave up.

But there was something about her, about the way her voice poured over me like honey that put me on edge.

I'm in deep trouble.

I should excuse myself and brush off her statement as a misunderstanding. *Should* being the key word. The last thing I needed in my life was someone like her to walk into it, but she was a stranger and something about the look in her eyes hooked me in.

Something that I curiously found myself wanting to discover more about. Even if it was just for one night. Besides, I never backed down from a challenge.

Oh and fuck it. What do I have to lose?

"Hi," I blurted out.

Smooth, Noah. Real, smooth. God, I'm so out of practice.

Her eyes shone with amusement. "Hi."

Keeping my gaze on hers, I drew out the chair next to me and placed my hand on her lower back, inviting her to sit. My fingers briefly brushed against the sliver of her exposed skin when I pulled it away as she slid onto the stool.

Even the smallest contact set my nerves on fire.

She propped one of her elbows onto the bar, resting her face in her palm and tucking her other hand under it. "I'm Mia." She offered. "What's your name?" I knew she was lying about her name, but I didn't blame her because I was about to do the same.

I held my right hand out. "Jonah."

She pulled her hand out from under her elbow and grabbed mine, my calloused hand enveloping her delicate one. "Nice to meet you, Jonah," she said, smiling.

I wasn't a jealous person by any means, but in that second, when the fake name I'd given her left her lips, I'd never been more jealous of a nonexistent man in my life. I even found myself, for an infinitesimal moment, imagining what my real name would sound like from her lips.

We lingered for a moment, looking into each other's eyes as if waiting to see who would give up first.

"Likewise, Mia." I raised her hand and brushed my lips across her knuckles. I noticed the sharp intake in her breath and the dark blush that crept up her face.

"Can I get either of you anything?" A soft, slightly accented voice snapped the thread holding our suspended moment.

Mia slid her hand out of mine, returning to her previous position, and turned her attention to Andrea. My eyes, however, remained on her as she gave our bartender her order. "Could I have another Macallan 18, neat? Please and thank you," she said with a bright smile.

I raised my brow at that and looked over at Andrea, who gave me a knowing look. Her gray hair was pulled up with a claw clip as usual, and she was wearing an oversized black blouse, the front slightly tucked into her dark jeans. Her older brother, Marco, owned the place and she'd been serving me my one glass of the same thing ever since I stepped foot here ten years ago.

A Macallan 18, neat.

This was just a simple coincidence, but out of all the things she could order, the fascinating woman next to me drank the same thing as me.

"And for you," Andrea started, even if she knew I never had more than one glass, but I cut her off before she revealed my name to the beautiful stranger next to me.

"Make that two. Thank you," I said, despite having barely made a dent in my first one.

Andrea gave us a quick nod and made her way to prepare our drinks. After handing them to us, she gave me a look and shook her head before letting out a huffed laugh and leaving to tend to another customer who had just walked in.

I grabbed the tumbler and brought it to my lips, taking a sip and hoping the bite from the whiskey would distract me from the effect Mia's closeness was having on me.

A thousand questions swirled in my mind, but I dismissed them. I had to fight my instincts to go into interrogation mode because I wasn't at work right now and doing so would probably make her run the other way.

Which was probably a better—smarter—option, but I didn't want her to leave quite yet. So I placed my glass back on the countertop before I drank the whole thing and went in with a safe question.

"What brings you to town?"

Surprisingly, the innocent question caught her off guard. I could tell she didn't expect me to lead with that line of conversation with the way her eyes slightly widened and the hint of worry that flashed in them.

The signs might have been imperceptible to others, but reading people was an integral part of my job and this stunning creature was hiding something.

She schooled her features back and tilted her head to the side, giving me another one of her killer smiles. If I didn't know any better, I would bet money that she had training.

"What makes you think I'm not a regular here?" She took a sip of her own drink and a droplet of whiskey spilled out, landing on her lip.

My eyes snapped to her mouth and the chatter around us fell to a quiet murmur. Her tongue swiped out to clear it away, sending desire coursing through my veins as I imagined how much better the liquor I'd savored a thousand times before would taste on her skin.

Before I realized what I was doing, I reached out for one of the legs on her stool and angled her to bring us face to face. Then I widened my stance and tugged her closer because for some reason I wanted to erase any space between us.

Something I'd never felt like doing before.

"I would have remembered you," I whispered as I placed my elbow on the bar and leaned against my fist, my index finger resting on my temple. I watched her carefully, studying her reaction to my confession.

A visible shiver rolled through her body, but instead of my admission taking her aback, her gaze raked down my white long-sleeved shirt to my black pants I'd put on this morning before checking out of my hotel in Sibaya.

The outside of her knees pressed up against my inner thighs as she fit her legs between my own and propped her boots on the front leg of my chair. Then she placed her hands on my knees and leaned her body toward me.

A whiff of her scent carried my way, an amber and woody floral scent filling my senses. It was heady and alluring.

As I held her gaze, her smile dimmed to be taken over by a look filled with so much heat that it rivaled my own.

So much fire that it set my firmly erected walls ablaze, threatening to crumble them into ashes.

"Care to make a wager?" she murmured, a hint of playfulness in her tone.

An amused smile tugged at my mouth, surprising me. People rarely stunned me, but she'd been doing just that since she walked in.

"What kind of wager?" I asked, arching a brow.

"Why don't you come closer and find out?" she suggested, leaning her body closer and for a moment, I debated over her proposition.

The intensity of her gaze was intoxicating. It made the hand resting on my thigh itch with the need to touch her. All I wanted to do in that moment was grab her face and kiss the fuck out of her.

She was beautiful and I bet she tasted divine.

That's when my logic set back in and I realized I needed to walk away. I started work tomorrow and had to stay focused. She was unpredictable and my life didn't have space for that.

My reasoning might be faulty, but I couldn't do this.

I broke eye contact and snapped our connection. I quickly glanced at the time on the register behind the bar and noticed it was almost one in the morning. I cleared my throat and said, "I have to go."

She parted her lips to say something, but I had already grabbed my brown leather jacket that was resting on top of the backrest and left before I could hear what she had to say.

The front doors to Faro closed behind me with a thud and the moment the salty breeze of the Mediterranean Sea washed over me, I let out a frustrated sigh. Gravel crunched underneath my feet as I donned on my jacket and headed for my car.

I wasn't proud of the way I'd just rushed out and left her, but this was the right thing to do.

Right?

I wasn't planning on actually leaving the parking lot until I made sure she left the bar safely, but being near her blurred too many of the lines I'd carefully constructed around my life.

And I didn't have enough strength in me to keep resisting her.

I shook my head in an attempt to clear the haze that clouded my judgment, even though I knew it was useless. I wouldn't be forgetting her anytime soon.

I grabbed my keys from my pocket and unlocked my car. I was about to step inside when a voice broke into the quiet night.

"Wait."

I stilled because I knew without looking who it was. I finally glanced over my shoulder to find her standing in the middle of the dimly lit parking lot. Her hair blew in the wind as she rubbed her palms against her bare arms to fight the biting cold.

She walked in my direction. "You didn't answer my question from earlier."

As she got closer, I noticed the goose bumps peppering her skin and her pebbled nipples straining against her thin top. I groaned and took off my jacket, then draped it over her shoulders before I took a step back to put a healthy distance between us.

"What question?" I asked, trying to stall.

She wasn't making it easy because she closed the distance until the tip of her boots met mine. Her fingertips snaked up my front until she hooked her forefinger under the gold chain I was wearing and tugged me down to her so close I could almost taste her.

My hands at my sides flexed and a pained groan rumbled through my chest as I waited for her next move.

Then, in the quietest, most sultry voice, she said, "Are you going to keep staring all night, or will you do something about it?"

I could smell the hint of whiskey on her lips and all I could think about was how ridiculously jealous—*again*—I'd felt when she'd licked that droplet off her lips. How much I wanted to be that droplet to know what it would be like to have her mouth on me.

Fuck, I wanted her. I shouldn't, but I did. *Badly*.

I should make the right decision, but for the first time in my life, I felt inclined not to. I kept my gaze locked with hers. "How about *you* find out?" I said in a low tone, our lips so close that on my confession, they brushed.

The hair at my nape rose as I watched for any hesitation.

When she didn't move, I wrapped my hand around her lower back and roughly grabbed the back of her head with the other. Whirling her around, I pressed her back against the back door on the driver's side and flattened my body against hers. Our fronts molded against one another, our lips a mere whisper away.

She sucked in a startled breath and I knew she could feel how turned on I was. My gaze bounced back and forth between her lust-filled eyes and said, "One night."

But the moment the words left my lips, I knew they were a lie.

"One night," she reciprocated.

The last tether of my control snapped and the second our lips connected, all the reasons why I shouldn't do this evaporated into thin air. The only thought my brain could conjure right now was how fucking good she tasted.

I knew it.

I slid my tongue against hers and she wrapped her arms around my neck to pull herself tighter to me. Having her kiss me with the same ferocity sent me into overdrive. Heat flooded my veins as my pulse kicked up a notch.

I maneuvered her away from the back door and threw it open. Pulling my lips away from her, I growled, "Inside. Now."

Once she did, I climbed into the back seat, joining her.

Then I immediately pulled her onto my lap, kissing her again.

God, she was fucking addicting.

How the fuck is this supposed to be one night?

With her hands on my shoulders, she grinded against my growing erection and my hands fell to her hips to urge her closer. I moved my lips from her mouth to pepper kisses along her jaw and down her neck while simultaneously bringing one hand up to pop the single button that was holding her top together.

Then I pushed the fabric aside and snaked my tongue down, wrapping my mouth around her peaked nipple. I licked over her nipple once before biting down, eliciting a low moan from her.

Her hands snaked up the back of my neck to grip the hair at my nape as she held me firmly to her chest, which sent even more desire coursing through my veins, knowing she wanted more.

So I swirled my tongue around to soothe the sting before moving to her other breast and doing the same, hoping to elicit the same reaction.

And I got exactly what I wanted.

"Fuck," she groaned before she pulled on the strands of hair to guide me back to her mouth. Her lips found mine in a passionate kiss as she worked her hips in a circle, rubbing herself against my covered cock.

I needed to be inside her and it was like she read my mind when her hands grazed down my chest and unbuttoned my pants. Out of breath, I pulled back to watch her slip a finger under the waistband and say, "I need you to fuck me."

No longer surprised by her candor, I let out a taunting small laugh and glanced up to meet her heated gaze. "Take me out then."

Without hesitation, she pulled the zipper down and slid her hand inside my boxer briefs, wrapped it around me and squeezed me tightly.

My head dropped back against the headrest and I let out a groan. *Fucking hell.*

My fingers dug into her hips as she stroked my cock up and down. She slid her hand up and brushed against the opening at the tip before tightly squeezing the sensitive skin there.

I shot up and grabbed the back of her head with one hand. "I said take me out, not play with it," I growled against her lips.

She smiled against my lips and squeezed again. "What if that's what *I* want?"

Instead of giving her an answer, I dropped my hand from the back of her head to her hip and bunched her skirt up to give me better access. I met her mouth again as I slipped a hand under her skirt, pushed her underwear to the side, and shoved two fingers inside her sweet cunt in one swift motion.

Her hold around me loosened and her eyes squeezed shut as she screamed, "Oh, God."

"Yeah, I tend to have that effect."

Her eyes fluttered open and she smacked my chest. "You're an asshole."

I brought my face closer and curled my fingers inside her in a languidly slow circle. Her eyes widened and I whispered, "And you're wet."

She whimpered as I removed my fingers out of her. Bringing my hand up, I pressed my fingers coated in her against her lips to show her. I watched in fascination as she dragged her tongue out and circled her hot mouth around my fingers to wipe them clean.

I swiftly took them out and crashed my lips onto hers with a hungry moan, needing a taste. A growl rumbled through my chest at the taste of her.

I was done waiting.

I snuck my hands back under her skirt and ripped her underwear off her. She gasped against my mouth, but quickly recovered and followed my lead. Reaching down, she slipped her hands under the waistband at my backside, helping me slide my pants and briefs down just enough.

My cock was finally free from its painful confinement and she began rubbing herself against it. The feel of her wet cunt gliding so easily against me with no barrier was so carnal it sent my brain into a blissful haze.

I wished I could see her cunt swallowing my cock, but there was no time for that. So after I positioned myself at her entrance, I grabbed her hips and thrust fully into her. She cried out so loudly, I almost came right then and there.

She squeezed her eyes shut and arched into me, rolling her clit against my pelvis. I groaned. "That's it, pretty girl. Keep riding me just like that."

She gripped my shoulders as I continued to fuck her while she rode me. We were both breathing hard and the smell of sex permeated the air. Our moans and grunts filled the car as she took my cock like a good fucking goddess.

Her breasts swayed up and down as she bounced on my dick and my head spun into oblivion.

"Ah fuck," she whimpered. "Right there." Her voice floated around me, but I was too far gone. So I focused on thrusting up into her again and again, hitting the same spot that seemed to make her lose it.

"God, you feel so amazing," I said to her before crashing my lips onto hers.

Sex had always been just sex, but this. Fuck, this was almost fucking magical.

Her cunt squeezed me and I slid my tongue inside to meet hers as she cried out. Her nails dug into my shoulders and her orgasm took over. I could feel her soaking my cock and that was all it took for my own pleasure to come crashing down.

I spilled into her and kissed her through the final waves of our orgasms.

Our lips pulled apart and we panted against each other's mouths.

This was....

Fuck.

When we both came down from our high, we finally looked into each other's eyes.

What a fucking sight she was.

Cheeks flushed, messy hair, and lips swollen.

"That was…" She trailed off, giving me a smile. And this one might have been my favorite out of all the ones she'd given me tonight.

"Yeah."

The air around us shifted, but unlike the uncomfortable silence that usually followed moments like these, this one was blissful.

She placed a soft kiss on my lips and lifted herself off me. As she moved to the side, I reached for the console and grabbed tissues. I wanted to do it but didn't want to over-step, so instead, I handed them to her. She cleaned herself off as I tucked my wet dick back into my pants, not wanting to rid myself of her yet, and pulled my pants up.

We both leaned against the back seats and stayed quiet for a moment. I didn't want her to leave, but she would have to eventually and I might not see her again.

I glanced over at her and found myself asking her something I told her I wouldn't. Something I promised myself *I* wouldn't. "What if I wanted to see you again?" I whispered, almost hoping she didn't hear.

She turned her head to the side and faced me, shock painting her features at my confession. "We agreed to one night."

"I know what we agreed on, but what if…" I trailed off,

not sure what exactly I was asking her for. My life didn't have space for a relationship. My job didn't leave room for one. But… I groaned internally. I didn't know.

All I knew was that one night with her wasn't enough.

Her silence tightened the flesh around my lungs and suffocated the previous peaceful air that had settled around us. But I didn't look away. I wanted to see the truth behind whatever answer she would give me.

"I'd break your heart," she said, letting out a soft laugh to dissipate the growing new tension.

I shook my head softly and whispered, "It's already broken."

I'd lost everything I'd ever loved.

My father didn't want me and my mother eventually left me.

Sorrow filled Mia's eyes and I looked away because I didn't want her pity.

I felt her move beside me until she hovered slightly over me and placed a soft kiss at the edge of my lips. "I'm sorry," she said as her goodbye before leaving the confines of my car and shutting the door behind her.

I didn't move and kept an eye on her as she stepped onto the sidewalk of the main street in front of the bar and hailed a taxi. Once one halted in front of her, she opened the door. I waited for her to step inside, but she paused, a hand resting on the roof of the small red cab.

I hoped she would chance a glance over here, but after a brief moment, she climbed in and shut the door behind her.

When the taxi pulled away from the curb, I stepped out from the back seat and climbed into the driver's seat. Later that morning, after I finished unpacking and settling into the apartment I had on the Academy's premises, I went to bed dreaming of the green-eyed pretty girl I met at a bar, wondering if I would ever have the chance to see her again.

Not knowing that I would come face to face again with her the next day.

With her as one of my new students.

Amalia

CHAPTER 4

PAST

"IT'S ALREADY BROKEN."

His words replayed in my mind so much I barely slept. I kept thinking about the way he looked at me. The way that one unruly strand of his lush brown hair rested on his forehead when he turned to face me. The way his dark brown eyes pinned my green ones as he waited for my answer.

The way the underlying pain in his voice made me feel something I'd never felt before and I didn't like it.

Because I wanted to say yes to his proposal. I wanted more than one night to learn his real name and what he was about. But that wasn't how I worked.

That wasn't what I was here for.

Even if he was the best sex I'd ever had.

Even if I could still feel him between my legs even after I'd showered and washed myself of him when I came back to the dorms well after curfew. Even if I could still feel the way his lips left mine bruised and how my scalp still tingled from how hard he gripped the back of my skull as he kissed and fucked me.

The urge to touch myself to the memory had been strong, but I didn't want to face a lawsuit from my colleague sleeping right above me on my first day here.

I'd tossed and turned until the early morning light filtered in through the curtains. I looked over at the clock on my small bedside table and noticed I had about two hours before we had to show up for our first class.

Hoping a run would help clear my mind before the day ahead, I quietly rolled out of bed and walked over to the small dresser where I had to make all my clothes fit. I grabbed a deep brown workout set and slipped into the bathroom, carefully closing the door behind me so as not to wake Stella—my roommate for the next year.

She'd been sleeping when I came back last night, which was a relief. I'd only briefly spoken to her when I'd arrived two days ago and she'd seemed cordial enough, but I'd rather avoid any questions about my whereabouts. Judging by her quiet nature, I didn't think she would have questioned me, but one could never be too careful here.

One thing I'd learned early on in this journey was that appearances were almost always deceptive.

I quickly changed into the matching set I'd picked—a

long-sleeved top and high-rise biker shorts—and threw my hair into a ponytail. After splashing my face with some water, I slathered moisturizer and sunscreen on my face before tiptoeing toward the door, making sure to avoid the one creaky floorboard.

I fastened my shoes on, grabbed my headphones from my duffel bag near the entrance, and slid out of the room, heading for the field at the back of the facility. Once outside, a gust of cold wind rolled over my body. I brushed my hands over my arms a few times to warm me up a little as I glanced around to see if anyone else was out here.

Relieved no one else was in sight, I put my headphones over my ears and took off, the music slowly pumping to match the rhythm of my beating heart.

As I jogged, I realized I hadn't had a chance to explore the premises since my arrival. So I took a left turn into an unbeaten pathway that eventually led into a forest behind the Academy.

Down the track, the path opened up onto a road that curved alongside the ocean. Echoes of waves crashing against the shore beneath filtered through the music. The soothing sounds acted as a balm and all my worries and uncertainties of what was ahead faded away.

I'd spent the last few weeks training and studying the material in advance for this year since I knew I'd need any extra advantage I could get. I'd always been a good student, but it hadn't been easy. Especially when it came to memorizing documents and a lot of this job required it.

Deciding not to dwell on the fact, I pushed myself harder as I looped around and back into the forest to head back before everyone woke up. Once I got closer and saw the Academy on the horizon, I slowed to a stop, chest heaving.

I turned off the beat drumming in my ears and wiped the sweat beading across my forehead with the end of my sleeve as I walked toward the back doors.

Once inside, I turned right and headed down the hallway toward my room, listing what I had to do in my head before going to class. I was so lost in the task that I hadn't noticed the man in front of me until I slammed into the hard body.

Fingers wrapped around my upper arms to steady me. A groan left my lips when I looked up and I realized who it was.

Just what I needed.

Asher Williams, the twenty-five-year-old son of the Academy's director and the most annoying person I'd ever met.

We had attended the same international school in Bemes and I had the unfortunate luck of having a few classes with him despite him being three years older since he'd dropped out for a few years for reasons that were still unknown.

I'd done my best to limit my interactions with him since he was well-known for his promiscuous reputation, but unfortunately for me, one drunken night after our high school graduation and a bad decision later, I'd found myself stuck with his constant flirtatious nature asking for round two.

I thought I'd rid myself of him after graduating and moving back home for university, but much to my dismay, he'd decided to follow in his family's footsteps and join the Academy despite most thinking he'd keep spending his father's money on a beach somewhere.

I'd known I might eventually run into him, but our class was big enough that I could have avoided him. To think I was almost to my room.

Guess my bad luck strikes again.

His eyes trailed down my body and he let out an appreciative hum. "Look who we have here," he said, gracing me with his signature smirk. "The one and only, Amalia Abara."

"Williams," I said in a clipped tone, shrugging him off me.

He shoved his hands into his pockets and stood to his full height. "What's a man have to do to get a text back from you?" he asked as he trailed his eyes down my body.

Asher had been trying to ask me out since that night, but I'd decided it would be simpler to just ignore him.

Out of sight, out of mind.

Until now.

I sighed and kept myself from rolling my eyes at him. "I have to go," I said and brushed past him, walking away.

"One day, I'll get you to say yes," he said right as I closed the door to my quarters behind me. I dropped my head against it, looking up at the ceiling.

To whoever's up there, keep him away, please.

"Sounds determined," a voice chimed, startling me from my supplication.

I looked over to find Stella sitting on her top bunk, already dressed with her laptop opened in front of her.

I shook my head and gave her a small smile. "You could say that."

She returned her attention to her screen and said, "You should get ready. We have to be in room 34B by eight a.m."

I looked down at my watch to notice that I only had fifteen minutes to shower and change. *Fuck.* I didn't realize I'd been gone for so long.

I tossed my headphones and watch on my bed and rushed to my dresser to grab our uniform—black cargo pants and a gray T-shirt. Stepping into the bathroom, I locked the door behind and climbed into the shower after throwing my workout clothes into the hamper in the corner.

After quickly washing my body, I dried myself off and changed into my clothes for the day. I brushed my teeth and washed my face before applying my skincare.

After looking at myself in the mirror and noticing the sleepless lines covering my features, I brushed a small coat of mascara over my long lashes and swiped some lip balm over my lips. Then I pinched my cheeks to give myself a bit of color to my cheeks and stepped out of the bathroom to find Stella already gone, a steaming cup of coffee sitting on my nightstand in her wake.

I might grow to like her.

I chugged a few sips, ignoring the burning sensation from the steaming liquid, rushed to slip on my sneakers, and scrambled out the door with five minutes to spare.

"Happy to see that I'm not the only one who's about to be late on their first day," a voice chimed next to me as I pulled a small satin headscarf past my forehead and fastened it to keep my wavy hair out of my face.

I looked to my right to find a pretty tall blonde with dark blue eyes smiling at me. She was wearing the same attire as me, her long hair pulled into a ponytail.

"I hope for both of us that's not the case," I responded as we rounded the corner and walked down the corridor that would lead us to room 34B.

She extended her hand and introduced herself. "Isabella Smith. But my friends call me Bella."

I took her hand in mine. "Amalia."

She let go of my hand once we got to the door and opened it for me, letting me in. Chatter echoed in the large room and I looked over at all the recruits forming a group in the middle of the room. "Oh, I know. Top of your class at Navarra and most coveted recruit this year. Your reputation precedes you," she said as we walked into the crowd to stand amongst them.

I scrunched my nose and glanced at her, letting out a small laugh. "I hope that's not a bad thing."

I'd spent the last few years training for a spot at the Academy and I'd worked hard to come here, but I didn't want the attention that came with it. Because attention meant expectations, and with expectations came the burden to be flawless.

I was far from that.

She gave me a small smile. "Not at all."

The conversations suddenly grew dimmer when the door on the other side of the room opened and a pair of footsteps grew closer to where we all stood. I couldn't see who it was yet in the midst of the sea of people standing in front of me.

"Also," Isabella continued as she leaned down closer to be at my ear level. "You should hide that," she whispered.

I glanced at her to find her pointing at my neck. Heat rose up my chest and I brushed a hand against the side of my neck, remembering last night. I was in such a hurry this morning that I hadn't noticed if the stranger from last night left any marks on my body.

Despite my secretly hoping he did.

She let out an amused chuckle. I tugged my shirt up, hoping to somehow hide whatever mark she was referring to, and turned my attention to the front.

Nerves slithered through my veins in anticipation of meeting our new instructor. His name preceded him and he was a legend here. I rarely admired anyone, but his accomplishments alone made me want to make a good impression.

I'd spent most of my life trying to find where I fit and figure out what I was good at. Teachers and people around me had always looked down on me, telling me I'd never achieve anything because I didn't excel in the department *they* deemed important.

My older sister had worked two jobs to support me and my brother after our mother had abandoned us when I was fourteen years old to *find herself.* So the pressure to succeed at something, *anything*, had weighed heavily on me. She'd given up so much to raise us, and I'd made it a mission to get better grades and find what I would do for the rest of my life.

It had been a daunting task, but when the Academy had a guest lecturer speak at Navarra during my first year there, I knew at that moment that I would do everything I could to get in.

Being here would grant me opportunities I wouldn't get otherwise and, besides, kicking ass for a living didn't sound too bad. As my therapist would say, channeling the anger I harbored against my dead-beat parents into something good was a step in the right direction.

The heavy footsteps came to a halt and everyone straightened their spines and put on their best faces, hoping to impress him.

A girl in front of me let out a low whistle and

murmured to the girl next to her, her voice barely above a whisper. "I'd heard he was gorgeous, but holy fuck."

I knew of Noah Brown, but since he'd allegedly refused to be photographed, I'd never seen what he looked like. But from the small glimpses I could grasp between the towering bodies in front of me, she was right.

I couldn't see his face yet, but my attention snagged to his body. His navy shirt molded to his arms, and the sleeves were rolled up, giving a delicious view of his forearms.

I'd promised myself last night would be the last time for a long time so I could focus on training, and he *was* my teacher, but that didn't mean I couldn't look.

He finally cleared his throat and the murmurs around me came to a full stop. "All right, everyone, welcome to the Academy. I'm Agent Noah Brown and I'll be your instructor for the duration of your time here," a strangely familiar deep voice said.

The girl in front of me moved, finally giving me a full look at the person standing in front of us.

My throat closed up and blood pounded in my ears, the whooshing sound blocking out anything that was being said next, if he was even saying anything because I could barely focus on breathing.

My lungs seemed to collapse inside my chest, making it impossible to take a deep breath as I awaited the inevitability of his gaze landing on me. And when his eyes finally met mine, my vision narrowed and memories of our night came crashing back in a full tidal wave.

His mouth on me, his cock inside me while I rode him, his lips devouring mine as I experienced the hottest night of my life.

And his parting words.

"It's already broken."

CHAPTER 5

PRESENT

FOR A FEW MOMENTS, WHEN MY EYES MET HIS, TIME STOOD still, the seconds stretching longer than I ever thought was imaginable.

Memories slammed against the walls I'd erected when I became Ines, threatening to crumble my carefully constructed new reality brick by brick. My heart slammed furiously against my ribcage and the walls of the rather large cell we were in felt like they were caving in, enclosing us in a much smaller place where infinite moments we'd shared in the past fought against our new realities.

Me as his captor and him as my captive.

Both prisoners of our new circumstances.

I quickly realized that I would need much better

defenses against him if his simple presence rattled me this much after years of building a barrier between who I once was and who I'd become.

Especially after he'd left.

My captive's eyes widened. "Amalia?" His voice was barely above a whisper and deeper than I remembered, but I recognized it nonetheless.

I found myself taking him in, telling myself that's what I always did with everyone I encountered so that I could store any details to my bank of information.

Yeah, right, my mind mocked me.

His bruised wrists were bound together with a rope chained to a pair of shackles hanging from the ceiling. His white shirt was torn, revealing various cuts on his torso, and blood matted the fabric of his shirt on his right shoulder.

I'd been told that one of Hamza's men had injured him when they'd intercepted him, but apparently no one had tended to his wound. Something I'd have to unfortunately take care of.

If he was to die on my watch, it wouldn't be from an easily preventable infection.

My gaze wandered over the right side of his face, taking note of the cut clumped with dried blood above his brow and fading bruise on his cheekbone. Other than that, his perfectly sculpted face remained intact despite the accident.

Some of his features might have changed and grown

over the years—the fine lines beside his eyes, the thicker beard on his strong, chiseled jaw and the few grays peeking through his thick brown hair—but one thing hadn't.

Ten years may have passed, yet his dark-brown eyes still ensnared me.

But I swiftly reminded myself that the man in front of me was the same person who I once thought was my everything, only for him to evaporate into nothing the moment he left.

I'd made my peace with it—or should I say ignored it like he never existed because it was much easier than to deal with the heartbreak that followed his abandonment.

But my name on his lips still had the same effect as it always had, the sound ricocheting around my body and dehiscing old wounds.

It'd been ten years, but all of a sudden, the pain of his sudden departure felt fresh. My chest squeezed and I inhaled in an attempt to regulate my pounding heartbeat.

The old Amalia would have been desperate to recapture how euphoric he'd made me feel, but I wasn't that person anymore. The rose-colored glasses I'd acquired when we were together, blurred into a darkness that now consumed me.

My conscience often fought with my new nature, my heart battling with my head with what my mission was. But I knew the old Amalia wouldn't find her way back until I closed this chapter. Unfortunately for her, we still had a long while to go before the Barrera cartel was no longer what it currently was.

I fought against the burn creeping up my throat and coerced myself to extinguish the fire threatening to over-take my insides at the reminder that he had been able to leave without so much of a goodbye.

Besides, at the end of the day, I had a job to do and he was in the way.

His gaze fought a wide range of emotions, but I didn't care—or at least I convinced myself enough that I didn't.

I took a small step back and crossed my arms, the skin of my fingertips itching to reach the blade sheathed against my thigh. "It's you," I stated flatly.

He raised his brow. "You sound disappointed."

"You're the last person I'd want to see and quite frankly, I would have preferred any other prisoner than someone who wasted a year of my life."

"You're hurting my feelings, pretty girl. Way to kick a man when he's already down," he replied, attempting to lighten the atmosphere.

The nickname seemed to have escaped him, but it didn't stop the irritation bristling under my skin at his attempt at familiarity. Like he hadn't run away without a word.

"Why are you on our territory? Who sent you?" I asked harshly.

A few days ago, while I was away to collect a shipment drop, Hamza called to inform me that DEA agents were sniffing around Bab Al Mansour and I'd told him I could easily take care of it on my own like I'd done many times before.

After infiltrating Barerra's ranks, I'd cut all communications with my team. They'd evidently been against it, but I'd known I wouldn't be able to cross the ledge into fully becoming Ines Bensaid, the new identity the Bureau had assigned me with, if I still had ties to any part of my life.

Including my family.

I'd told them the one thing I knew would strain our relationship so that I wouldn't have to explain my whereabouts and simply destroyed the burner phone the Agency had given me.

They'd sent a few agents to create a line of contact, but unfortunately for them, I'd already embraced my role as Barrera's sicario and got rid of them before they could endanger my cover.

I'd had only one goal in mind for the last five years and whoever got in the way needed to disappear.

By all means necessary.

No agents had dared come after me again until a few days ago, but strangely, Hamza had persisted in taking care of this one himself. Something about Barrera requesting one of them be kept alive.

Loose ends weren't a part of his ways and I'd always been his best soldier to tie them. I hadn't been told who it was, but I never expected my new prisoner to be the same man I'd once loved.

Noah had never told me much about his past and I'd heard whispers here and there at the Academy that his first and *only* partner had been killed when they grew too close to bringing Barrera under tangible sources. But I'd been either too naive and too in love to care.

It made a lot more sense as to why he was here now, but I still didn't understand why he ventured on this territory in the first place or why Barrera didn't simply get rid of him.

I would.

Even if it was for purely selfish reasons.

Noah's brows pulled together. "Who sent me? *Your* territory?" he said, a puzzling look on his face. "Why are *you* here? There was nothing about—"

"Why I'm here is none of your concern," I said, cutting him off.

He shook his head and a cough rattled his chest. "It kinda is in light of my current situation," he deadpanned as he tugged on the chains.

"I'll see what I can do about that after you tell me why you're jeopardizing my assignment."

He huffed out a small laugh. "Always bargaining. Glad to see you haven't changed."

"You don't know me," I said, my tone dry as I tried to soothe the urge to let out my frustration on his face.

He lifted a single eyebrow and let his gaze drift down my body. "I beg to differ, pretty girl."

One moment, I was standing a few feet away from him, and the next, my dagger was pressed up right beneath his chin, my free hand holding the back of his head forward. "Do not call me that ever again," I seethed, looking up at him. Before I could stop myself, I added, "You lost that right a long time ago."

A flash of hurt dimmed his features, but it disappeared as fast as it came. I waited for his expression to morph into panic like all my previous victims had when I had them at my mercy in their final moments.

But it wasn't fear that painted his gaze like I'd expected.

Instead, amusement shone in his irises as he leaned into my touch, his skin tensing against the sharp blade. That only had me pressing the edge harder against his neck, a droplet of blood blossoming against his tanned skin.

It slowly trailed down the curvature of his neck, but he still didn't flinch.

The faintest smile curved his full lips. "Careful now, *pretty girl*," he drawled. "You wouldn't want to go against your dear boss's wishes."

"I don't answer to anyone but myself," I said through gritted teeth. It wasn't exactly the truth, but he didn't have to know that.

Barrera had appointed me as his enforcer and I mostly executed my own wishes to get the answers I needed, but he still ordered me around like one of his lower soldiers and I had to feign to obey every once in a while.

If he ever found out why I was really here, let's just say what I did to prisoners was a mere play compared to what he'd have done to me for being a rat and my body probably would never be found as I swam in Oued Aguz.

I moved my attention back to Noah, waiting and watching. Silence coiled between us like a living, breathing element that sent frustration raging through my veins. My chest grazed against his with every breath as we stared at each other.

Our lips were merely a brush from one another, his breath fanning across the parched skin of my lips. I could practically taste him.

We exchanged a quiet push and pull with neither of us giving an inch. His expression looked inquisitive as if he was searching for something, while mine battled between pushing the blade further into his thyroid to rid myself of him once and for all, and the nagging invocation of the stain he'd left on my mind, reminding me that once, I'd loved him.

I shook myself out of it because, frankly, I had better things to do.

I exhaled the breath I didn't notice I was holding and begrudgingly released my hold on him. Brandishing my knife upward, I cut the rope tied to the chains above his head and stepped back, watching him land on the cement ground with a loud thud.

"Behave until I'm back," I ordered as I looked down at him on his knees in front of me.

When he glanced up and his gaze found mine, a small flicker of satisfaction brushed against my breastbone. But it was briskly replaced when I noticed how weak he looked. No matter how far I'd gone or what I'd done to get here, my past self occasionally snuck out.

I hated myself for caring even in the slightest, but he was still Noah.

The same person who used to be part of some of my favorite memories.

But those same memories I once treasured had long turned bitter.

I should've known better at the time.

People always left.

Their memories only festered until they turned into ashes.

I let out an exasperated sigh. "Bathroom's in the corner and I'll see that someone gets something to eat sent to you," I threw at him. "And before I forget," I added before I raised my fist and connected it with the injured side of his face.

His head whipped to the side from the sudden impact, the bones of my knuckles crunching against his cheekbone. "What…" He paused to spit, a mix of blood and saliva landing on the cobblestone floors. "What was that for?"

I raised my hand, my knuckles stained with splatters of his blood, and patted his cheek. "Just doing my job."

People would grow suspicious if I'd visited a prisoner and came back unmarked. This was insurance. And a little payback if I was being honest.

He said nothing more as I turned on my heels to walk away.

As I moved to lock his cell, I briefly chanced one last look at him, finding him rubbing against his abraded skin. When the bolt slammed shut, he lifted his head and our eyes met again.

I paused for a moment, a tumult of emotions running through me. Then I left.

Just like he'd done.

Noah

CHAPTER 6

PAST

I WAS ABOUT TO REPLY TO THE EMAIL THE DIRECTOR SENT me earlier this week when someone knocked on my office door. It cracked open and revealed Alex, the new trainer I'd be working alongside this year.

We hadn't officially met since I only got in late last night, but I already knew everything I needed to know about him. Top of his class—not as good as I was, but good enough that I approved his application—which meant he would be competent enough not to screw up, but unfortunately for me, he was too cheery for my liking.

"Sorry to interrupt, Mr. Brown," he started as he stepped into my office uninvited. Annoyance bubbled in my veins at his intrusion. He gave a bright smile that I was sure charmed a lot of people. It only fueled my irritation.

He shut the door behind him and walked over to my desk, where I was still seated. Placing his hands behind his back, he continued, "I just wanted to introduce myself and say that I'm very much looking forward to working with you. I've heard—"

I tuned out the rest of his sentence. It was always the same when anyone met me for the first time. I didn't need to listen to him list my accomplishments and how eager he was to learn from me.

When his chatter quieted, I focused my attention back on him and noticed his outstretched hand. I stood from my seat, towering over him on the other side of the desk. He wasn't short by any means, but I still had a few inches over him.

Then I did the professional thing to do, gave him a curt nod and reached over for his extended hand and shook it. "Mr. Avery," I said as I let go of his hand. Bracing my palms against the wooden surface in front of me, I added, "Next time, wait until you're let in before coming into my office."

His smile faltered and he cleared his throat. "I-I didn't mean…"

"I'll see you in class, Mr. Avery," I said, cutting him off.

"Yes, sir," he replied before hurrying out of the room.

I let out a sigh and hunched over my computer to quickly reply to the offer I'd gotten every few months with the same answer I'd always given.

Thank you for the offer, but I'm satisfied with the position I currently hold and I'm not looking to fulfill a new position at the moment.

For the last two years, Director Williams had been offering me a unit chief position back in Bemes. Although it would be a much better pay than what I earned here as a training officer and I would be closer to my mother, who always reminded me I should visit more, I just didn't want the change.

I'd been at this job for the last decade and I liked stability. I didn't want to have to acclimate to new people, a new role, or a new city.

After clicking send, I locked my computer screen and looked at the clock to see that it was almost 8:00 a.m. So I left my office and headed for the training room. I paused in front of the double steel doors, looking through one of the small windows inside each door to watch the group I'd have to train for the next twelve months clustered together in the middle of the room.

I frowned when I noticed Avery talking with the students at the front of the group. He erupted into laughter at whatever one of them seemed to have just said.

I shook my head.

Fraternizing with students was discouraged, but I guessed he must have missed that part of the rule book before he came to work here. Either that, or he was choosing to ignore it.

Something I'd have to discuss with him after today's session.

Finally, I took a deep breath and pushed the set of double doors open.

Here we go.

As soon as I entered the training room, heads turned in my direction. When they realized who I was, their spines straightened and a hush fell over the room. It became quiet enough that you could hear the sound of my footsteps echoing in the room as I walked to the center of it.

The sound of a low whistle and murmurs broke the silence that had descended around us as I approached and took place in front of them. I even got a few wide eyes from some of the students standing right in front of me.

I'd been teaching at the Academy for almost ten years now and had gotten used to the reaction when people discovered what I looked like. I was younger than people who had filled my role previously, and I wasn't oblivious to my looks. So I simply brushed it off like I'd always done and cleared my throat.

"Listen up, everyone," I said loud enough for everyone to hear. "My name is Noah Brown. I'll be overseeing most of your training here." My eyes swept across the room, my gaze jumping from trainee to trainee to assess each of them until…

My stomach dropped when my gaze locked with hers. Her eyes slightly widened, recognition flashing within them.

No fucking way.

Even if she was mostly hidden behind the people in front of her, I instantly recognized her. The woman from last night was in my classroom. As a recruit.

As *my* fucking recruit.

This was exactly why I didn't step out of my routine because things like *this* were bound to happen. Of course, the only time I decided to be selfish and do something for myself, the woman I hadn't been able to stop thinking about since last night ended up being one of the one hundred and fifteen initiates.

A snicker pulled me out of my thoughts.

My gaze darted to where it came from, my eyes landing on a blond recruit standing tall in the middle of the crowd, his arms crossed over his chest and an amused expression painting his features.

Not for long.

I stepped forward and the crowd parted for me. I walked up to him. His face fell. I leaned my face down until only a few inches separated us. My eyes narrowed, and for a moment, I just stared at him.

"Name?" I asked quietly.

His smile dimmed at my question. He must have thought I already knew his name based on the current expression on his face. No one was ever that important.

I kept staring at him and his throat bobbed up and down as he swallowed. Then he cleared his throat and said,

"Williams, sir. Asher Williams," he said, his voice slightly cracking at the end.

"*Asher*," I started, emphasizing his first name. Recruits were always referred to by their last name, but in his case, I'd decided it would have to be earned. *If ever.* "Care to enlighten me on what's so funny?"

He peered at the trainee next to him for backup, his eyes flicking back and forth between the brunet and me. He looked away, leaving him to his own devices. He brought his gaze back to mine and cleared his throat again. "It was nothing, sir."

"Think of that next time you interrupt me. Got it?"

He shifted in his place and nodded.

I straightened and turned around, walking back to my previous position.

"Now where were we," I said, all of the trainees' attention back on me. I went over the basics—rules, schedules, and program expectations if they wanted to make it at the end of this.

I'd managed to do most of it without looking at her, but right as I moved on to the training part of today, I couldn't help but chance a glance at the girl from last night.

Only to find her already watching me.

For two hours, I kept my attention away from her.

Or at least I tried to. But it inevitably kept going back to her every few minutes and I still didn't know her name because I didn't bother with introductions, too restless to get today over with.

I'd been standing at the back, observing the class as Avery ran them through defensive tactics before he finally let them pair up. To my discontent, Williams immediately beelined for her.

It looked like he pleaded with her for a few minutes before she finally relented and waved her hand before her, gesturing for him to lead the way. He gave her a flirtatious smile before getting into position.

She rolled her eyes at him and did the same.

He suddenly moved to close in on her, hoping to catch her off guard, but she managed to step out of his way. He laughed and I heard him whisper to her, "I see you like to play hard to get even in a fight."

Green fumes sprouted in my chest at their familiarity. I tore my gaze away from them to try and tame them, turning my attention to another pairing of two guys—a man with his brown hair tied in a half-bun and a blond with his hair buzzed short that looked to be twice his size. They were going at each other like they held a vendetta against one another.

The blond one rushed forward, his fist moving to hit the other trainee square in the jaw, but he put up his hands up to block the shot just in time. He then retaliated by aiming a few leg kicks at his opponent's legs until he brought it farther up that his foot hit the blond's ribs.

I watched them spar for a few more minutes until a loud thud resonated in the room. And it came from behind me.

Tendrils of anger started to form when I realized *who* was behind me.

If that bastard hurt her…

I whipped around, only to find *her* holding him down in an armlock. I held in my smile as I watched this Asher guy struggle under her grip, his face turning beet red by the second as he kept trying to get himself out of her hold instead of submitting.

She applied more pressure and leaned down to whisper something in his ear, the hint of a smile gracing her lips.

I like her.

Asher finally tapped the mat and she let go. He rolled away from her and peeled himself off the floor, standing straight and dusting his clothes to right them, his breaths harsh and his face still red.

She held out her hand for him to shake and he reluctantly took it, a strained smile on his lips. Then he turned on his heels and headed for the water dispenser, grabbed a paper cup and filled it with water. His gaze flitted to her again while he brought the water to his lips, but he immediately looked away when he saw me watching him.

A few minutes later, I dismissed them for the rest of the day. While most of everyone stayed behind, she was the first to bolt out of the room.

And against my better judgment, I went after her.

She rounded the corner and headed for the hallway that

led to the dorms, but before she could reach her destination, I opened up a nondescript door, wrapped my hand around her elbow, and hauled her into what looked like a storage room.

She barely had time to react before I slammed the wooden door shut.

"What the—" She stopped mid-sentence when I flicked the lights on and her eyes landed on mine. "Jo—Mr. Brown?" Her eyes widened, and she stumbled back, but my grip on her didn't let her go far.

"What are you doing here?" I questioned, my voice tight.

Her brows pinched together, but she didn't respond.

The muscle in my jaw ticked as I repeated through gritted teeth. "I asked what are you doing here, *Mia*?" I demanded. My tone was accusatory, but deep down I was furious. More at myself than I was at her, but in this moment, they both blurred together.

She ripped her arm from my grip. "If it wasn't obvious already, I'm here to train. And my name is Amalia."

Realization slowly dawned on me. I pinched the bridge of my nose, closed my eyes, and threw my head back. This was already a worst-case scenario, but now it was even worse than I could have ever imagined.

Not only did I sleep with one of my students, I slept with the one that the Director personally selected for me to watch over. I hadn't had the chance to look over her file after he called me because I'd wanted to assess her in class before I knew of her accolades.

I shook my head. "You're Amalia Abara," I stated.

She crossed her arms over her chest. "The one and only."

"Of course you are." I let out a laugh of disbelief.

God, I was fucking stupid. Of course it had to be her and the revelation felt like a slap in the face. Fire erupted in my chest as I looked at her.

"Did you know who I was at the bar last night?" Before she could get a word in, I continued my line of accusation. "Is that why you approached me?" I rubbed a hand through my hair before dragging it down over my face. "Did you think it would help you get favors if you slept with me?"

The moments the words left my mouth, I regretted them.

She reared back at my accusation as if I had back-handed her across the face. "Excuse me?" She narrowed her eyes, the green in her irises turning ablaze. "I won't stay here and let you talk to me that way, so I'm leaving," she said, her tone harsh.

She pushed me out of her way, but the second her fingers wrapped around the handle and she opened the door, my hand darted out and slammed it back shut.

My breathing grew heavy and I knew what I was about to do would be a mistake, but I had to apologize. I'd stepped out of line and that wasn't who I was. My hand still rested on the door, while the fingers of my other one skimmed against the hand she had resting at her side.

"Amalia," I whispered.

Tension crackled between us as she turned around, but she didn't look at me. So I brought the hand from above her head and tugged her chin up, forcing her to meet my gaze. She stared up into my eyes, the glint of fire still there, but I could tell it wasn't from anger.

She was upset and I was the reason behind it. I didn't like it.

"What do you want? Throw more insulting questions at me?" she asked harshly.

I brushed my thumb back and forth along the side of her hand. "I'm sorry," I said quietly. "I was out of line and I shouldn't have said what I said. I didn't mean any of it, Amalia."

The blazing hurt in her eyes dimmed at my words and for a moment, time seemed to stop as we stared at each other. Conflicting emotions flooded me when she looked at me, my mind battling with indecision.

I released her chin and gently cradled her jaw in my hand, the feel of her skin somewhat soothing against my hardened calluses. Her lips parted ever so slightly, and an intense desire to kiss her, to feel her lips against mine one more time instantly hit me.

One more time wouldn't hurt, right?

The pad of my thumb swiped against her bottom lip, and she sucked in a breath. The sound acted as a tether, grounding me back to reality and the gravity of what I was about to do.

I dropped my hand like her skin was hot coal, stepped away from her and left, knowing this was the right decision to make.

I didn't trust myself around her, which meant I needed to avoid her as much as I could. I couldn't avoid her during class, but surely I could limit my interactions with her and stay away from her outside of it.

Yeah, I could do that.

Everything would be fine.

But even I knew that was a lie.

Noah

CHAPTER 7

AMALIA WAS THE LAST PERSON I'D EVER EXPECTED TO SEE and despite ten years being gone, she was still just as strikingly beautiful as she'd ever been.

The serrated knife I'd driven into my heart when I'd left her felt just as fresh as the day I'd put it there. I didn't have many regrets in life, but she was my most salient one.

I knew I'd made a mistake the moment I'd landed in Bemes after abruptly leaving the Academy. But I hadn't had a choice.

I'd wanted to reach out, to go back after everything I had to deal with was over with and beg her to forgive me for leaving without a goodbye, but I couldn't. I'd known it was a cowardly move, but I just…

Couldn't.

Maybe her being here was a sign, but it couldn't be one I read too much into. I had to focus on getting out of here and accomplishing what I came here to do.

Her presence unsettled me even more when I realized she was working for my father. Omar Barrera didn't hire women to work for him unless it was to entertain his business associates. But by the jab she'd given me before leaving, that was definitely not what she was here for.

She must have done some terrible things for my father to appoint her to any rank, let alone employ her as his enforcer.

My mind mulled over our conversation, but it kept latching onto a small part that had bugged me ever since she said the words. She had called my father's territory theirs.

Not his, *theirs*.

That fact left me with two potential conclusions. Either she was too good at her job even when the others weren't around or the job had gotten to her. If the latter was true, it meant that if I wasn't careful enough, Amalia could unravel the truth and jeopardize my plan to bring my father down.

Which might turn out to be a tad bit more difficult with being a prisoner and all.

I waited until her steps quieted and I heard the entrance door to the basement shut to move. I removed the ties around my wrists and my legs protested as I pushed myself up.

I brought a hand up to massage my throbbing jaw while

I explored the cell I was held in. I studied the space to see if there had been any changes made since I'd last been here.

It wasn't as large as I remembered it to be, but the smell, aside from the stench, was still the same—musty and damp with a hint of honey. No matter how many times he'd stuck me in here to "build my character," I'd never figured out where the smell of honey came from.

My finger brushed against the cold stones making up the back walls until they nudged against the shallow marks I'd left behind a long time ago. Wisps of ancient memories flickered at the edges of my vision, the echoes of his words still bouncing against these walls to haunt me.

"Such a disgrace."

"I can't believe you're the only child I have and this is who I have to give my whole empire to when it's time."

"Your mother should have gotten rid of you when she still had the chance."

I could still see the look of disdain on his tanned and harsh face as he looked at me curled in the corner of this cell. I could still remember the endless nights spent sleeping on my stomach on this same hard floor, pain biting each of my thoughts until it became too unbearable to stay awake.

The physical scars may have faded, but the memories never seemed to. I'd tried to shove the images away, to free myself of his constant reminders that I hadn't been the son he'd aspired me to be, but it had never been that easy.

I'd struggled to rid myself of the stains his words left,

the marks his rage painted me with. I'd tried really hard by being the best at everything, by trying to fight the parts of him in me when it bubbled too close to the surface.

My father only ever loved one thing. It wasn't me or my mother, or even his family. The only thing he ever cared about was his title and the money his businesses and organization brought him.

When I was younger, I'd convinced myself that once I passed my initiation, things would change. He'd become the father I'd always imagined he'd be. The love that people tell you every parent has for their child would finally turn on and it would just click for him that I was more than just a means to an end.

But I'd been foolish to ever think that would happen.

Truth was, my father had never been a father to me. He'd never cared about anything that related to me except my taking over if anything were to happen to him. I'd known that since I was a child, but I reminded myself that things were different now.

I might be his prisoner, but I would find a way out because I wasn't the weak kid who'd always cower against his father's wrath. I was my mother's son and I would fight my way out, one way or the other just like she'd done all those years ago.

I kept looking around the cell, inspecting every brick for any loose foundation. When I was younger, I used to spend hours doing the same thing, only to never find anything, but it'd been almost thirty years since my last time here, so one could hope.

But I wasn't known to have much luck.

At least I knew where I was on the property. I didn't know much about my father—bonding wasn't really his thing—but I knew one thing for certain. He was sentimental about this house, and I highly doubted he'd made many renovations since my uncle, my mother, and I escaped or ceded any land of his.

I mean, he didn't have to.

My father's world was divided into five territories run by three notorious families—the Alaouis, the Slimanis, and finally my father's, the Barreras.

The Slimanis had long relinquished most of their territories to my father, his soldiers running the majority of their operations. He'd tried to do the same to the Alaouis, but they were currently his only rival still withstanding.

And it wasn't for his lack of trying.

This part of the cartel had never been made public knowledge because each clan kept their operations concealed and hidden through their multibillion companies. The Alaouis had their jewelry behemoth corporation to use for their money laundering and *subject* acquisitions while my father monopolized the world of luxury textiles.

My job at the Bureau gave me one of the best clearances and I still wouldn't have known this if it wasn't for being born in it. Omar had been training me to overtake everything right until the day I left, but from the way we'd parted ways, I doubted he'd had me in mind to carry his legacy.

The only legacy my father had left me with was a simple mantra. It was the same one that I repeated to myself as I closed my eyes, gliding down the wall on the far back. I tipped my head back onto the cold wall, thinking of my next steps while listening to the small droplets of water hitting the hard floor to the beat of a measured cadence.

I have to get out.

It must have been two or three days since I'd woken up for the first time, but I wasn't exactly sure since it had been eerily quiet after Amalia had left me with a throbbing jaw.

Besides, it wasn't like I received regular visitors or had a window in my cell to indicate how long it'd been. The only source of light I had was from the few flickering light bulbs along the hallway wall.

But this wasn't new to me. I'd tried to clock the days and weeks in the past, but eventually they all blurred together.

The notion of time here always seemed to disappear. Hours quickly became days and before you knew it, you were passed out from dehydration and hunger.

My stomach growled at the thought of food. Amalia had been true to her words and a tall, skinny kid who couldn't be older than fourteen years old had left some food in my cell. He'd barely looked at me when he slid the plate through the cell's bars before hurrying back to wherever he'd come from.

I'd watched him disappear, hoping he wasn't going through the same things I'd been through as a child because that was a worse punishment than being stuck in here.

I'd left the single piece of stale bread and the beans concoction sitting underneath it untouched, the tray in the same place he'd placed it. My father's favorite weapon was most definitely not poison, but it had been years since I'd last seen him. Things could have changed, so one could never be too careful.

I hadn't eaten or drunk anything in probably over a week, but I'd survived longer at the hands of my father.

My eyes snapped open at the faint sound of footsteps approaching. I quickly stood up and faced the cell door, preparing for whoever was coming. Through the iron bars, I watched the basement door be yanked open. Unsteadiness rose in my chest when a group composed of two men I'd never seen before and Amalia stormed toward my cell.

What the fuck is going on?

When they stood in front of the cell door, I knew straight away from the look on their faces they weren't coming over to have a simple chat and spend quality time. At least, not the type of quality time I'd be very fond of right now.

The taller of the two men appeared to be in his thirties,

with light brown skin and a short, trimmed dark brown beard. He was wearing navy dress pants with a white button-down shirt. Remnants of sweat glistened on his bald head, which meant it was most likely early afternoon because that's when the heat here was at its height.

I studied him carefully while he stood there doing the same. He looked familiar but not enough to ring a bell. He gestured for the man behind him to open up my confines. The young man, who looked at least ten years his junior, moved in front of him and fumbled with the bolt to unlock the door.

He had fair skin, his forehead and cheeks slightly sunburnt, with a full head of curly red hair. His black shirt was smeared with dust and his light brown pants were frayed in various parts.

I glanced over at Amalia, trying to read what was about to happen, but the look on her face this time was one I'd never seen before. I hadn't heard or seen her since I'd woken up what must have been at least a week ago and the faint sliver of light she had shining in her green eyes last time seemed to be fading away, a looming darkness in its stead.

"*Wa tla9na, Sabiri*[1]," the man behind snapped in my native language, urging the redhead to rush.

I recognized his voice from a few days ago when he'd been with Amalia when I'd woken up from my slumber. He

---

1. Hurry up, Sabiri.

was also the same man who'd called my name during the ambush that killed Dale.

By the look of it and the fact that he knew my name, he must be someone high-ranked because my father would never tell anyone about me unless it was absolutely necessary. If he was, then I must have brushed paths with him when I was younger. But I'd locked away a lot of that time as far as I could at the back of my mind.

As soon as the lock was unfasted, he walked in leisurely, Amalia following close behind. The young redhead scurried behind them, dropping the clasp to the ground in his wake, the clinking sound filling the heavy silence looming over us.

They stopped a mere few feet in front of me, while the boy stayed behind them, his hands clasped in front of him as he fidgeted in place. He didn't have any weapons on him, but I'd noticed the tall one had a silver Beretta tucked in the back of his pants when he came in. And I knew Amalia had a least one weapon.

"Ah, Noah. It's good to see you," the tall man greeted me as he drew closer, but the smile he gave me didn't reach his eyes.

"It seems you know my name, but I don't have the displeasure of knowing yours." My gaze didn't falter from his as I cataloged where everyone was to figure out if there was any way I could make a run for it.

He peered over at Amalia and let out a laugh that grated against every single one of my nerves. "He's got jokes," he said, then turned his attention back on me. "My name isn't really of importance, but if you must really know, I'm Hamza. Pleasure to meet you." He held out his hand for me to shake as if this was a normal introduction between two people.

My gaze flicked to his outstretched hand before meeting him head-on again. "Can't say I feel the same."

He dropped his hand back to his side and his jaw clenched, but he quickly recovered and let out another snicker. "Bensaid," he called over his shoulder, still staring at me. "You didn't tell me he was funny."

She gave him a non-committal shrug, not that he could even see it.

"What do you want?" I snarled.

"Can't I just pay a visit to my favorite prisoner?" he mocked, the lines around his mouth tightening as he toyed with a golden band on his ring finger that I hadn't noticed before but one I would recognize anywhere.

For generations, whoever led the Barrera cartel gave his right-hand man, his most trusted advisor, the same ring that was engraved with the family crest—the face of an Atlas lion.

We might not exist, but we'll always make sure to be heard.

I used to think that the statement was powerful and I took pride in being a part of something like that, until I discovered what really lay underneath the beast my father had created when I was thrown into the throes of his world.

I also recognized it because it used to belong to my uncle Reda.

"What is it that you really came in here for?" I demanded again, my tone harsher this time.

He was wasting my time and I didn't have the energy to spend it talking to an asshole who was on a power trip. I knew I was pushing his buttons and that he didn't like the challenge in my tone, but I decided to keep going, hoping he'd make a rash decision that would give me an opportunity.

I raised a brow. "What is it, *Hamza*? Scared?" I challenged.

He chuckled darkly and inched closer, close enough that his next words were whispered low, only for me to hear. "You've changed quite a bit"—he paused, coming even closer, and I could see he had my name right between his teeth—"Little Barrera."

My lips curled up in disgust at the condescending nick-name one of my father's soldiers used to give me when he wasn't around, to remind me how much of a failure I was to my father.

Flashes of a face that used to visit me in my cell at night to beat me black and blue whenever my father was too busy to do it himself flooded my mind. Then recognition clicked at who Hamza was.

Acid pooled in my veins as I pushed the images out and looked out of the corner of my eye to assess Amalia's reaction, realizing she hadn't heard him.

I would have to eventually tell her, but my father's name wasn't something I was particularly proud of.

Hamza backed away, a satisfied smile curling his lips into a sneer. Fury pounded through every inch of my body, decimating any phantom pain that remained from what he'd inflicted on me all those years ago.

I launched off the wall as the rage took over. Grabbing his collar, I brought him toward me and swung, landing my fist into his nose. He spluttered back, cursing as he held his bleeding nose. Blood seeped through his fingers and landed on his pristine white shirt, spoiling its front.

I went in for another punch but didn't make it far. I was jerked backward, an arm wrapping around my throat and squeezing. I moved my palms up to wrap them around my opponent's forearm and dropped down to haul them over my shoulder.

They landed in front of me with a loud thud, and our gazes clashed.

Amalia.

Before I could fully register it was her, her foot hit me hard in the ribs, sending an electric shock through the left side of my body. I ignored the pain and grabbed her foot to push her away, but she retaliated by uppercutting me in the stomach.

I didn't want to hit her, but she was making it difficult not to defend myself.

She exploited my hesitation to her advantage and used the flat of her hand to smack me in the ear. My balance became unsteady from the impact and I tumbled forward, my palms landing on the ground to steady me.

My vision faltered for a moment from the impact to my eardrum. I blinked to right it and looked at her just in time to see her knuckles aiming for my jaw. I stopped it before she could make contact and grabbed her wrist to maneuver it behind her back, holding it there. Then I tugged her back to my front, my arm squeezing her throat as I put her in the same position she had me just a few minutes ago.

"I wouldn't do that if I were you," she choked through gritted teeth, her nails from her free hand clawing at my skin. She brought her elbow back, hitting right on my bruised ribs to try to get me to release my hold on her.

I brought my lips against her ears and huffed out, "You aren't giving me much of a choice."

The sound of a gun going off resounded against the walls, a bullet ricocheting against stone and dust falling over our heads from the impact.

"Enough," a loud voice boomed.

I eased my hold on her windpipe as we both looked up to find Hamza holding his gun in his hand, the barrel aimed at the ceiling. Was he crazy? The bullet could have hit her or the kid from the rebound.

"Don't make me aim the next one at you," he added, streaking blood covering the bottom half of his face.

I shifted my gaze to the kid, finding him tucked in a corner, trembling from the commotion we caused.

Now I felt bad. It wasn't technically my fault, but the

last thing I wanted was to scar someone with more bad memories than I was sure he'd already experienced if he worked in any position under my father.

So I withdrew my hold against Amalia. I was only letting her go because I felt pity for the kid, but otherwise, I would have kept going. I hadn't sparred with her in a long time and I would be lying if I said I hadn't missed it.

She didn't immediately move, instead reaching for her boot. I only saw a fleeting silver reflection before a sharp pain radiated across my thigh. I looked down at my leg to notice a tear in my black pants, blood blooming from the small cut she'd just inflicted.

I stared at her, stunned, because she just fucking *cut* me.

She got up and sheathed the blade back into the side of her black boot. She brushed her hands on her front. "Let's go," she commanded. Hamza opened his mouth to say something, but she stopped him. "I said, let's go," she repeated, her tone more demanding as she walked out of my cell.

He looked over at me, his nostrils flaring. "I came here to get you a nicer living arrangement, but guess you need a little more time in here."

I laughed dryly. "I'd rather stay here, but thank you so much for your consideration."

He pointed his bloody finger at me. "You're lucky to be who you are," he snarled, then turned his attention to Sabiri. "Lock him up."

"*Wakha, Sidi Hamza[2],*" Sabiri replied, his voice barely above a whisper

On his way out, Hamza grunted and kicked the bucket I'd used to relieve myself over the past few days. I'd placed the tray on top of it to contain the smell, but they both toppled over, urine and the slop of beans mixing and spreading across the wall and on the floor.

The stench of ammonia caught my nostrils and I scrunched my nose, brushing a finger underneath my nose to help alleviate the burning smell. Sabiri shuffled to put the lock on the door and lock it with a key before he hurried toward them.

Once they shut the steel door, I groaned and scooted myself toward the back wall. I rested my back against it and reached for the hem of my shirt, tore a piece from it and tied it around my thigh.

All I had to hope for now was that it didn't get infected before I got out of here.

I was furious that she'd cut me but still impressed none-theless. She never backed down from striking my nerves and I liked it, I always did. That's what was so frustrating about her.

No matter how many times I'd told myself that I had to stay away, it just pushed me to want more.

---

2. Yes, Mr. Hamza.

Noah

CHAPTER 8

PAST

EVERY TIME I POUNDED ON THE HEAVY BAG, MY KNUCKLES stung from the cuts already there with how often I came here at night over the last eight weeks to clear my mind.

No one ever used this room since it was a little far out at the back of the main building, which meant it was perfect for me.

The sound of my fists hitting the leather, over and over again, echoed through the room and provided a short relief for my mind, but it had never been loud enough to drown out my thoughts.

But at least, the harder I hit, the more occupied my hands were from doing something stupid like sending her a text message—her number was in her file—or knocking on her door.

I kept pummeling my fist against the punching bag, letting this *craving* I had for her melt into anger. Anger at these foreign and *intense* emotions Amalia stirred in me. At the confusion I felt between the urge to both push her farther away yet at the same time wanting to grab her face between my palms and crush my lips to hers every time she walked into the room.

Anger that I wanted a woman I shouldn't want.

I sounded like a broken record and it felt like she might be the only solution to fixing this problem I seemed to have. I shouldn't be this obsessed with someone when I barely spent any time with them.

Maybe I needed her to reject me or say something that would shut whatever malfunctioning gate of emotions she appeared to have fucking turned on. This proximity I had to her every day was not good for me because it kept making me realize one thing I didn't want to think too much about.

I didn't want to feel whatever the hell I was feeling for her. It wasn't even because of her, she was… perfect.

But I wasn't, I was…

Tainted.

Besides, this wasn't healthy. I meant, really. This *feeling* distracted me in class because I could barely stop myself from looking at her any chance I got. And I didn't get distracted.

That kind of thing didn't happen to me. I was clear-minded and focused.

Yet she fucked that up too and even the hardest workout

bag didn't seem to stop the frustration I felt against not being able to fix whatever issue I seemed to be experiencing.

"Agh," I screamed in frustration as I picked up the pace, letting loose a cascade of punches on the heavy bag, each strike harder than the last.

The blaring ring of a phone sounded throughout the room, temporarily pulling me out of my chaotic thoughts. I threw one last punch and briefly collapsed against the leather before backing away from it, shaking out my hands.

I then walked over to the wooden bench where my duffel bag was sitting and grabbed my phone. I answered on the third ring, not looking at the caller ID. "Brown," I answered, annoyance still coursing through my veins.

"Is that any way to greet your mother, Noah?" My mother lightly scolded me over the line and the sound of her voice reminded me of how much I'd missed it.

I closed my eyes and sighed. *"Lo siento, mamá[1].* I didn't know it was you. Everything okay?" Her voice sounded a little weaker than usual, but I brushed it off because knowing her, she was probably overworking herself at the diner even though she didn't have to.

"Does a mother need something to be wrong to call her dear son?" I could hear the smile in her voice and it calmed whatever restlessness that was drowning me.

Nothing settled me more than hearing her voice. That

---

1. I'm sorry, mom.

was my mother's superpower. No matter how far apart we were or how long it had been since we'd last talked, she always soothed whatever I was feeling.

"No, but it's late and the middle of the week, so I just wanted to make sure."

"I'm fine, baby. Now talk to me about you. I miss you," she said and guilt gnawed at me. It had been a few weeks since I'd last called her, but with training, it completely escaped me to do so. She spoke again. "How's the new class? Are you nice to them? I told you many times not to be too hard on them. They need kindness too, baby." The lilt in her accent grew stronger with each question. It always happened when she got too excited or she was scolding me.

" *Yo también te echo de menos, mamá*[2]. They're fine and I *am* nice. How are you? Will you finally take me up on my offer and retire?"

My beautiful mother, who was already in her late fifties, didn't need to work. I'd told her too many times to count now that I'd be more than happy to take care of her, but she refused to retire for some odd reasons.

I'm not too old to work. Your mama still got it, she'd say whenever I'd bring it up. One thing about my mother was, you couldn't argue with her. I'd tried every once in a while even if I knew her response would stay the same.

But that didn't stop me from adding money to her

---

2. I miss you too, mom.

account every month without her knowledge. She probably *did* know, but she'd never mentioned it.

"Noah," she said in the tone she always used before she gave me a lecture.

I chuckled and shook my head. "Right, you still got it."

"Damn right I do, baby," she replied, laughing, and I joined her. I didn't laugh very often, but when you had a mother like mine, her laugh was too infectious not to join her.

"How is it at the diner?" I asked as I sat on the bench, grabbing a towel from my bag to wipe the sweat off my face and neck.

My mother and I had moved back to Morocco from Colombia a few weeks before I turned twenty after I'd gotten an offer to train at the Academy. I'd always refused before because I hadn't wanted to leave my mother behind or ask her to give up the life she'd built for us there to come back to a place that held so many bad memories for both of us.

The agent that kept knocking on my door, Theo Alvarez (also known as the biggest pain in my ass), had been so relentless that I'd eventually agreed under two conditions— that the Bureau guaranteed my mother's safety and that she could go back to a place we'd made home whenever she wanted.

So they'd moved her into a small town right next to Bemes and she'd been working at the same local diner ever since.

"Oh, you know, it's been the same for the last thirteen years."

"Right, but make sure you get enough rest. You always tend to work too much," I tell her, worried.

"I'm fine. Besides, I could say the same about you, Mr. I never take vacations."

I stifled a laugh at the nickname and held my hand up even though she couldn't see it. "That's fair."

She was quiet for a moment, but I knew her too well to know that her next line of question wouldn't be something I was particularly fond of. "Now tell me, when will you give me any grandbabies? I'm not getting any younger, you know? If you need help finding someone, I could—"

"*No, mamá.* No fixing me up, *por favor*[3]. You know I don't have time to date."

Her heavy sigh told me exactly how she felt about my answer.

Besides, it wasn't like I could tell her about the girl who occupied every inch of my mind because I shouldn't be thinking about her that often.

I was about to change topics when I felt the heat of a heavy gaze on the back of my neck.

I looked over my shoulder to find Amalia standing right by the entrance. She looked surprised to see me here.

"Mom, I have to go. I'll call you later, okay?" I told my mother in Spanish as I kept my gaze on Amalia.

---

3. No, mom. No fixing me up, please.

"All right, baby. Visit sometime, ¿*Vale*[4]? I love you."

"Love you too," I replied before hanging up.

I pocketed my phone into the side pocket of my bag and brought a leg over the bench, straddling it. "Has anyone ever told you it's inappropriate to eavesdrop on someone's conversation?" I asked her, clenching my fingers against the wooden edge.

"It isn't really eavesdropping if I didn't know you'd be here," she said, removing her shoes and placing them inside near the door.

I groaned internally. "What are you even doing here?" I muttered, watching her cross the rubber-matted floor and make her way toward the heavy bags where I just was.

A small frown appeared on her face. She pulled white hand wraps from the side pocket of her bottoms and began weaving them through her fingers. "It's a gym. What do you think I'm here for?"

"You *shouldn't* be here," I snapped before I could stop myself. "It's way beyond curfew. You're supposed to be in your quarters."

She shrugged and pressed a fist to the bag. "I was never really one to follow rules."

"I can tell," I murmured under my breath.

She ignored me and gave the heavy bag a few testing jabs before shifting her weight and picking up her pace.

---

4. Okay?

How she even had the energy to do this after the day I'd put them through was beyond me.

Amalia's heavy breathing slowly filled the quiet room and before I could stop myself, my gaze wandered over her body. Her hair was pulled back into a ponytail and she wore a simple black workout set, but anything on her could never be *just* simple.

Her shorts did nothing to hide the delicious curvature of her ass, one I hadn't gotten to see that night, and her top gave me a glimpse of her luscious breasts that I would give anything to play with one more time.

My eyes fixated on a droplet of sweat that trailed from her neck and down to her cleavage, disappearing underneath her bra. All I could think of right at this moment was what her skin would taste like.

I wouldn't put it past myself to get on my knees and beg for it because I still dreamed about her taste every night, despite trying my hardest not to. But could you really blame me when she looked and tasted as divine as she did?

Something about her always seemed to capture all my senses and held me hostage. I still couldn't put my finger on what it was, but I knew it was past simple physical attraction. Because it wasn't just that. It felt like something bigger pulling me to her like she was an orbit and I simply couldn't help but gravitate toward it.

"Are you going to keep staring at me or…?" she asked without looking at me, landing a jab against the bag.

Shit.

I snapped back to reality and chastised myself. I heard her chuckle as I snatched my gaze away. Embarrassment burned my skin and I reached inside my bag to grab my shirt that I'd taken off earlier. I slipped it over my head and grasped my bag, moving to leave, when an irritated groan came from her.

I raised my gaze to find her smacking a palm against the leather in frustration before she shook it off and got into position again. She started whatever sequence she was doing before again, only for me to quickly realize she was going through one of the more complex combinations I taught in class a few days ago.

She was executing it perfectly, until she got to the trickiest part and missed. She stabilized the bag with both of her hands and did it again, only to slip again at the same place.

I should leave, I tried telling myself as I watched her do it over and over again, her irritation growing every time she failed to complete the pattern.

I cursed myself and stalked over to her. I stopped a few steps behind her to avoid getting hit and without over-thinking it, I pressed one hand on her back, the other to her stomach.

She immediately tensed under my fingertips, stopping mid-strike. She stabilized the bag before whirling around. Her fist was aiming for my face, but I grabbed it just in time to stop it from colliding with my nose. Then I lowered it and let it go just as quickly.

"What are you doing?" Amalia asked bitterly, glaring at me.

"You're doing it wrong, so I'm helping you," I countered.

"I didn't ask for your help," she fired back.

"But you need it," I replied, confused at her animosity. I moved toward her again, but she stepped back, her back colliding with the bag behind her.

"I don't *need* you."

I wanted to laugh at how absurd her aversion to my help was. Of course she didn't *need* me. She was great, better than most people I'd ever encountered while doing this job. But she needed to be corrected if she wanted to do the combo perfectly.

That's all I was trying to do.

Frustration chafed beneath my skin. "God, you're so stubborn. Why do you always refuse to be helped?" I asked. Why couldn't she just let me give her advice when she clearly could use it. She did the same in class.

She clucked her tongue. "Ah, right," she drawled. "Because trying to help me is taunting me and *yelling* at me more than you do anyone else in the class since I got here. Helping me is making everyone underestimate me from how many times you correct me in front of everyone for the tiniest mistakes I make."

Taken aback, I frowned. "I don't yell at you," I started, but she crossed her arms over her chest, giving me a "you're kidding right?" look. I ignored her and continued,

"I simply correct you because even the tiniest mistake, as you so call it, could end in you being hurt." I didn't know when or how my voice had grown louder, but the echoes of my last few words boomed around us.

I thought she knew I was harder on her because I saw the tremendous potential she had and I'd rather focus my attention on her than waste my time on people who didn't care about this as much as she seemed to.

I took a deep breath in, reined in my exasperation, and looked at her. I held her eyes, unrelenting. "Just let me help you, *please.*"

She waited a moment before letting out a heavy sigh. "Fine," she grunted out as she faced the heavy bag again.

My heartbeat drummed in my ears as I wrapped my hands over both of hers, her back now flush against my front, strands of her hair tickling the tip of my nose. She sucked in a sharp breath, which only brought her closer.

I couldn't have fucking put myself in a worse position if I tried. Not only that, but my brain insisted on focusing on how her skin felt against mine again, how she fitted perfectly against me.

I breathed in to calm my overspeeding heart, but this up close, I caught an overwhelming whiff of her musky vanilla scent mixed with her sweat, sending my senses into overdrive.

God, I'm a fucking mess.

Swallowing hard, I smothered the effect she had on me just enough to actually help her like I'd intended to. I proceeded to talk her through each part of the combination, teaching her tricks to make it easier to land every punch with precision.

Once I was done, I reluctantly let go of her and stepped back a few steps. I jutted my chin forward, indicating for her to do it on her own this time. She nodded, got into position, and started the sequence.

When she got to the part where she usually made a mistake, she landed the first hit successfully and completed it almost to perfection.

"Better. Now do it again," I ordered.

She peered at me over her shoulder and opened her mouth to say something, but I repeated myself before she could. "Again, Amalia."

She groaned and turned around, following my command. She puffed out heavy breaths as she went through the motions again, improving each time.

We'd been at this for the last hour and it was almost midnight when she finally landed every hit exactly how I'd just taught her. I smiled to myself, a hint of pride filling my chest. "That's it, Amalia. Just like that."

Suddenly, she finished the set in a hurry and turned around. "All right, I'm done for the night," she panted, her chest heaving. She started undoing the wrappings around her hands and moved past me, but I didn't let her get far.

"Hey, what's wrong?" I asked, grabbing her wrist and pulling her in.

She kept her head down and avoided my gaze. *Something she never does.*

I grabbed her chin between my thumb and forefinger, lifting her eyes to meet mine. There was a flash of something in her eyes, but she averted her gaze before I could decipher it.

"N-nothing, I'm just tired. Like you said, it's past curfew, so I should go," she stammered out, yanking her wrist out of my hold and hurrying away from me again.

Shit, did I say something wrong?

"Amalia, wait," I said, reaching for her once again, but my foot must have caught on something and I tumbled to the ground, inadvertently bringing her down with me.

I wrapped my arms around her body, cradling her into me to shield her from the fall as I landed on my back. The sudden impact drove the air from my lungs and I closed my eyes, groaning internally.

Of course shit like this happens to me.

When air finally filled my lungs again, I immediately asked, "Fuck, are you okay?"

She hummed and slightly nodded against my chest, soothing my worries that I hadn't caused her to be hurt. For a mere second, her head rested against my chest as we lay there to catch our breaths. But when I finally loosened my grip around her, she pulled back, her hands pushing against my chest to help her up.

Her ponytail had slightly come undone over the last hour and loose strands fell over her face as she looked down at me. Her face was only inches away from mine, the tips of her hair brushed against my skin. My right hand came up, pushing a few stray locks behind her ear while I rested my other one on her thigh.

More of her face was revealed to me, which was when I noticed how *flushed* she was. I would have brushed it off to the intense workout she'd just had if I hadn't known what she looked like when she was turned on.

Is that why she wanted to leave?

She raised her gaze to meet mine and in an instant, everything around us faded, my awareness honing in on the glint in her eyes. I could make out every speck of gold in her green irises and my breath caught in my throat at how fucking pretty she was.

My heart increasingly slammed faster against my ribcage, to the point of reaching unhealthy levels. As if my body was operating of its own accord, I slowly, *gently*, trailed my fingertips from the side of her face down her neck while maintaining her gaze.

When she didn't stop me, I followed the curvature of her exposed collarbone and kept going down, tracing the outside of her right breast. My thumb featherly brushed over her nipple that was straining against the fabric, like it demanded my full attention.

She shivered under my touch and I continued my path down until my hand landed on her other thigh. My eyes darted to her lips and she must have leaned down further because they were now only a breath away.

It vaguely registered in the back of my mind that this was the second time since I learned she was a student of mine that we'd found ourselves in this position. But this time, I didn't want to pull away.

I wanted to bury myself in her and remember what she felt like.

She opened her mouth to say something, but no words came out. She licked her lips and tried again, my name coming out of her mouth in a whisper this time.

A low growl slipped past my lips at the sound and my gaze darted back to her eyes to see her studying me. The previous glint I'd noticed in her eyes earlier was now replaced with a hunger that I was sure matched mine.

I pushed up and pressed my lips to hers tentatively, her eyes closing at the contact. When her lips didn't move against mine, I pulled back, flames of shame that I'd misread the situation licking at my chest. "I shouldn't have, I'm sor—"

Dazed, she opened her eyes, leaving the words stuck in my throat because in the next moment, her hands grabbed the sides of my face and she kissed me.

She was kissing me, her soft lips moving over mine. I felt an instant rush of relief that she wanted the same. It felt… overwhelming.

Kissing her felt like the wind had gotten knocked out of me, like the earth spun on its axis as our lips met and I was slammed onto my back, the taste of her driving the air from my lungs.

Yet simultaneously, it felt like she breathed life back into me.

I slid my hands around her back and up to her neck, sliding my fingers into her hair and tugging her closer. I licked the seam of her lips, coaxing them further open, and with every swipe of tongue, she rocked her body against mine.

It took everything I had in me not to throw her on the floor, undress, and fuck her until the only thing she could say was my name over and over again in ecstasy.

Lick her everywhere until all I could taste for days was her. Then do it all over again because I knew that once would never be enough. I'd known it that night two months ago and the thought was only being reinforced with the way her sweet moans filled every nook and cranny of my brain.

"Amalia," I groaned into her mouth.

Her teeth nipped at my lips as she breathed out a, "What?" before kissing me again.

"We should—" I said against her lips between kisses. "We should stop."

Her lips paused on mine and when I opened my eyes to look into hers, a frown appeared between her brows. Her bruised lips turned down as she lifted her face away from mine.

Before she could misinterpret my words, I moved my hand to cup her cheek, my thumb brushing over her puffed up lips, aiming to replace the scowl there with a smile.

"Let me be clear," I said, moving my thumb up to gently swipe over her cheekbone.

My eyes flickered between hers as I finally confessed what I'd been denying myself since I met her. Fuck the consequences, I'd deal with them later as long as it meant I could have her. Even if it was just for a little while.

"I want you. In more ways than one." My hand moved to the back of her head, my fingers gripping her nape and bringing her head down. I pressed a kiss to her lips before pulling away but kept our lips a mere breath away. "I want to see you. I want to fuck you again and again," I whispered against her lips before nipping at her bottom one and kissing it again. She inhaled a sharp breath and her chest moved up and down, up and down. "But I want to take my time, and not on a gym floor."

She let out a small laugh and it felt like the greatest reward to draw a smile from her, because *God* she was a fucking sight when she smiled.

She groaned. "Fine, when you say it like that," she said before placing a brief kiss on my lips. She then pushed herself up, removing her weight from my body, and I instantly missed her on top of me.

She stood and I rolled to my knees in front of her. My hands trailed up her bare legs and to her hips, holding her. My lips hovered over her front and I looked up, locking my gaze with hers and watching a blush bloom onto her face.

"It'll be worth the wait, I promise," I whispered against

the fabric of her biker shorts before moving my mouth upward and pressing a kiss to her covered hip bone.

Then I stood, my body brushing against hers in the process. I stole one last chaste kiss on my way up—I couldn't help myself—then put a healthy distance between us before I went back on my words and had my way with her right here, right now.

I'd barely gotten a taste and I was already insatiable.

She moved to grab her things and I walked over to the bench to grab mine. When I turned around, her eyes were cast downward, her irises slightly widening.

I adjusted myself in my gym shorts and marched over to her. "Eyes are up here, pretty girl," I teased, something I rarely did anymore, and wrapped my arms over her shoulder, bringing her into my side.

She chuckled and smacked my chest as I pressed a kiss to the top of her head. Once outside, I kissed her for a few more minutes before we parted ways. She made her way back to the facility where her dorms were while I walked to my apartment situated a few blocks down the road from the Academy.

After I showered and lay in bed attempting to fall asleep, all I could think of was when the next time I'd get to have her all to myself would be.

Amalia

CHAPTER 9

PRESENT

I'D BEEN SITTING ON THE UPPER FLOOR OF ZAKARIA'S penthouse for the last fifteen minutes, patiently waiting for him to show up so that I could quench my boredom.

I'd landed in Azilah two days ago after Barrera had insisted I visit the farms he owned in the Anfa mountains, which were east-south of the city. He'd ordered me to check on the progress of our products, making sure harvest would be ready on time and that none of our farmers had stolen from us like what had happened during the last reaping.

I'd tried to argue that I'd just been there last month and me visiting again would be pointless, but he'd brushed my valid point and just raised his voice, saying that I was under his payroll.

I would have reminded him that I hadn't seen a *rial*[1] since I'd started working for him, most of my money coming from the stash the Agency had given me when I started and the deals I'd made over the years with smaller drug dealers on the side to keep Barrera's cartel actually functioning.

But I'd decided against it, not wanting to bother having to hear his pestiferous voice grate on my nerves any longer.

I'd noticed Barrera had been more tense recently, but I still couldn't fully figure out why. At first, I'd thought it was a result from the loss of his only son, Matheo, but Barrera wasn't sentimental.

He'd lost his wife, Faouzia, two years ago and had barely flinched when I'd given him the news. All he'd said was to make sure she'd be properly buried and to find a nice place next to her parents for her grave.

I'd grown accustomed to his reckless decision-making process over the years, but he'd always at least consulted with Hamza before making any final decisions.

Now, especially over the last two weeks, his decisions had increasingly become more impulsive and he'd been equally more trigger happy than usual with anyone who even dared look at him the wrong way.

Come to think of it, both Barrera and Hamza seemed to

---

1. Old Moroccan currency. It was used between 1880-1921, but the word is still commonly used when describing money whether in stores when purchasing items or when conversing with others about money.

be a lot more on edge than usual and that asshole Hamza seemed too familiar with our prisoner.

I knew Noah had been on the case investigating the cartel years ago, but although he'd gotten close, he'd never been able to overthrow Barrera's operations after his partner and his partner's wife died in a tragic fire.

My gut had always told me that nothing about that fire seemed accidental, but the incident had happened before my time at the Agency. The files were sealed so even when I'd tried to access the files on the investigation of their death before going undercover, I'd been denied access.

I had clearance for everything Noah and Agent Aguerd had compiled, except the investigation on the fire. I'd brushed it off to bureaucracy, but maybe I should've dug deeper.

Barrera's change in behavior might have been because we'd taken an Agent prisoner, but it wasn't like this was the first time we'd had that happen. Now, the others were either much easier to turn if we'd made their pockets a little heavier or I'd been simply tasked to get rid of them after a few days.

Which Barrera hadn't asked me to do yet, something that had never happened in the three years I'd worked as his enforcer. I hadn't asked any questions and it was a slight relief since killing him wouldn't bode well for me when I went back to my position at the Agency at the end of my assignment.

Are you sure that's the only reason? My mind deadpanned.

I pushed the mocking remark away and walked over to the banister. I leaned my forearms against it, my dagger hanging from my fingertips. It swayed from side to side as my eyes scanned over the space to make sure nothing was out of place.

On the left of the all-white minimalistic marble kitchen, plump cushions dressed in warm and rich tones, an array of brown and gold pillows to match were atop long wooden frames arranged around three sides with intricate designs carved onto the front and side panels.

A rectangular low brass table stood in the middle, two matching smaller side tables sitting on each side of the center segment where the other two shorter sofas met. A few ottomans were placed at the end of each side segment, their tones matching the draping of the sofas.

A large overhead gold brass lantern, adorned with hand-crafted details to match the other elements in the room, hung from the high ceiling, cloaking the ground floor in warm patterned shadows.

I'd studied the floor plans and Zakaria's routine over the last few months every time I visited the cannabis fields. I'd hacked into his security systems so that I could access his cameras and make sure he wasn't present when I came over to learn the ins and outs of his apartment. I also didn't want to bother picking the lock every time I stopped by.

My gaze flitted over the mantel to the large brass clock

that matched the tables in the living room, to see I had seven minutes left until he came home. Which still gave me plenty of time to do what I came here for and catch my flight back to the compound.

I was technically in the region for official business, but since I had some extra time to spare, I'd decided to pay Alaoui's underboss a little visit to teach him a lesson about hindering my shipments. So once my scheduled visit had been over, I'd driven the eighty-six miles that separated our territories.

If I had been anyone else, Adil Alaoui's men would have flagged me the second I crossed over and hunted me down, but since my role in Barrera's cartel was to remain anonymous, it worked quite well in my favor.

Besides, nobody would suspect a woman to be the one behind all the bodies the Barrera cartel left behind. Well, at least in recent years.

Right on time, footsteps approached the front door and I walked into his large dressing room. After the jingle of his keys plopped down on the entryway table, I began counting the seventy-two steps he would take to his bedroom to shower after his time at L'Oasis, a cabaret he religiously visited every Wednesday.

I waited for the sound of his footsteps to hit the clay curved staircase on the left side of the living room, but instead, the echo of a thud and Zakaria's groan reverberating against the tiles made its way up to where I was on the upper floor.

My brows pulled together, confused.

What the hell is that?

I moved to reach for my back pocket, but before I could grab my phone to see what was happening downstairs from the cameras I'd installed there on my initial visit here, I heard him move again, finally making his way upstairs.

I watched him closely from the slight gap formed between the ajar door of his walk-in closet and its hinges. Zakaria stripped from his tan suit, throwing the discarded clothes somewhere to the side of the room until every inch of his naked body was exposed, his flaccid cock dangling as he turned to admire himself in the large mirror next to the bathroom door.

I rolled my eyes and reined in the bile burning my throat on its way up. *Pathetic.*

He then walked into the bathroom and closed the door behind him. The sound of his shower stream came on and I took the opportunity to take my phone out to see what he'd dropped downstairs.

Maybe it was cargo that I could take as a bonus payment from my visit. He didn't care about having his men steal from us, so why not repay him the same courtesy.

Pulling up the cameras, I tapped on the screen that showed his living room.

You have got to be fucking kidding me.

Instead of a duffle bag, most likely filled with bags of cocaine like I'd presumed, a man with his hands bound behind his back was lying unconscious on his side like he'd been carelessly tossed. Half of his body rested on the patterned tile floor while the other half was right on the edge of the rug.

The man in question couldn't be older than mid-twenties. His clothes were torn and disheveled, cuts and fresh blood painting almost the entirety of his body. Black matted hair stuck to his bronzed skin, a large bleeding gash right above one of his bushy brows peeking through his dark strands.

The shower cut off and I brought my attention back to the task at hand. I pocketed my phone and grabbed my dagger. Steam billowed into the room as Zakaria cracked the bathroom door open and I padded into position, ready and waiting.

He was completely oblivious to my presence as he stepped inside the closet with a towel fastened around his waist, so when he walked past me, I brought my dagger down hard and sliced against his right Achilles tendon.

His screams pierced my ears, and the corner of my lips briefly quirked up in satisfaction as I relished the pretty sound. I never thought I'd enjoy someone's suffering, but being in this field for so long, I'd learned to enjoy it instead of dreading it, especially when they came from someone who'd earned their fate.

"*Wa n3al din moh*[2]," he shouted as he fell to the ground, crying out in agony as he reached for his feet. Then

---

2. Ah, motherfucker.

he brought his hands up to his eyesight and his screams hitched to a higher note.

I took a moment to savor the look of horror casting over his face at the sight of the blood dripping down the sides of his hands, trailing down his forearms.

Then I stood, arms at my sides. My knife dangled from my fingers, blood dripping from the tip and adding itself to the fountain gushing from Zakaria's severed heel.

He lowered his hands when he took notice of my presence and when he found me staring at him, his facial expression morphed into surprise.

Most likely from finding a woman at the other end of his misery. That look on men's faces when that happened never got old.

"Who the fuck are you?" he yelled between angry sobs, trying and failing to stand up.

"My name is none of your concern," I said quietly. "What's important here actually concerns *you*."

"Do you fucking know who I am, *kah*—" I stepped on his injury, cutting him off, and an agonizing scream filled the air, replacing his demeaning insult.

I shook my head and cleaned the bloodied tip of my boot against a clean part of his towel.

Men and their inflated sense of worth to call a woman by her name.

I approached and loomed over him, noticing the shift in his eyes. He was preparing himself to attack me, but before he made the grave mistake of underestimating me, I pressed my foot over his throat and leaned down so my weight could bear onto him.

Tears loomed in his eyes from the pressure and I dragged the tip of my knife over his face until it found the hollow part of his cheek. I titled my head and raised a brow, grinning. "I do know who you are, but why would that matter when I have you at *my* mercy?" I asked mockingly.

His words were muffled since my foot was still crushing his windpipe.

"Oh yeah, sorry about that." I shifted my foot to relieve some of the pressure but pressed the tip of the blade harder against his skin. "You were saying."

"What the hell do you want?" he spat out.

"God, thank you so much for asking," I deadpanned. "It's just you keep stealing from me and I thought I'd stop by to say hello and introduce myself so you remember not to do it again because I quite hate it."

"I never fucking stole from you," he grunted, tears free-falling down his cheek and onto the side of my dagger.

"Here's another thing I hate: liars," I confessed, making a shallow cut on his cheek to test the tensility of his skin.

"*Ya rabi*[3], I'm not fucking lying, you crazy bitch," he screeched. "I don't even fucking know you."

My chest twisted violently with annoyance. "See, actually," I drawled, pressing my sharp dagger a little more into

---

3. Oh, god.

his skin. "We have a friend in common that tells me you're the one who's been stealing weapons from my shipments."

His eyes swam with confusion, so I added, "The name Mehdi ring a bell?"

His pupils dilated and his nostrils flared at the name, a sense of understanding washing over him. He cursed in Arabic under his breath.

"Ah, so you do know who I work for," I stated.

"Listen, you *bitch*," he scoffed in disgust, attempting to glare at me through his pain. "If Alaoui finds out you're on our territory, he'll—"

I cut him off. "He'll what? Kill me? Gosh, I'm so scared, especially when you have no clue who I am or how to find me. And you know if you step one foot on Barrera's territory, he'll unleash a war against your pathetic little cartel before you can ask God for mercy."

He pressed his lips together.

That's what I thought.

"So next time your foolish mind decides to hijack my shipments and steal cargo that isn't fucking yours, think of the gift I'm about to give you so that you remember not to lie when asked a simple fucking question."

I technically wasn't allowed to kill freely unless ordered to since there was a system in place, some old rule to keep some sort of peace. Although I wasn't a stickler for rules, I knew I couldn't kill him since terminating another cartel's underboss would only create drama.

So I did the next best thing I could do that would most

likely only leave me with a harsh warning not to do it again.

With that, I pulled my other hand up and gripped his jaw to steady him. He trashed under me and jerked forward, but before he reached me, I slid my dagger from one of his cheeks to the other, cutting through the skin and muscle and carving until the line of his lips extended closer to his temporal bone.

A blood-curdling scream erupted around us as blood spurted from the gash and warm liquid poured over my skin. His pleas mixed with every curse word in *darija* you could think of faltered into quiet cries, his hands flying back and forth between his face and his heel, unsure which wound to tend to.

I sighed, my shoulders relaxing, and stood. The sight was quite enjoyable, but I didn't have time to stay over and enjoy it longer like I wished I could. So I walked back into his room and paused for a moment.

I let out a deep sigh and moved over to the pile of clothes he'd discarded earlier. I picked up his suit jacket but didn't find what I was looking for. I then made my way downstairs to the other possible place he might have left it.

I passed the still unconscious man and walked over to the entryway table. Once I found what I was looking for tossed next to his car keys, I jogged back upstairs to where he was still lying in a pool of his own blood, his towel now wide open and exposing him.

My stomach recoiled at the sight as I stood at the entry

of the closet. "Consider this a favor," I said before tossing his phone into the growing crimson pile he was wasting and walking away.

I knew I didn't have much time before his reinforcement would show up, so I quickly stopped by the bathroom to wash my hands and blade, not wanting to spend the journey home with his filth on my body.

I tied my hair again into a ponytail and changed into a clean pair of black cargo pants and a white tank top that had been in the small duffel I'd stashed under Zakaria's bed earlier while I'd waited for him to come home.

Once done, I shouldered my bag and rushed downstairs to leave. Sheer curiosity halted my steps when I reached the limp body. I crouched down, my elbows resting on my knees, inspecting his features more closely to see if it would spark any recognition.

Nothing.

I knew he didn't work for the Alaouis because I knew everyone in their ranks, both official and unofficial. So what was he doing here and what had he done to get this treatment from Zakaria?

The fact that he wasn't dead could only mean one thing. He was still valuable.

I hadn't planned on taking his prisoner, but he might have information that could be helpful. As if I'd conjured him from the depth of his consciousness, he stirred, a pained breath leaving his lips. His eyes fluttered a few times but didn't open.

They must have drugged him with something potent for him to still be under its effects. I could drag him out, but that would only attract many unwanted peering eyes that I didn't have time to deal with.

In a hurry, I reached for the side pocket of my bag and grabbed the nasal spray, then peeled it out of its package. I rolled the stranger on his back as much as I could since his hands were still tied and tilted his head back. After inserting the tip of the nozzle into one nostril, I pressed the plunger firmly to release the naloxone into his nose.

Time felt like it stretched infinitely as I waited until he fucking finally jerked awake.

"Wh-what happened?" he whispered, his voice hoarse like he hadn't used it in days.

I turned to his side and cut his restraints before helping him sit, but he wavered, so I slapped him across the face.

He brought a hand up, rubbing the reddening area. "What the fuck was that for?" he tried shouting, but his voice cracked at the end.

I opened the zipper of my duffel and grabbed a hooded jacket. "Listen, we don't have time for explanations or formalities. Put this on and get up," I ordered him, throwing the piece of clothing to him.

It fell in his lap and he looked at it, bewildered.

"Did you not hear me? Hurry or this place will be swarmed with more of the men who brought you here. I don't think you want that to happen, do you?"

His gaze met mine and a haunted look shadowed his

eyes. I didn't know what they'd put him through nor did I care, but my warning must have woken him up from his trance because he tugged the jacket over his head, wincing while doing so.

He pulled the hoodie over his head and moved to stand, only to fall to his knees.

God, I'm already regretting my decision to take him with me.

I switched my bag to my other shoulder and reached for his right arm, wrapping it behind my neck. He was much taller than my five-foot-seven frame, but I used both hands to grab his waist and helped him make another attempt at standing.

Once he was up, I hurried us out the door and to the service elevators that led to the back doors because if Zakaria had enough energy to call anyone, they'd use the main door to get in.

The service elevators needed a special key that each owner of a penthouse owned, and to my scarce luck, the building only gave one to each tenant, which I'd grabbed from his wallet on my way out.

When we made it to the back streets, we walked to where I'd parked my car and helped him inside. The overnight *3assas*[4] walked over to me and before he could say anything to try to help me pull out of my parking spot, I

---

4. Person (usually a man) who watches over cars on the street and "helps" you park them in exchange for a small fee of your choosing.

stashed a purple bill in his hands and climbed into the driver's seat.

I plugged my phone into the rental car and shot a quick text message to the pilot, warning him about the addition to our flight plan. Then I tossed it in the cup holder and beelined for the airport hangar where Barrera's private jet was waiting for me to take off.

Amalia

CHAPTER 10

PRESENT

SURPRISINGLY, THE STRANGER NEXT TO ME HADN'T SAID A word during the whole journey to the airport. I'd expected questions or some sort of resistance when we arrived, but he'd simply nodded when I ordered him to come with me.

Better the devil you don't know than the one you do, I guess.

We'd made it just in time to the hangar to board the jet and we were now about to take off. Our travel time was only for an hour, and I couldn't wait to get back. I hated being away since I couldn't keep my eyes on everything and Hamza's men always seemed to mess things up whenever I was gone.

Last time I'd left for longer than twenty-four hours, I'd found one of my prisoners, one I still needed information from, dead because they were bored and wanted something to play with.

I could only imagine what they'd done to Noah in my absence. A pit formed in my stomach at the thought, but I blamed it on not having eaten since this morning and not because I didn't want anything happening to him.

I ignored the looming thoughts whenever I dared to conjure his name and moved my gaze toward the stranger sitting in front of me. He seemed lost in thoughts, a haunted look on his features as his index finger's brittle nail scraped repeatedly against the beige leather captain's chair he was seated in.

What the fuck happened to him?

I didn't want to care, but he was so young and reminded me so much of my little brother Ángel. Of his innocence that ended up being tainted by the blows of reality.

I hadn't talked to him or my sister, Antonia, in years, but it didn't take away the fact that I still missed them.

A few months before I was set to leave, I'd drifted away, slowly leaving their calls and text messages unanswered until they showed up one day at my doorstep demanding an explanation.

I'd told them that I needed some time apart and wanted them to stop blowing up my phone. Of course they didn't buy it, so I'd brought up the only thing that I knew would get them to back off once and for all. I'd told them that I'd rekindle with our mother and that I wanted to spend more time with her, something we'd promised each other we'd never do even if she reached out and begged us on her knees until they bled.

After my admission, they'd told me that if I ever came back to my senses, then we could have a rational conversation. Until then, they didn't want to hear from me if I had any connection to the woman who'd abandoned us because she'd preferred leaving track marks on her body for a temporary high than taking care of her kids.

My siblings and I had always been close, especially after our father left us the moment Ángel was born and our mother followed a few years later when my brother turned three. The hurt from being estranged from my siblings still resurfaced on rare occasions as I lay alone in bed to catch a few hours of sleep, but I always pushed it aside, reminding myself that Amalia was supposed to be gone.

At least until all of this is over, I told myself.

But what if I'd been gone too long that the only person left after all of this was Ines? I'd ingrained myself so much into my role that I didn't know whether I was still acting or this was who I'd become and would stay as for the rest of my life.

The sound of a ringtone pulled me out of my thoughts. My brows furrowed when I noticed it wasn't the one from my regular phone. It was coming from my burner phone and only one person had access to that number, which they weren't supposed to use to call me.

I unfastened my seat belt and stood, grabbing my bag from under my seat. My burner phone kept ringing as I turned and walked toward the back of the plane, passing the beige sofas that matched the front seats where I was just seated.

The plush leather lined the right side of the plane back to the bathroom where I was headed, another set of smaller chairs facing each other with a glossy wood table in between on the opposite side.

I stepped into the bathroom and closed the door behind me. The ringing stopped for a moment, only to resume for a second time. I reached for the bottom of my bag and grabbed the small black flip phone.

"Why are you calling? You're supposed to wait until *I* call you," I answered, seething.

"Wow, it's great to hear from you too, Amalia," the voice on the other line greeted me, teasing.

He was the only one who addressed me by that and although it was rare in between to hear someone call me by my real name, it never failed to feel like driving a knife into an old wound.

I brushed it off, knowing I didn't have time for his usual candor since we were minutes away from taking off. "I'd rather not hear from you unless I choose to subject myself to it, Nassim, so do me the courtesy of not wasting my time right now."

He cleared his throat and I waited for his next words but stayed quiet for a moment, which was extremely unusual for him. His continued silence sent something I hadn't felt in a very long time traveling up my spine.

Apprehension.

I closed my eyes and sighed. My fingers pinched the bridge of my nose as I pressed him. "What is it?"

"You need to leave."

My eyes blew open. "*Leave*? What do you mean leave?" I asked, confused.

"There's been a change of plans. You have to abandon your assignment and leave Barrera's compound. I'm flying out of Cartagena tonight and need you to meet me at the safe house in two days," he stated. Gone was the lightness in his tone.

Despite being one of the most ruthless men I'd ever met, Nassim always had an annoying cheerfulness to him. Something must be really wrong if he wasn't delivering a joke with his news and even more so if he was changing our plans months ahead of the time we'd originally planned for.

Uneasiness moved and wrapped around my gut, squeezing tightly. "Why? What happened?"

"I'll tell you when we meet."

"Nassim. Now."

"Listen, I can't explain right now and I need to get things in order before my flight later. So please, Amalia, just trust me."

I fought against the retort sitting at the tip of my tongue because he'd only asked me to trust him once before and he had yet to break his promise.

The first time Nassim and I had met, I'd almost killed him.

I'd been in Bemes for an important weapon shipment collection that was coming from Colombia. Our Dutch suppliers weren't able to keep up with our high demands, so we had to look overseas for a new distributor.

Barrera had appointed Hamza to be in charge, but after months of dragging, I'd grown tired of waiting. Our cargo was growing scarce, so I'd handled it. Just like I handled most things nowadays because for a cartel that had been around for decades, they surprisingly didn't run as smoothly internally as one would have thought.

After spending some time researching and vetting other cartels, I'd made contact with Daniela, who ran the arms operation for the Aguilar cartel and we'd brokered an exclusivity deal where they'd supply us with weapons and we would let them use our ports for distribution.

It was late at night and I'd been waiting for their first shipment when a black motorcycle pulled up a few feet away. The rider had barely parked and unsaddled his seat, when I branded my gun out and shot him, grazing the outside of his thigh.

I'd adopted *shooting first and asking questions later* the moment I stepped into Ines's skin, but never to kill because they might hold crucial information that I could use.

With one hand holding his injured thigh, he'd held the other one up in surrender.

The intruder yelled something, but I couldn't hear him

146

because of his helmet. He moved to remove it and I shot the gravel at his feet. He jumped back and dropped his helmet to the ground, holding both of his hands up. "I come in peace," he grunted out.

I squinted, trying to make out his features, but because of the docks' low visibility, all I could make out at a distance was that he had mid-length dark hair because it was blowing in the wind and he wore a silver band on the ring finger of his left hand.

In my line of work, I'd become hyper aware of people's body language and I could tell even from afar that he wasn't lying, but it didn't matter. He was overstepping on private territory and I had an important package coming.

Whoever this was needed to leave, so with my gun still on him, I shouted, "Leave. This is private property."

Instead of doing as told, he straightened himself up, wincing and cursing in Spanish. Then, he said, "I have a proposition for you, Amalia."

My eyes widened and my finger moved back to the trigger. He didn't look like someone from the Agency and there was absolutely no way I'd made a mistake and blown my cover.

"You have me mistaken for someone else and I won't repeat myself. Leave or I'll shoot. And this time, it'll be at one of your vital organs."

With his hands still up, he took a step toward me. "I know who you are, Amalia, and you'll want to hear what I have to say." He took a few more steps. "My name is Nassim Taleb-Aguilar, and my father was Reda Taleb."

My ears perked up at the name because I'd recently overheard a heated argument between Barrera and Hamza, where he'd threatened his right-hand man would suffer the same fate Reda had if he went against orders another time.

When I didn't say anything right away, he took another step, closing the distance, my gun pressed against his sternum. "You can trust me."

I knew I probably shouldn't trust this stranger, but the sincerity shining in his eyes told me I should give him a chance.

And I had.

That night alone, I'd learned more about the cartel than what I'd gathered during the first year and a half I'd spent alongside Barrera. We'd only met twice again in person after that during my visits to Bemes since he lived in Cartagena and didn't want to be found out. It took some convincing on his part, but I'd eventually agreed to help him with his plan.

We'd had a few obstacles since we started working together, but the one thing he'd never wavered on was his word.

I groaned. "Fine," I finally agreed, deciding to let it go and trust him once again. The pilot's voice came on the intercom, letting us know that we were ready for takeoff. "I have to go," I said before hanging up on him and tucking the phone back into its hidden compartment.

I was fucked.

Not only would leaving be extremely difficult to do, but, to my dismay, I now had another person to account for. The other option would be to leave Noah behind, but I knew that wasn't a possibility, no matter how much I'd like to.

I had no idea yet how I would escape without bringing attention to myself, but I knew I had to figure out a plan and quickly.

I heard the hum of the plane as it slowly taxied onto the runway and exited the bathroom. On my way back to my seat, I stopped by the small refrigerator in the corner to grab two water bottles and whatever snack options were available.

The refrigerator would normally be more packed since a flight attendant was usually part of the crew when I traveled with Barrera or Hamza, but whenever I was alone, I asked for her not to be here because the one they always hired was too chatty for my taste and her incessant voice grated on my nerves.

The stranger I'd taken prisoner didn't look up when I approached, still in the same position I'd left him in, like he'd barely noticed I'd been gone this whole time. I sat down, shoved my bag back under the seat, and fastened my seat belt.

I placed the water and the two Merendina on the glossy wood table separating us, hoping the small chocolate cake hadn't expired, but his gaze was set far away, his nail still grated over the leather.

"Your seat belt," I said, hoping to get his attention, but he still didn't look my way.

The plane came to a slow stop at the start of the runway, and the pilot called "ready for departure" over the radio. The engine wired louder and the man in front of me still hadn't moved.

Frowning, I repeated myself, this time much louder, "Your seat belt."

His finger stopped its movement as he finally snapped out of whatever world he'd gotten lost in. He looked over at me, the same lost look still drowning his brown eyes.

"Yeah, sorry," he whispered. He shook his head and moved to fasten his seat belt just as the plane accelerated on the runway, taking off. His head then drifted to the side like it did when he sat down earlier, his hand moving back to where he had it before.

My next words slipped out before he could resume his patterned sequence.

"What's your name?"

My question seemed to have taken him by surprise by the way his attention snapped back to me, his eyes wide. He let out a deep sigh and said, "No one's asked me that in a long time. They called me Number 7, but my name is Gabriel."

He'd just confirmed what I'd suspected all along.

He was one of Zakaria's courier workers. The Alaouis

were known to use young men and women—anyone they could put their hands on or who owed them money—as a mule to smuggle their drugs across the Mediterranean. They used other ways to get their drugs across international borders, but this was their main method.

It was highly cost-effective for them and the easiest to stay below the radar. No matter the human cost.

It made me sick to even think of because I knew that if the mule couldn't swallow the drugs, they implanted them surgically, without anesthetic.

There were many questions I could ask him about Alaoui that would help me gain an advantage, but something deep down told me to give this kid a break from it all. Even if it was just for an hour.

Instead, I gave him a curt nod. "I'm Ines."

Something about him made me keep going, so I pushed the water bottle and one of the sponge cakes closer to him. "Eat. It isn't much, but that's all I could find."

I would try and get him real food when we landed, but it would be much harder since I couldn't show any care toward him. He was supposed to be a prisoner, not a stranded that I'd benevolently taken in.

He reached for the hood over his head and slid it off, sticking his hands into the jacket's pockets. He titled his head to one side, examining me. "Why are you being nice?"

I arched a brow and fought the unexpected urge to laugh. I'd been called many things over the last few years, but nice had never made it even close to the list. "I'm far from being nice. Eat or don't, but I won't carry you when you pass out."

He considered what I'd just said for a moment before reaching for the water and unscrewing the cap. "This isn't drugged, right?"

"I have better things to do than lace a water bottle."

Satisfied with my response, he started gulping the water, like he'd been stranded on a deserted island for days and this was the first water he'd come across.

"Hey, slow down before you throw everything up," I warned him.

He brought the half-emptied water bottle down, placed it on the wooden surface, and grabbed the sweet. "I haven't had these since I was kid," he said, a hint of melancholic nostalgia in his voice.

An unexpected sorrow washed over me at his tone. Who I used to be might have become foreign to me, but one thing I'd promised myself was to never let Ines become heartless past a point where she'd treat victims the same way as the ones who'd taken them.

I'd killed a lot of people over the last five years, but they'd never been innocent. I didn't know Gabriel's story, but something in my gut told me he'd been put in this situation involuntarily out of necessity and not because he was guilty of a heinous act.

I didn't say anything and watched him closely as he ate the sponge cake, taking small sips of water in between bites. My eyes roamed over his features, really taking him in for the first time.

Aside from the weighted history he seemed to carry over his shoulder and the beating he'd just had, he wasn't bad-looking. Although matted, I could tell that his dark hair was shorter on the sides and slightly longer at the top, but not by much. The cut above his left brow had stopped bleeding, a few trails of dried blood running down from his cut to his temple and disappearing into his hair.

His left eye was swollen shut, bruises in various stages of healing covering his under eye. There was a shallow cut on his lip and another set of bruises on the left side of his face.

Zakaria had left no expense in whatever lesson he was teaching him. I'd known of Zakaria's brutality and if Gabriel's face and ginger movements were any indication, I could only imagine the canvas of bruises and welts on his skin hidden underneath the clothes he was wearing.

He downed the remnants of his water bottle and the hint of tattoos peeked underneath the fabric that had slid slightly with the movement, but before I could decipher what the words at the bottom of what seemed like a larger tattoo were, he dropped the bottle onto the table and reached for the other one.

He must have just realized I'd been observing him this whole time because he stopped himself short, his fingers hanging midway. "Sorry," he apologized, taking his hand back.

"It's fine," I told him, my tone coming out softer than I'd heard it in a long time. Most likely because I knew that once we landed, I would have to put him into a cell and treat him like anyone else. He'd once again become a prisoner, just at the hands of someone else. So, at that, I offered, "There's a shower in the bathroom at the back of the plane. We land in less than an hour, so if you want to use it, I'd do it now. There's no change of clothes, but I suggest you keep the same ones you're wearing now."

He stared at me for a moment before speaking, "What's the catch?"

Something about his question caught me slightly off guard. I'd expected him to jump at the opportunity, but instead, he'd questioned everything I'd offered him so far. "Where I'm taking you isn't nice, so you might as well enjoy the last few moments of liberty you have," I said truthfully, not wanting to waste my time lying.

I would try to find a way to get Gabriel out, like I'd done to many other kids Barrera captured, but right now he was the least of my worries. He might have reminded me of my little brother, but I had to bury the thought away.

We didn't have long before we landed and whatever ounce of niceness I'd shown toward him would have to evaporate, like it had never been there in the first place.

I still had two days to spend at the riad and any change to who Ines was would trigger Barrera and I didn't want to raise any suspicions.

It took Gabriel a moment to let my words sink in before

he accepted them, giving me a curt nod. He then unfastened his seat belt and stood, moving to walk away but paused midway.

He looked at me. "For what it's worth, thank you," he said with a small smile, the faint hint of a dimple appearing on his cheek before it vanished as fast as it appeared.

He moved again and I watched him as he headed for the back. His gaze roamed over the space, his fingertips skimming the surfaces before he finally disappeared into the bathroom.

While he showered, I reached again for my duffel bag and retrieved a cloth, ropes and a gun, then placed them on the table in front of me. By the time the plane touched down, Gabriel was bound and gagged, something he didn't fight me on.

"Let's go," I said in a muted tone once the plane was parked, reaching down to grasp his arm.

I pulled him to his feet and pushed him in front of me. Once I heard the mechanism of the aircraft's door being unlocked to open the door, I brought my gun up and slammed the butt against the back of his skull, sending him tumbling to the ground.

Noah

CHAPTER 11

PRESENT

I'd been in this cell for the last two weeks and still hadn't found any ways to escape or had figured out what my father wanted from me.

When it came to him, it didn't surprise me that I still hadn't seen him. In the past, he'd always waited until I was almost unconscious before he'd paid me a visit, and now that I was older and no longer at his mercy, he definitely wouldn't come around, knowing I'd fight him back.

I'd been observing the guards who came every once in a while to check on me—which was an indication that I was the only prisoner down here—to see if I could persuade any of them to turn, but so far I'd had no luck. They'd come by, confirm I was still breathing, then leave, occasionally leaving a piece of stale bread and a small brass cup filled with warm water inside my cell every few days.

Another wave of exhaustion was looming over my head and my entire body hurt from the inside out, especially after the latest beating I took earlier. I'd mostly been left alone since the last time I saw Amalia, but for some reason, over the last two days, Hamza's lackeys had paid me more visits than they'd had since I'd been taken captive.

I'd initially fought them back, but I'd soon learned that they took a perverse pleasure in my resistance, so I'd stopped, which made them leave a lot faster. They weren't the strongest opponents I'd faced, but repeated beatings would take a toll on anyone, especially since I hadn't fully healed from the accident or knew the extent of my injuries.

I looked down at the bloodstained gauze wrapped around my thigh. The only grace I'd gotten had been Amalia caring for the wound on my leg instead of letting it get infected and potentially lead to sepsis from the exposure to the dirty old cell I was currently living in.

A few hours after she'd left with Hamza and that kid Sabiri, she'd returned to my cell and tended to the wound she'd inflicted, barely saying a word. She'd only spoken to me once to order me to take my pants off so she could have better access. Then she'd stitched my leg in a time record, bandaged it, and left.

During the whole time she'd been here, I'd wanted to explain myself since we hadn't really spoken ever since the night I'd left. Yet I couldn't find the courage to do so. I'd been a coward then for leaving without a word and still was one for not explaining myself now.

But I found myself stuck where to even begin. Nothing I came up with seemed good enough. I knew telling her the truth would be a great way to start, but which truth did I even start with?

The one where I lost the most important person in my life and felt hopeless and scared? Or the one where the person she was now working for was none other than my father?

Both seemed like the beginning of an uphill battle.

I'd have to wait until I got out of these four walls so I'd be able to make her listen to me. Because I knew she would run from me if I asked her to talk, not that I'd blame her. She had every right not to want to listen to what I had to say, but I'd make her. I'd lost her once. I wouldn't let it happen again.

No matter the cost or how hard I had to fight, I'd get her back.

And she helped you, my mind wishfully thought, but I pushed it aside, not wanting to read into it and end up disappointed.

I'd been lying on my back, looking up at the ceiling and counting the cracks in it for the hundredth time. A gnawing hunger ate at my gut and I managed a dry swallow to tamp it down. I'd been ignoring it over the last few days because if I gave in to it, I'd step into a helpless and desperate territory.

I couldn't allow myself to if I wanted to come out of this alive.

Besides, I'd gone through much worse when I was younger.

When you were born to be the heir of the cartel, your life consisted of one thing—surviving all the trials you were subjected to until initiation day.

On a Barrera's twelfth birthday, you'd be given a target to eliminate. If you succeeded, you were trained to take over until the old *Ra'is* passed, whether by natural causes or if he'd been killed.

If you didn't complete the task, *you* were terminated.

What I hadn't known at the time—hadn't known until I joined the Bureau—was that the target for each initiation was to kill the current drug lord so you'd take over. The cartel wanted to see if you'd be willing to go to extreme lengths for the role and to prove that there was no one you couldn't kill.

Talk about a twisted fucking way to prove it.

But uncovering that information made me realize three things. My father had killed his to be in power, I'd been set up to do the same to mine, and the fact that I had to kill my father was most likely the reason why he'd wanted me dead.

Not that he'd lacked reasons to. I was sure he had a long list of them.

I'd always been relieved that I'd never had to go through the initiation because, although I wanted my father gone, I'd never wished to be part of his world. It was something I'd been forced into from the moment I'd taken my first breath.

If by some omniscient force I'd known about the life I'd be born into, I probably would have prayed to never take it because I could have avoided a lifetime of carrying a pain that never seemed to go away.

I was forty-three years old now and the weight of my name and its legacy had never lifted.

It had gotten better, with therapy, my medication, and a lot of hitting inanimate things, but there was a lingering feeling in the back of my mind that was always there, threatening to take over and drown me.

And sometimes when that happened, I just wanted to let it.

Because wouldn't that alternative be infinitely more peaceful?

My exhaustion was now at a threatening distance, and I closed my eyes, hoping to give myself an ephemeral moment of peace, but not long enough to let it drift me away.

I woke up hours later, realizing that despite me fighting it, the exhaustion had taken over. I didn't know for how long I'd been sleeping since there was nothing here to tell the time of day, but it couldn't have been for more than a few hours.

My eyes flitted open, and a shiver ran down my spine. At first, I thought I'd no longer been immune to the chill of the cement floor. But when I moved, I realized that the water leaking had somehow made its way to where I'd lain.

"*Tfou*[1]," I cursed under my breath.

The whole back of my shirt was now soaking wet. I couldn't believe I hadn't woken up when it reached me. Before it made its way to the bottom half of my body, I got up and removed my shirt. I squeezed the excess water out as I walked to the iron door to hang it between the bars, letting it somewhat dry up before I put it back on.

I'm so over this captive shit.

I walked to the back of the cell and plopped down against the wall, the bitter cement digging right into my spine. "I need to get out of here," I murmured, the echoes of my plea bouncing back to my ears.

I closed my eyes when a voice said, "You and me both."

I jerked back, moving my head to look around but not finding anyone there. "Great, now I'm hearing things," I whispered to myself.

I hadn't eaten or drunk much water since being here, but I hadn't been here long enough to be hallucinating already. That usually came around week three or four, and

---

1. Damn it.

at the time I was six years old, so surely I should be able to sustain for longer now.

I rubbed my eyes and shook my head from side to side. Then I dropped my head back, branding what I'd just heard as a figment of my apparently creative imagination.

"*Matat7lemch a khoya*[2], I'd actually much rather be in whatever was happening in your brain than here," the muffled voice said again.

My eyes flew open and I shot to my feet. I definitely *did* hear that.

"Who are you?" I asked, standing in the middle of the room, waiting to hear it again.

When whoever it was didn't speak, I began to think I really was hallucinating, but I rarely spoke *darija* aside from swearing. I could understand it and get by if I needed to, but I definitely wouldn't have talked to myself and made a full cohesive sentence.

I moved to sit, but the person—a man—spoke up again, "Gabriel."

I sifted through my brain, wondering if I knew the name, but it didn't ring a bell.

"That doesn't really tell me much," I responded, focusing on what he'd say so I could pinpoint where it came from.

I'd never had the chance to visit the outside of this cell when I'd been kept here, but whenever I'd been dragged in,

---

2. You're not dreaming, bro.

I'd never noticed a cell next to mine. There was a large door on the left wall outside of my cell, but I'd always thought it was broken or contained a closet on the other side for storage. Besides, in all the times I'd slept here, I'd never seen or heard another prisoner.

Any of the cartel's hostages were kept in a different wing on the other side of the property. My father hated me but not enough to showcase it to the world because me being held in a cell for *misbehaving*, as my father liked to call it, would have been used as a leveraging point to show weakness within his ranks and my father would never let that happen.

He scoffed. "I mean, there isn't much to tell. Do you want a biography or something?"

The voice came from my left, so I stepped closer, my ear resting against the wall to hear. There was a slight rustling on the other side of the wall.

"I wouldn't be opposed to it," I replied, my hand skimming over the wall for any opening because I could hear him so clearly now, you'd think we were both in the same room.

He huffed out a laugh. "Well, when it's asked so nicely," he deadpanned. "My name is Gabriel Al Naji and I am twenty-three years old. Parents are dead and I have a sister that I haven't seen in years because the cartel took me from her." He let out a humorless laugh. "That enough for you?"

I sat up near the corner where the back wall met the left one. While he'd been talking, I'd found a small fissure toward the bottom of the wall. I'd rolled onto my stomach and tried narrowing my eyes, but it was too small to see through to wherever he was on the other side, only big enough to let the sound travel between our two cells.

"I'm sorry," I said sincerely. I unfortunately knew a thing or two about loss and even though I'd been born into the cartel and suffered at its hands, I knew that was nothing compared to what the families put their prisoners through. I didn't know which one had taken him before he landed here, but they were all equally horrific as the next.

"It is what it is."

I nodded in agreement even though he couldn't see me.

"How long have you been here?" he asked.

"This time, at least two weeks. But it could be more or less, who knows? Time isn't the easiest to tell here." Before he pushed me on what I meant by *this time*, I asked him the same. "What about you?"

"I just got in today," he said so casually as if we were on vacation and he'd just landed. "But I spent almost twelve years at the last place I was held in. This already seems like a resort compared to where I used to be," he explained, giving more information than I'd asked for.

His answer confirmed what I'd presumed. I hadn't heard any sounds or movement until today, so my guesses were that he'd either been completely unconscious until now and they'd left him unattended or he'd been put in his cell while I'd been sleeping.

"Don't get too comfortable. They like to pull you into a false sense of security before striking," I warned him, knowing that if he had a decent experience so far, they were just gearing up to put him through the worst.

Whoever this kid was, I hoped he'd make it out of here alive.

I opened my mouth to ask him why he was here, what his cell looked like to see if it was similar to mine, or if it was constructed differently so that we might be able to find a way to escape, but he interrupted me.

"Do you have family out there?" he asked, changing the subject.

I wanted to shift the conversation back but decided against it. If I pushed and asked him too many questions, he might retreat and grow suspicious. Instead, I answered him.

"No, I don't." I paused and drew slightly away from the wall, bending my knees to rest my forearms against them, my hands hanging in between. I didn't say anything for a moment, but after a short pause, I spoke again, "At least none of that matters."

My throat thickened with a wave of emotions I'd buried and the back of my eyes burned when I thought of that time. Of the day on which I'd gotten *the* call that was still vividly ingrained in my brain.

The day when I'd lost the most important person in my life.

The person who'd spent her entire life making it up to

me for my father's mistakes and the person who taught me that being loved wasn't conditional to what you could do for them.

That you could be loved unconditionally for just existing.

Noah

CHAPTER 12

PRESENT

WHEN YOU LOST SOMEONE, YOU WERE SUPPOSED TO FEEL sad. To feel like a part of you had been ripped apart and that you'd never be able to get it back.

But all I had felt was a numbness I couldn't even begin to describe before it was decimated by anger left in its wake. Hot and burning anger that I'd lost the only person I had in my life who cared whether I lived or died. That cared whether I was happy or sad.

That did the best she could to heal the wounds I'd been inflicted with during my childhood by getting us out and giving the best life she could with the little she had.

My mother passed away ten years ago, and the anger had tempered, but the freshness of the blow hadn't. I used to think that the further I got away from it, the less it would hurt.

That the pain would disappear and I wouldn't have to feel this constant pressure inside my chest that never went away, the one that just lingered and threatened to take over the moment you gave it an ajar opening.

And when the pain took over, it felt worse than the day that it'd happened.

Dedifferentiated chondrosarcoma.

I had no idea what those two words meant, but I knew one thing. Those two single words took away one of the most important people in my life.

Two words.

Against one life.

I stood at the edge of the cliff and looked down at the angry waves crashing against the rocks below that matched my thundering heartbeat. Cold wind whipped through my clothes, making the fabric snap against my skin.

I welcomed it.

It was the only thing that seemed to tether me to reality at the moment.

I didn't remember how much time had passed since I'd learned the news or how I'd gotten here because it seemed as if the concept of anything but those two words had vanished the moment I'd gotten the call.

My mother had died a few hours ago from a cancer I never knew about. She'd never told me. I had to learn it from a stranger who informed me she'd passed away peacefully in her sleep at the hospice she'd been admitted to three weeks ago.

I'd even spoken to her not too long ago and she didn't tell me.

She didn't tell me.

Why?

Why didn't she tell me?

Why didn't she let me say goodbye?

Why didn't she let me come take care of her?

Why? Why? Why….

I felt lost.

And scared.

And angry.

And lost.

She was my person. And I'd lost her.

I screamed, the sound so guttural it made me drop to my haunches, my fingers gripping my hair. How was this possible? Why did this happen? She wasn't supposed to leave me.

I knew realistically this day would eventually come, but I always thought it would be so far in the future that I'd be better equipped for it. If there's even such a thing as being ready enough to lose your mother.

I always thought I'd at least get to spend her last few moments by her side, that I'd get to say goodbye and give her the peace she deserved.

I waited for the tears to come, but all I could feel was the intense tightening of an iron fist around my heart, branding it with irreparable scars.

I couldn't breathe.

My vision became blurry and I closed my eyes.

My chest was heavy with each inhale.

I can't breathe.

She'd sounded tired during our last conversation a few weeks ago and I thought it was just because she worked too much. I should have pushed and asked, should have jumped on a plane and gone to see her and make sure she was okay.

Why didn't I go?

Why didn't I call her more to ask how she was?

Why didn't I fucking answer her last phone call?

She'd called me this week, but I'd been too fucking busy being happy to answer. I'd told myself that I would call her later. That I'd maybe tell my mother about her. *Maybe even fly us so the two people I loved could meet.*

I thought I'd have time.

But I'd been robbed of it.

"Hey, you okay?" Gabriel's voice pulled me out of the memory.

"Yeah," I answered.

I'd learned to remember the good memories instead of the only bad one, but whenever I thought of that day, it always felt like driving a freshly sharpened knife into a wound you'd thought had healed.

Instead of feeling like a dull hit, the aftermath spilled

endlessly, making the pain you'd experienced resurface all over again.

Especially since my mother hadn't been the only person I'd lost that day.

I heard Gabriel open his mouth, but the sound of heavy footsteps coming down the steps and approaching the door to the basement caught my attention.

Muffled voices sounded from behind the closed door, indicating that it was multiple people coming in, which meant it wasn't just a guard checking in on how things were going.

Fuck.

I rushed to get my shirt and pulled it back on, the fabric still wet. I ignored the sticky feeling of it against my skin and made it back to my previous spot. "People are coming," I whispered to Gabriel. "If you were unconscious, pretend you still are."

"Wha—" he started, but I cut him off.

"*Now.*" I'd barely gotten the word out when the door cracked open. I hastily rested the side of my head against the wall to my left and pretended to be asleep before whoever they were came in.

I wasn't sure how many of them there were, but regardless of who or the amount, if I wasn't awake, they were less likely to rein me into trouble because every time a group had visited, I'd either gotten knocked around or stabbed.

Not that I really minded Amalia stabbing me.

The footsteps were approaching, and I noticed they

hadn't closed the door behind them, which meant they intended to bring someone out. None of them spoke as their steps grew closer, but they didn't stop at my cell.

Something was wrong because silence was never a good thing. It always meant things were about to get worse.

Usually death.

I internally winced from the memories the sound brought as metal keys clinked together, breaching the deafening silence. A few seconds later, the hinges of a metal door screeched open.

I wanted to see what was happening but knew that someone could be standing in front of my cell watching, so I kept my breathing even as I heard them step inside whatever the place on the other side of the walls was.

The footsteps grew closer to where I sat, the sound echoing off the cold stone walls. Then they stopped.

Some sort of object tapped against the concrete before a voice I hadn't heard in years spoke up. A dreadful chill shot down my spine in response, a myriad of memories assaulting my mind, but I pushed against them because now wasn't the time to reminisce about the terrible old days he'd put me through.

"*Tga3ad*[1]," he demanded of Gabriel, who must have followed my advice and acted as if he was still unconscious.

"I said wake up." My father's tone was much harsher as

---

1. Get up.

the sound of the object he was holding—most likely his wooden staff—collided with something more dense, a thud echoing to the side of my cell.

He whipped his rod again and I heard Gabriel sputter out a strained curse before asking why.

There was another loud thud against flesh before Omar spoke again, "Alaoui might do things differently, but here prisoners don't ask questions. They follow commands."

"Get him," someone else said in Arabic and I immediately recognized Amalia's voice.

I wasn't oblivious to the fact that she worked for my father, but Gabriel was just a kid. I didn't care what he'd done or how he'd landed there. He shouldn't be suffering at the hands of a cartel, especially not my father's.

I *knew* her. She wouldn't hurt a kid, but I hadn't seen her in ten years and who knows how long she'd been working for Omar. So I might be mistaken. She might have changed from the person I'd known and fallen in love with.

But I refused to let myself believe that. I wasn't a hopeful type of person, but for her, I'd be the most optimistic person on the planet if it meant there was an infinitesimal hope that my Amalia was still in there.

Commotion broke on the other side, a cacophony of grunts and heavy breathing, until another thud, this time much louder than the previous ones, resounded next door.

I finally opened my eyes, deciding I had to do something even if I was behind locked doors.

Doors slammed shut and footsteps came down my way.

I stood and walked over to the metal barrier just in time to see two men turning a corner and walking down a somber hallway.

I recognized one of them—Sabiri—while the other I'd never seen. He seemed to be around the same age as Sabiri, but where Sabiri had fairer features, this one had dark hair and brown eyes so dark they were almost black.

They dragged whom I assumed was Gabriel's limp body by his armpits across the concrete floor, Amalia right on their heels. She briefly glanced in my direction, her gaze hard before looking away.

Another kid, this one much taller and bulkier than the other two, walked out. He stepped to the side to let the last person get through, his wooden staff dragging at his side.

My father.

My heart clenched with a mixture of emotions that I'd thought I'd long buried. Decades had passed since I'd last laid eyes on him, on the man who'd inflicted much pain in me, but the wounds still felt fresh, time merely dulling their sharp edges.

His presence was like a looming shadow, casting darkness in every room he walked into. It felt suffocating, the weight of the murkiness he left in his wake pressing down my chest, sucking the air out of my lungs and making it hard to breathe.

He didn't have a single wrinkle on his suit and his expensive loafers barely had a dirt mark on them. The harsh lines on his face had grown older. Creases lined his forehead from the permanent scowl on his face and fine wrinkles decorated the side of his eyes.

He had his medium-length graying hair slicked back. The beard he always kept maintained was now dusted salt-and-pepper and longer than I'd ever seen it.

You would think that the passage of time would have softened him, that he would at least look at me and perhaps his gaze would be tinged with a hint of regret or remorse for what he'd put me through.

But I shouldn't have expected more than what he'd granted me with.

He simply walked past me, barely awarding me a glance. But despite the brief exchange, it didn't stop the coldness in his eyes from rooting me in place.

Even after thirty years and all the work I'd done to try to rid myself of the hold he had on me, I still felt like I had to walk on eggshells around him, afraid to set off another explosion of anger.

But a voice in my mind screamed at me that I was no longer the boy he'd terrorized.

The shock of seeing him finally washed off and I realized they almost had Gabriel out the door.

"Hey," I called out, approaching the iron bars and gripping the cold metal with one hand.

They all stopped in their tracks, but only Amalia and my father turned around. She pinned me with a glare, but I diverted my attention to my father.

I met his gaze dead-on, not letting the emotions

churning in my gut to be showcased on my features. "Take me instead. Whatever you're about to do to him, you can do to me," I said coldly.

He disregarded my request and moved to turn around, but I rammed my hand against the bars, a metallic clang reverberating through the confines of my cell.

"I'm talking to you," I said through gritted teeth.

He whipped around and slammed his wooden staff against the metal grid right where my fingers were, but I removed them a second before his rod made contact.

"Stand back, *boy*," he growled, his voice dripping venom. He peered at me with his weathered light-brown eyes, his bushy gray eyebrows forming a single frustrated line.

My jaw clenched at him calling me *boy*. That's what he used to call me whenever he was displeased with my behavior, right before he'd beat me black and blue with the same rod.

He stepped closer when I didn't respond. He leaned in, laughing dryly. "Glad to see you still listen, *son*." He'd whispered the last word only for me to hear before spatting at my feet, a look of disgust on his face.

Being this close was a grave mistake on his part. I might have once been unable to hurt him back then, but those days were long gone.

Using his weakness to my advantage when he moved to turn away from me, I lunged forward and grabbed the right end of his staff with one hand through the opening of the cell bars.

Caught off guard, my father stumbled backward, his eyes wide, and I used the small distance he'd created to swiftly whip the wooden rod around and over his head, my free hand reaching for the other end.

Then I brought the staff over his front and pinned his back against the surface of the cell door, jamming the object against his throat and tightening my hold in a vice grip.

"How's that for listening," I growled under my breath, blocking out the sensation of his nails breaking the skin of my forearms as he tried to relieve the pressure on his windpipe.

For a moment, only the sound of labored breathing and the harsh rasp of metal against flesh filled the air as my father flailed around, trying to get away from my grip. Omar's face turned ashen from the lack of oxygen, his body growing limp.

I didn't care if I killed him, but a sudden sound cut through the ragged breathing and grunts—a sharp and unmistakable click.

With my grip unrelenting, I looked up to find the glint of a barrel trained steadily in my direction. I met Amalia's gaze and I couldn't find an ounce of warmth looking back at me.

"Let him go," she ordered through gritted teeth.

I tightened my grip against my father's throat, awarding me with a bullet whizzing past my ear.

"I said. Let. Him. Go. Or the next bullet won't miss."

I released my grip and removed the weight on his throat, letting my father crumple to the floor. I stood straight with his staff in my hand, my chest heaving from the exertion as he lay in a heap at my feet. He gasped for air, desperately trying to get oxygen back into his starving lungs.

A small satisfaction ran through me as I watched him be the one catching his breath for once. I prepared for the aftermath and threw his staff back at him. My father staggered to his feet, his breathing still labored as he lunged for me but the evident iron bars stopped him short.

Omar's face contorted in rage and the burning fire in his eyes intensified the perverse gratification of seeing him so worked up coursing through my veins.

Instead of cowering from his frustration, I stood firm and crossed my arms over my chest. My eyes held his with a steely resolve and I gave him a cold smile.

"*Weld el kelba*[2]," he growled under his breath, his fingers grabbing onto the bars and shaking the immovable cell door, the hinges groaning from the force he was applying. "Keys," he asked no one in particular.

When no one moved, he whipped around even more enraged. "I gave an order."

---

2. You son of a bitch.

The taller of the boys fumbled through his pockets in search of said keys, his fingers trembling. The seconds ticked by and he was apparently taking too long for my father's taste because Omar stepped forward, his hand shooting to seize the kid's throat, barely reaching it since my father was no match with his five-foot-six frame.

Caught by surprise, the kid stumbled backward, his back hitting the wall behind him. He didn't struggle against my father's grip, knowing better, and let my father look through his pocket.

The boy's face turned red until Amalia's voice boomed in the hallway. "Barrera, *enough*," she said in a harsh tone.

My father released his hold on his victim's throat and redirected his wrath toward her, but before he could say a word, she interrupted him.

"We have to leave and finish what we came here for in the first place. Remember?" she said, gesturing with her gun toward Gabriel's body still slumped.

Surprisingly, my father's expression simmered down. He grabbed the bottom of his jacket and straightened himself. Then he glared at the kid who had been on his knees catching his breath after my father had released him.

He reached for my father's staff and handed it to him. Omar seized it forcefully from his fingers and walked down the hallway toward Amalia, not sparing a glance in my direction.

My gut churned, waiting with bated breath. If he dared touch her, I didn't care how impossible it would be to tear this iron door down, I would do it and kill him for laying a hand on her.

He took me by surprise again and just breezed by her, exiting the basement without a word.

I looked over at Amalia to find her eyes trained on me. I could tell she was wrestling over something, but I didn't know what. And with everyone in the room, it wasn't like I could just ask what was on her mind.

Not that she'd open up to me like she used to even if no one was around.

She finally looked away but right before she disappeared through the door, I caught the hint of a smile on her face, but it was so brief, I might have simply imagined it.

Amalia

CHAPTER 13

A POUNDING HEADACHE LOOMED AT THE BACK OF MY SKULL and all I wanted was to hit the person responsible for it. I had everything perfectly planned and Noah had single-handedly ruined it in one impulsive—and stupid—fell swoop.

As entertaining as it was to watch Barrera struggle so pathetically, a scenario I'd often envisioned exacting upon him on many occasions, Noah still managed to fuck up my plans from the confines of a barricaded cell.

Once I'd landed in Bab Al Mansour last night, I'd called Hamza and ordered him to send one of his lackeys to collect Gabriel. Meanwhile, I took my car that I'd left parked in the hangar before my flight and made my way back to the Barrera mansion, using the time to work out my next steps.

I certainly couldn't call the Bureau since I'd gone rogue. The goal of my assignment hadn't changed, but how I got there most definitely went against anything I'd learned in training at the Academy.

So I spent the thirty-minute drive making all the necessary arrangements to have everything fall into place and prevent myself from getting killed in the process of my own extraction.

After I'd managed to get a trusted contact of mine at the Royal Palace to convince the Crown Prince to visit The Oasis, one of the most coveted nightclubs in town, for an early birthday celebration, I'd then spent the early hours of this morning carefully planting conversations that Barrera would overhear about the event that would be held in honor of Moulay Ahmad.

The prince was turning twenty, which meant one important thing to Barrera. He was young and malleable, unlike his father, his Royal Highness.

Earlier this afternoon, Barrera had finally taken the bait after hearing Sabiri mention the Crown Prince. He'd immediately found me and asked I accompany him to pick an outfit at the marketplace in the old city.

I didn't want to raise suspicions, so I'd agreed, putting a delay in my plans to get Gabriel out of the cell next to Noah's.

I should have known better than letting one of Hamza's

subordinates take care of him. Because instead of putting Gabriel in a cell with all the other prisoners on the other side of the property like I'd asked, he'd taken him to the old cell that was adjacent to the one Noah was currently staying in.

I'd rarely used his cell before since it was on the opposite side of where my room was on the property, except when I required additional space for my interrogations, especially when I could leverage the hook on its ceiling.

Besides, I preferred using the building where all the other prisoners were so that they could all hear every torturous scream when I had a discussion with one of them. It helped make them more talkative when their turns came.

Hamza and his crew had apprehended Noah while I'd been away and Barrera had insisted we confine the new hostage there although it was actually my decision.

I'd asked Hamza's soldiers because I didn't want an agent mingling with our prisoners and the place was secluded from the rest of the property, so only authorized people could go in there.

I'd only ever kept one prisoner at a time there, so it made no sense to me as to why they'd taken someone else there, making my job so much more difficult.

Since I couldn't risk Gabriel overhearing, knowing that sound carried easily between the cells despite their distance, I'd eventually found a way to get Gabriel out of there without raising suspicion.

But of course another hurdle appeared in my way in the

form of a painstakingly frustrating handsome man who decided to strangle Barrera when we were almost out the door.

I reined in my frustration as I led the way to Doc's office. I'd briefed Barrera earlier about Gabriel potentially having information on Alaoui that might be useful to us and that he might also still be concealing contraband.

I'd been under the assumption that I'd be taking care of it on my own when Barrera had simply nodded after I'd delivered the information, but when I'd made my way to Gabriel's cell, he'd appeared with Sabiri and two other teenagers I knew he'd most likely took off the streets to *work* for him.

When I'd asked what he was doing, he'd told me to stop asking questions and lead the way. Instead of challenging his authority, something I had no issue doing, I'd opted to do as asked.

I'd been tempted to stand my ground but knew that might lead to questions I just didn't have time to answer. The hours until I had to leave all of this behind ticked by and wasting any resourceful time wouldn't help me come out of this alive.

I didn't particularly want Gabriel to be put in the direct line of vision of Barrera and suffer in the process, but if it was the temporary price to pay until I got him out, I was prepared to do so.

I didn't feel remorse very often anymore, but as I watched Sabiri and the other boy whom I'd never seen before today drop Gabriel's unconscious body on the examination table, the emotion whirled inside my ribcage.

I shook myself out of it and dismissed the boys, Barrera having already retreated to his room to get checked by his personal physician. Then I turned my attention to Doc and said, "I need you to check him for swallowed packages of cocaine. He most likely overdosed last night and seemed fine after I gave him a dose of Narcan, but we need him alive."

He looked at me impassively the entire time I relayed all the information I knew he'd need.

No one really knew much about the older man since he rarely spoke unless for one-worded responses or if he needed a clinical confirmation. He'd already been the cartel's physician on call a few years before I joined the ranks and I always felt like something about him was off.

It might have been his bushy mustache that covered most of his upper lip or his disturbingly pale green eyes or maybe even the greasy gray hair he always had pulled into a low ponytail.

I still couldn't pinpoint exactly what it was about him, so I simply limited my interactions to a bare minimum.

He gave a curt nod and immediately got to work, reaching for scissors and cutting through Gabriel's torn-up top. With his scissors still in hand, he glanced up at us with a look of indifference.

"Right," I said, taking it as my cue to leave. I walked

out of his office and headed for my quarters to prepare the last step of my plan.

Barrera had left for The Oasis about an hour ago.

He hadn't made a grand public appearance since his son died a few weeks ago, so he'd taken Hamza and a lot of his men with him, only leaving a few guards behind since I was here to watch over everything.

This was exactly what I needed and why I'd opted to bring the prince in town. I'd known Barrera wouldn't have attended Moulay Ahmad's birthday celebration no matter how beneficial his endorsement would be if he'd had to travel to another region for it.

I'd meticulously timed the extraction when I knew all the remaining guards who had stayed behind would gather in the living room to watch the football game. The country's national men's team was playing for some sort of qualifying round and there were only a few minutes left to determine if they'd make it through.

Which meant that all the men were now rooted to their seats, giving me a short window of time to leave.

I grabbed my guns from the small table I was sitting in front of and slid them into my shoulder holster. Standing, I grabbed my leather jacket from the back of the wooden chair and pulled it on, zipping it up.

Then I swiftly walked out of the room, listening for any

sounds. The property had gone quieter, the faraway sounds of the boys in the living room drifting my way.

Hurry up, my brain urged me and I tamped it down with a vexed, *I know.*

With the keys of the cell in hand, I made my way down the stairs and crossed the courtyard, passing the large fountain in the middle. I quickly glanced through the ajar back doors to see if all the guards were still accounted for in the living room.

After I confirmed all seven men were there, I hurried the remaining steps toward the building where Noah was held. I unlocked the front door and walked down the dimly lit hallways until I reached the narrow concrete staircase that led to the basement.

Once I made it down the steps, I looked at my watch and noticed I had four more minutes before the game ended. I quickly unlatched the three locks on the basement door and carefully cracked it open to minimize the screeching noise it made.

When I stepped into the hallway that led to his cell, Noah stood and watched me warily as I approached. He looked over my shoulder, most likely to see if we had company. When he realized I was alone, his gaze traveled back to mine.

"Came to pay me a visit?" he asked teasingly, the corner of his lips tugging up in a smirk.

"Sarcasm isn't your style," I deadpanned.

"And being held captive is?"

With no time to waste, I paused in front of his cell, unlocked the bolt attached to it, and dragged the bars wide open. "We're leaving," I ordered, ignoring his quip.

His brow shot up. "What are you talking about?"

I bit down on my molars and reached for his wrist, ignoring the jolting shock when our skin made contact. "*Noah*, we have to go. We don't have time," I said urgently, tugging him forward.

Thankfully, he didn't resist.

I dropped his arm and shook my hand out before turning around to make our way out, Noah right on my heels.

"Where are we going?" he asked just as we reached the exit.

I halted abruptly and spun around, catching him off guard as my front collided with his. He grabbed my upper arms to steady me and despite the fabric separating his touch from my skin, the same irritating zap of electricity rang through my body.

Ugh, stop it.

"Let's go," I gritted out, yanking myself out of his grip and turning around to leave.

"Not until you tell me what the hell is going on?" he insisted, not moving.

I closed my eyes in frustration. I was already regretting my decision to bring him with me and we hadn't even made it out yet. I faced him again, locking my gaze with his.

"I don't know if you remember, but I *did* say we didn't have much time. Which includes time for questions. You can either come with me or die here. I couldn't fucking care less, but you better decide fast before we *both* end up dead," I said, turning away from him.

I'd barely reached for the door handle when he stopped me again. "Amalia," he whispered.

I swear to God I'm about to put a bullet in his head.

I opened my mouth, but before I could tear him a new one, he seized my arms and yanked me back with urgency. With a swift motion, he pressed his other hand firmly over my mouth and pulled my body flush against his, pressing our bodies tightly against the cold stone wall.

Furious, I moved to push him off, but he held me firmly against him, his eyes hard on mine. He leaned his head down until his breath fanned over my ear. "You can thank me later," he said as I heard the faint shuffle of footsteps outside.

He pulled back, his lips brushing against my skin in the process, and I had to suppress the shiver the contact initiated.

Something must definitely be wrong with my system because what the hell were all these reactions my body was having to Noah? Not only had I not seen this man in ten years, I wasn't particularly fond of him, so why was I fucking reacting to *anything* in regards to him?

Pull it together, Amalia.

In the tense stillness of the moment, we both held our

breaths, our eyes locked on one another, waiting for whoever was outside to pass us by unnoticed. After what felt like an eternity, Noah hovered over me and cautiously glanced through the small window of the door.

"He's gone," he said, letting go of me.

"I figured."

"A *thank you* wouldn't hurt."

I ignored him and looked at my watch, realizing the game was over and we'd lost our safe window to leave the premises without a hitch. I reached for my boot and pulled out a spare pistol.

I was good but not stupid. There was no way we would get out of here with me being the only armed. And I hated to admit it, but he was a pretty good shot, and we'd need it.

"There are seven guards on the property tonight, and one more guarding the large entry gate. My car's in the garage, so keep low and avoid being seen." I placed the gun in his palm and added, "And for the love of God, don't do anything stupid."

"Why are there only seven guards? That's not normal."

Since we were already running out of time, I didn't spare a thought to how he knew that and answered him, "Barrera's out tonight. He went to the Crown Prince's twentieth birthday bash with Hamza and most of the crew." What I didn't reveal was that I was the one behind it. He didn't need to know that.

"Any more questions?"

"Later, but for now, lead the way, pretty girl."

Ignoring the nickname, I looked out the window and when I confirmed that no one was outside, I opened the door and kept close to the wall, navigating us toward the garage. Once inside the brightly lit multi-car garage, I beelined for my vehicle and popped the back open.

"Get in," I commanded, pointing at the trunk.

"No, I'll drive," he said, already making his way to the driver's side of my compact SUV.

I wiped a frustrated hand over my face and glared at him. "Noah, I swear I'll leave you behind to fend for yourself if you keep pushing against everything I ask of you."

He opened the car's door. "Amalia, whether we like it or not, they'll know we're gone within the next few minutes. You're a better shot and I'm a better driver, so get in the car. Now *you're* the one wasting time."

The fucking audacity of this man. My patience was running thin, but he had a point. It was just a question of minutes before they realized that Noah was gone and I was too.

I slammed the trunk closed and hurried to jump into the passenger's seat. Noah got into the driver's seat and turned the engine on. The garage door slid open as he approached it and he merged into the gravel road that led down to the iron gates at the front.

I knew the doors would open automatically after scanning my license plate at the front, but it didn't stop my heart from wanting to leap out of my chest as we drove toward the front gate.

I hadn't felt this way in a long time and I couldn't say I'd missed it.

I started thinking we were in the clear, but just as we reached the exit, the car barely passing the iron gates, the sound of a gunshot erupted behind us.

"Stop the car," someone yelled.

I glanced over my shoulder to find one of the guards standing in the middle of the gravel driveway with his weapon drawn up.

Noah yanked on the stick shift and stomped down on the pedals, tearing off into the night just as the guard who sat in a chair outside to the side jerked awake. The older man fumbled for his old rifle, but it was too late because he was already far in our rearview mirror.

Noah raced down the long, deserted street that connected the rest of the world to Barrera's property, but a few moments later, headlights cut the darkness around us.

I threw a glance behind us and said, "We have company."

"I hadn't noticed," he deadpanned as two more cars emerged, joining the party. Their headlights loomed close with each passing second and then bullets started flying.

Before I could instruct Noah where to turn, he slammed on the brakes and sharply veered the car into a dirt path off the road, the car skidding around the corner with a deafening screech that drowned the sound of gunfire.

I held back a shriek, almost flying off my seat. I tightly

gripped the handle above the window as he sped down the dirt path.

How the fuck does he know where to go?

We always masked prisoners coming in so they wouldn't know how to get out and there were no blueprints out there of Barrera's property since he'd bribed the city's officials to keep everything off record.

"Where are you going?" I asked, holding on tightly. The car bounced and jolted over the uneven terrain, the three cars joining the road behind us one by one.

"Hang on," he warned a moment before he merged onto the main thoroughfare, the city's neon lights flickering in the distance. He hurtled down the boulevard, weaving between cars that were most likely heading for a night out, but the three black SUVs were still trailing us.

With every passing moment, tension mounted and Barrera's men were closing in on us, their bullets unrelenting.

Noah clutched the steering wheel, his eyes fixed on the car ahead. One moment, we were behind it and in the next breath, he swerved hard to the left, his foot pressing down the accelerator as he shot past the vehicle that was in front of us.

The nearest SUV on our tail mimicked the movement, following us on the opposite side of the road.

What the hell is he doing?

My eyes narrowed on the road in front of us. "Noah,

watch out," I screamed as I spotted a construction site ahead, a barricade of orange cones and flashing lights.

"I know," was his only answer as we closed down on the site in our path.

"*Noah*, what are you doing?" I yelled as we were about to enter in a head-on collision with the site.

He ignored me and kept his focus ahead.

At the last possible moment, Noah swerved back to the right side of the road, almost hitting the car now behind us. The sound of tires screeched as they skidded across the pavement and honking resounded in the night air.

Oh, he's fucking crazy.

I glanced behind to find the SUV that was trailing us had slammed its brakes a moment too late, colliding straight into a parked excavator.

One car down. Two more to go.

"You're fucking crazy, you know that?" I said, turning my attention to him.

"Better crazy than dead." He briefly looked over at me with a satisfied smile, but it was short-lived. His eyes widened, an alarmed look painting his features.

Everything that came next happened in a blur. Noah yelled, "Watch out," and reached over for me with one hand to pull me down in the same breath, trying his best to cover me from his side.

The car skidded off its lane as the passenger window next to me exploded, shattered glass raining down on us.

Noah quickly righted the car, but the SUV veered in our direction, metal scraping against metal.

"Barrera, pull the fuck over," the driver shouted in Arabic, but Noah floored the gas pedal even more, the speedometer almost reading the hundred miles mark.

Barrera? What is this guy on?

I would have blamed my misunderstanding on the fact that *darija* wasn't my native language, but I'd mastered it before coming to work for the cartel, so there was no way it was that.

I must have just misheard with all the adrenaline coursing through my body.

I glanced over at Noah, but he didn't look at me. Instead, he had a grim expression on his face, his jaw clenched, but I didn't have time to dwell on this any longer or we'd end up dead.

I peered into the side-view mirror, noticing there were only two men in the car that just shot at me. "When I tell you to, slam on the brakes and slightly weave into their lane," I instructed Noah as I grabbed my gun and checked the chamber.

He gave me a quick side-glance before looking back at the road. "What?"

"Stop questioning me and just trust me."

"Fine," he gritted out.

I focused my sole attention on the wing mirror, waiting for the perfect moment. I waited with bated breath as the second SUV weaved through cars and drew closer until they were far enough for what I'd planned.

"*Now,*" I shouted and Noah did as I'd told him.

The driver hadn't expected me to be this close range and didn't pull away fast enough before I raised my weapon and fired two bullets—one for his head and the other for his companion.

The driver slumped forward, his head lolling as it collided with the steering wheel, the sudden impact causing the horn to blare and join the symphony of the chaos already ensuing outside.

Their vehicle veered off across the lanes, cars behind honking and doing their best to avoid it. It kept its course until it collided with a street lamp post, the airbags deploying.

Noah muttered something unintelligible under his breath, pulling my attention back to him. Before I could register anything, the car lurched forward as something rammed into us from behind, almost sending us careening into the truck in front of us.

As Noah regained control, they struck again, the impact sending shockwaves through the vehicle. I peered over my shoulder, noting movement in the front seats, the gleam of a rifle being loaded.

Police and paramedic sirens cut through the air. We were about ten minutes away from the expressway and we had to both get rid of the car before we reached it and evade the authorities' radar. The last thing either one of us needed was to end up in a prison cell, only to then be sent back to Barrera.

Using the sleeve of my leather jacket, I wiped at the broken glass on the windowsill. Then I unfastened my seat belt, tightly gripped the grab handle, and leaned the upper half of my body out.

I fired once but missed when a hand tugged me back.

"Are you out of your fucking mind?" he shouted, his voice sharp with urgency as he yanked me back to my seat.

I whipped around, my frustration boiling over at the fact that he made me waste a perfectly good shot. I tilted my head. "Would you rather do it?"

His grip on the steering wheel tightened. "As you can see, my hands are a little occupied at the moment," he gritted out just as a bullet ricocheted against the back bumper.

"Then let me do this," I said and moved for the window again.

He tugged me back down to my seat, his hand gripping my thigh. "No. I'm not risking you dying because you wanted to play the hero."

My irritation spilled over, ravaging a path through my veins. "I'm not playing the fucking hero," I bit out. "I'm trying to make sure we don't end up fucking dead or worse back at Barrera's. I don't know about you, but I'd rather not be held captive as a traitor."

The truck previously in front of us changed lanes and Noah sped up.

"Come here," he said.

"What?"

"I said, come. Over. Here," he repeated, reaching under his seat with one hand and adjusting his seat back.

I finally realized what he meant, my eyes widening in comprehension.

"Absolutely not."

"*Amalia*," he said, tugging at my hand.

Letting out a frustrated breath, I climbed onto his lap, making sure I didn't block his view of the road, and straddled him, holding his shoulder with my free hand to remain steady.

Not wasting time pondering over the fact that I was *straddling* him and we were this close after years, I leaned out the window and started shooting, one of Noah's arms holding me steady.

The first bullet only lodged itself into the windshield, but the second shattered it, lodging itself into the shoulder of the passenger with the rifle in its trajectory. I then lowered my gun, aiming my next shots down.

I struck the right front tire, the vehicle screeching from the imbalance, but it didn't stop them. I shot again but discovered I'd run out of bullets.

"Fuck," I groaned and immediately reached for the inside pocket of my jacket for a spare magazine. I quickly ejected the spent magazine and replaced it, my fingers moving briskly until it slid into place with a click.

I reemerged and unleashed the next bullets into the left

tire until their vehicle abruptly came to a stop. Now both of their front tires were flat, jamming up the cars behind them. A sense of relief washed over me and the driver slammed his hands on the dashboard in frustration.

Our car lurched forward with newfound speed as Noah slammed his foot down the accelerator, then briskly turned a corner toward a quieter and smaller street, away from the main roads.

I finally breathed out, throwing my gun into the passenger seat after turning the safety on and slumping as if every ounce of energy I carried had been depleted, my hand resting against Noah's chest.

I could feel his heart beating under my touch, matching mine as we both caught our breaths. His hand around my waist squeezed as he leaned into me, his chin resting right above my collarbone that had been exposed earlier when I'd opened my jacket.

"Good girl," he breathed out against my skin, his exhale hot on my neck.

The praise snapped me out of my momentary lapse and I clambered off his lap, taking my gun and dropping back onto my seat with a heavy thump.

We sat in a heavy silence and I could feel him looking at me, wanting to say something, but I cleaned my gun to distract me and kept my eyes on the road.

After a few changes of streets to make sure no one else was following us, Noah merged into the expressway that separated Bab Al Mansour and Bemes, the city lights slowly fading in the background and cloaking us into darkness.

He didn't ask where we were going or for directions and I didn't offer the answers. We drove for a little while in a tense silence and I waited until we were far enough away from the city before I spoke up, "Pull over. I'll drive."

Unlike all the other times, he complied without questioning. After pulling over onto the side of the highway, he exited from the driver's side and I took his seat, moving over the console to do so. I plopped down and adjusted it while he made his way to the passenger's side.

Once we were both settled, I eased my car back onto the road and headed for the safe house that was a forty-five-minute drive up north of Bab Al Mansour, in a university town that wouldn't draw too much attention since new students were in the process of coming in to settle in for the new school year.

The highway was mostly deserted except for a few occasional cars passing us, heading for the city behind us.

As I drove down the road, I kept sifting through the information that wasn't adding up, but one thing in particular kept nagging at me. I'd planned to wait until after we'd met with Nassim and we were almost to the safe house, but I needed to know.

I glanced over at Noah and finally asked, "Why did one of them refer to you as Barrera?"

Noah

CHAPTER 14

PRESENT

HER QUESTION HUNG HEAVILY AROUND US, THE WEIGHT OF it sitting against my chest.

I knew I'd have to tell her one day, that my revelation might change everything between us forever. I just hoped that despite my lies, my next words wouldn't create an irreversible rift between us that I wouldn't be able to mend.

I hesitated for a moment, unable to meet her gaze. But then, with a heavy sigh, I finally let go of the one truth I'd kept buried inside, the admission breaking free like a dam succumbing to the weight it'd been holding over for too long.

"Because I used to be one," I admitted, my confession suffocating the air around us. I chanced looking over at her to find her brows pulled together in confusion. "Omar Barrera's my father."

Her eyes searched my face for answers and when my expression didn't falter, a wave of understanding washed over her, melding with hurt and betrayal that threatened to swallow me whole.

I would give anything to turn back time and meet her again for the first time, to right my wrongs and make sure the look on her face right now would never have a chance to make its way there.

She closed her eyes and turned away from me, her attention back on the road. My stomach sank with each passing second she didn't speak.

"Say something," I pleaded, needing her to say or scream something, *anything*. Anger I was prepared to deal with because anger meant she still cared. But indifference, her silence, that I didn't want to fathom its repercussions.

I *needed* her to be angry. I *needed* to know that deep down, no matter how much time had passed, she still cared.

Maybe it was foolish of me to think that despite my constant betrayal and lies, she'd still want anything to do with me, but a foolish heart reached for hope and I wasn't ready to give that up.

I didn't think I ever could.

It felt like hours had passed when she impassively said, "All you seem to have ever done was lie to me, so no, I don't have anything to say to you."

"That's not true," I started, my voice strained with guilt. "I didn't lie about everything."

I kept my focus on her, hoping she'd talk to me. But she stayed silent, her eyes remaining on the road and refusing to meet my gaze. I eventually turned my attention to where we were going, stealing glances at her from the corner of my eye every once in a while.

It was a few minutes before midnight when we passed a white town sign that read *Ben Sbih*.

We drove for another few miles before she left the paved road and turned into a dark narrow alley. Amalia navigated through a labyrinth of narrow alleyways, passing a group of kids playing football in the streets, until a one-story property, its rammed earth facade weathered with time, came into view.

She came to a stop behind a motorcycle already parked there, turned off the engine, and said, "We're here. Let's go." Her hand reached to open her door, but my hand shot out to grasp her arm. She immediately jerked away from my touch. "Don't," she said coldly, still refusing to look at me.

"Amalia," I whispered, urging her to look at me, but she ignored me and stepped out of the car, leaving me behind.

I thought I knew what heartbreak felt like when I'd promised her I'd return that morning, only to leave and never see her again.

It had taken me a while after my mother's passing for

the true weight of losing Amalia to settle in. But when my emotions kicked back in, I'd spent months feeling like a knife was constantly being twisted into my chest whenever anything reminded me of her.

But this somehow made whatever I'd felt back then like child's play.

My heart was pounding in my ears, the blood rushing too quickly to my head. All I could feel was an immense pressure sitting against my chest, but I refused to let it win, no matter how overwhelming it tried to be.

This wasn't over.

The sound of someone slamming against the hood of the car startled me out of my thoughts. I looked up to find Amalia standing outside, an aggravated expression on her face.

"We don't have all day," she called out, her voice cutting through the night.

Without a second glance in my direction, she spun around and strode toward the white iron front door. She reached for the back pocket of her pants to retrieve a key, then moved to unlock it. With a groan of protest, the door swung open and she disappeared inside, leaving it ajar behind her.

With a heavy sigh, I stepped out of the car and made my way over to her. When I stepped over the door's threshold, I found myself greeted with an unexpected sight—the glint of a gun barrel.

It wasn't the first time I'd met the end of a barrel, so I

chose to disregard it, instead focusing my attention on the figure holding the weapon.

With the entryway hallway cloaked in darkness, his features remained mostly obscured, but I could still discern that he was around Amalia's age—or maybe even mine. He had on a long-sleeved shirt, dark straight pants, and a beanie over his head despite the suffocating August humidity.

The lights were suddenly turned on. "Lower your gun, Nassim," Amalia's voice rang out, tinged with impatience. "He's unfortunately with me."

I didn't let myself dwell on her "unfortunately" and watched as this *Nassim* reluctantly lowered his gun, his expression tense as he eyed me.

"Who is he? You didn't tell me anything about us having company," he inquired, his gaze still on me.

Amalia shed her jacket and hung it on a hook farther down the hall, leaving her in only a black tank top. She then approached us and leaned her shoulder casually against the wall behind him. "You didn't exactly give me the opportunity during our last conversation," she replied dryly.

I hated not knowing how they knew each other, hated how familiar they sounded with one another. I had no right to be jealous, but it didn't stop the resentment.

"Do you trust him?" Nassim asked, glancing at her over his shoulder.

I waited with bated breath for her answer, although

deep down I braced myself for disappointment. After everything that had transpired between us and my latest admission, why would she say yes?

Her gaze flickered briefly to mine before settling back on the stranger who was still standing between her and me. "No," she admitted as I'd expected, but it didn't stop the expected disappointment from washing over me. "But *you* can for whatever you have planned. Something tells me he has more at stake in this than I originally thought."

Nassim furrowed his brows at Amalia's response and turned toward me. Shifting his gun to his left hand, he extended his right one toward me and gave me a small smile. "Nassim Aguilar," he introduced himself.

I accepted his outstretched hand and firmly shook it once. "Noah Brown."

Amalia shook her head, a sigh of disbelief escaping her lips. "Now that we're all acquainted, we have matters to discuss."

With a nod of agreement, Nassim tucked his weapon in the back of his pants before motioning for us to follow him farther into the house. I gestured for Amalia to take the lead, trailing closely behind her.

The interior was a surprising contrast to what I'd expected for a safe house or its drab exterior, warm hues welcoming us inside. Traditional decor adorned the stone walls, and a vibrant rug lined the hallway that led to the main living area.

A half wall divided the space, revealing a small kitchen

to the right with an iron back door that mirrored the one at the front, likely leading to some sort of courtyard.

On the other side of the divide, the living room was set up in a traditional Moroccan seating arrangement. Over the large matching rug to the one at the front were two low cushions that lined the walls in an L shape. At the center, a low wooden table was ladened with an array of bread, butter, honey, and a silver teapot, its fragrant mint tea wafting through the air.

Nassim wrinkled his nose in distaste as we settled around the table. "What the hell is this smell?"

"That would be me," I replied flatly. "Didn't really have much time to shower between being held captive for the last three weeks in a damp cell and then brought here against my will."

Amalia, who was sitting next to Nassim on the cushion facing the entryway, rolled her eyes. "You're welcome to go back."

Nassim's gaze bounced back and forth between Amalia and me as he reached behind him to place his gun on the wooden surface in front of us. He then grabbed the teapot and asked, "Tea, anyone?" with a smile playing on his lips.

Bewildered, I just stared at him because why was this stranger being this cordial by offering mint tea and smiling minutes after having a gun pointed at my head.

When no one answered his offer, he poured himself a glass and said to himself, "Guess that'll leave more for me." After taking a leisurely sip, Nassim reclined against the pillows, his hand hanging as he toyed with the teacup.

Amalia met his gesture with a glare, but he seemed completely unfazed by her demeanor.

"Relax, Amalia. You're always so serious. You just got here, and it's quite rude to refuse when someone offers you tea, you know."

"Don't tell me to relax, Nassim," Amalia interjected, her tone sharp with impatience. "Just cut to the chase and tell me why you had me come here."

His gaze shifted between us, his expression thoughtful as he seemed to contemplate his next words. Finally, he leaned forward, setting his glass aside with a sigh.

"All right," he began, his tone now serious. "Barrera's planning to move on Alaoui's territory and expand Adil's *special* operations." He paused, allowing the weight of his words to sink in before continuing. "He sent out a hit on his head for fourteen million *rial* three days ago."

Amalia's brow furrowed, her gaze fixed intently on Nassim. "That doesn't make sense. Why would he contract someone else to kill Alaoui when he could've just asked me? Are you sure about the intel? Who even told you this?"

She fired each question without giving him time to answer, but he let her as if he was used to her way of processing information.

Which meant he *knew* her and I didn't like that.

When she was done, he met her gaze squarely, his expression turning somber. "I wouldn't tell you to leave and meet me here if I wasn't sure. My contact sent me this the day I called you." He reached into his pocket, retrieved a folded picture, and placed it on the table in front of her. "I haven't confirmed yet if you've been made, but when one of my guys told me a hit had been posted for Alaoui's head, I knew something was wrong."

She peered at the picture and her features darkened at the sight of whatever was on the table.

Nassim spoke again as I grabbed the photograph from the table. It was a grainy print of Amalia and another man, talking at the docks in Bemes. She was handing him something, but it was too blurry to tell exactly what it was.

"We need to move quicker than we'd planned," Nassim continued. "Your cover might not be blown, but if there are talks about you betraying the cartel, it's just as bad. Barrera already has a monopoly in the country. If he overthrows Adil, we're fucked. He'll have too much control for us to do anything about it."

The gears turned in my head as I processed everything he'd just said, but I still didn't understand what was his connection to Amalia or his interest in my father. I could tell he wasn't from the Bureau because I would have known about an operation aiming to come after my father's empire.

I might have let go of my need to bring Omar down, but I still monitored his whereabouts and what he was involved in. That's how I found out about what happened to Jamal and his wife.

Placing the picture back on the table. I turned my attention back to him. "Who are you?" I asked curtly. I knew I was being short, but I couldn't care less right now. I was itching to know his connection to my father and most importantly to my Amalia.

"I could ask you the same thing," he countered.

"I asked you first," I insisted.

I expected him to push back or give me an elusive answer, but instead, he leaned back against the pillow behind him and met my gaze head-on. "My father used to be Barrera's right-hand man back in the seventies and eighties. He had to flee the cartel years before I was even born and I'm back to finish what he'd started."

His revelation hung in the air, the implications sinking in slowly as I processed his words.

"You're Reda's son?" My question came out barely above a whisper, memories of the past flooding my mind.

Shortly after we'd boarded the plane that night, exhaustion and the pain medication my mother had given me after stitching my neck up had pulled me into a deep slumber.

I'd woken up hours later in Colombia with a new last name and a new life. I'd learned later on that my uncle Reda had been in contact with someone in the Aguilar cartel and had eventually been able to broker a deal in exchange for sanctuary within their ranks.

Reda and I had had a relatively close relationship, but he'd always been secretive and vague about his private life.

I'd actually thought there was something between him and my mother and they just didn't want me to be aware of it.

But when my mother and I had left Colombia years later, he hadn't come with us. He'd insisted on staying behind, claiming he'd had business to tend to and that he couldn't leave it behind.

Guess this is what he meant by that?

Nassim furrowed his brows. "How do you know my father's name?"

"Because he's part of the reason I'm still alive today."

Noah

CHAPTER 15

"I don't understand. What do you mean he's part of the reason you're still alive?"

"I knew your father," I started, but Nassim cut me off.

"How did you know him?" he rushed out, his gaze searching mine for answers.

"Let him finish," Amalia interjected, her tone strict.

I briefly glanced over at her before focusing my attention back on my newfound cousin. Nassim sighed and gestured for me to go on.

"I knew your father," I repeated, my voice steady as I prepared for the second time tonight to reveal the connection I had to the cartel, a tie I'd spent my entire life severing.

I didn't particularly want to reveal to more people who

my father was, but we had a common target and I needed Nassim to trust me.

"Reda Taleb was *my* father's right-hand man."

His features contorted in a whirlwind of conflicting emotions. "Your father?" he echoed, the words hanging in the air between us like a heavy cloak, suffocating.

I gave him a curt nod and cleared my throat. "Omar Barrera's my father," I affirmed. "But only by name. Reda was more of a father to me than mine ever was."

Nassim's eyes widened in disbelief as his fingers instinctively found their way to his temples, pressing firmly as he shook his head. After a few moments, he finally brought his gaze back on me.

"Wait. Are you the little boy in the picture my dad always used to carry in his wallet? I always asked him who it was and he just kept telling me that it was someone from his past that he deeply cared about."

"That's something you'd have to ask him."

Nassim's features suddenly sombered, his eyes full of sorrow. I knew what that look meant because it was the same haunted look I'd sported after I'd lost my mother.

A phantom ache wrapped around my rib cage as I waited for Nassim to confirm what I thought, regrets of years lost and moments never shared washing over me.

The more I looked at Nassim, the more I saw their resemblances. From the shape of his eyes and the way they crinkled when he smiled, even their personalities were extremely similar.

And the more I looked at him, the more I saw a ghost of the man who'd shaped my childhood alongside my mother.

For a long time, it had always been just me, my mother, and him. I'd thought of reaching out on multiple occasions after we'd moved away, but I didn't want to jeopardize his secrecy.

I'd almost done it when my mother died, but I couldn't find it in me to tell him that she'd passed away. I'd hoped he'd find out on his own and reach out, but that had never ended up happening.

"He passed away last year," Nassim said, his voice strained. "Car accident. He died on his way to the hospital and I never got to say goodbye."

I gave him a nod of understanding. "I know what that's like," I whispered. I could feel Amalia's gaze boring into my skin, but I didn't look her way and kept my eyes on Nassim. Before either could ask what I meant by that, I redirected us to the topic at hand. "What's your plan?"

Nassim didn't question my changing the subject and explained what he and Amalia had been working on for the last year. I initially thought they had a solid plan in place, but the more he revealed, the more frustrated I became.

Once he was done with his explanations, his eyes stayed on me, waiting for me to comment. Silence stretched between the three of us as I glanced back and forth between him and Amalia before my gaze landed on Nassim.

"So your plan is to essentially kill my father, take over, and become the new *Rai's*?"

"Yes."

I huffed out a laugh of disbelief. "You're out of your fucking mind. I thought you had a better plan than that. Do you not think Barrera won't have you killed the second you're in his line of sight?"

My gaze slid to Amalia. "Especially you."

She'd essentially committed the highest treason you could against the cartel. The moment she was in my father's reach, he would have her executed and there was no way I'd let that happen. She absolutely could take care of herself and handle her own, but I was also acquainted with what my father was capable of.

I couldn't care less if it made me sound like an asshole, but I wouldn't let her put herself in harm's way. I wouldn't risk losing another person I loved, especially not at the hands of my father.

"I can't believe you agreed to this," I mumbled, bewildered. She'd worked for my father for who knows how long. Surely she knew this would never work.

Her gaze twitched with irritation. "I did because it's the best shot we have. I've worked for your father for the last three years and he certainly won't recuse himself. The only thing that'll stop him is if he's six feet underground. If we don't put someone in power ourselves, the cartel will fall into Hamza's hands since Mateo's dead and he's just as bad as *your father*."

The way she'd said the last words felt like getting punched in the gut. I could hear the resentment in her voice and I hated it. But a small part of me focused on the fact that this was the first time she'd shown some kind of emotion since I'd told her. She wasn't indifferent anymore and I'd hold on to that like a lifeline.

She spoke again, "Besides, I doubt *you* want to be the next *Ra'is*, but what do I know, with all your lies, you just might."

I had no plans of taking over the cartel from my father. No matter how much I wanted his reign to be over, I wouldn't put myself in a world I'd never wanted any part of in the first place despite it technically being my legacy.

I wished their plan were better than barging into the *riad* and killing my father, but we were out of time, especially after the picture Nassim had gotten of Amalia and the hit my father had sent on Adil's head.

We were looking at a few days at most before things would become a lot harder to handle if my father gained control of Alaoui's assets and territory.

My eyes cut back to Nassim. "I still think this plan is incredibly stupid, but I'm in. Except I have two conditions."

"Name them."

"She stays with me at all times and my father can't be killed if I'm not present."

From my periphery, I noticed Amalia's eyebrows shoot up in bewilderment. "Stay with you at all times?" Amalia's laugh was harsh. "You don't get to make decisions for me," she hissed.

My eyes didn't leave Nassim. "Those are my conditions or I walk, and you need me," I stated, holding my ground. I knew Amalia didn't like my first condition, but I didn't care. "I might not have seen the man in almost thirty years, but he's still the same."

I knew my father well, just not in the way most kids knew theirs. Years might have passed, but deep down, he was still the same man. His ego had always gotten the best of him and my presence would unsettle him.

He'd never anticipate me coming after him, let alone overthrow him. Even after I almost choked him to death during our little reunion.

A sigh left his lips before he conceded, "Deal."

Amalia's head cut sharply toward him as anger emanated from her. "*Nassim*," she interjected, disbelief evident in her tone at him agreeing with my demands.

He looked her in the eyes. "We need him. I won't have time to rally up everyone we need on such short notice. So I can use all the extra hands I can get and it's his father," he explained. "And if my own cared for him, then I trust him."

"Fine," she mumbled in irritation.

"As for your crew issues, I know someone who can help," I told him. "He'll be on board when he knows who's involved."

There was someone I trusted implicitly, someone I knew would help once I told him who we were after, especially after the events that transpired a few weeks ago involving his wife.

More importantly, he also deserved to finally know the truth I'd been hiding from him. I'd thought I had done a better job at protecting him against my father, but learning that he'd known for years that I'd concealed his parents' murder made me feel like I'd failed him.

On top of that, the fact that my dead half-brother almost killed his wife made it even worse. While he might struggle to forgive me for keeping my connection to my father, I clung to the hope he'd understand. If he didn't, then I'd keep trying until I earned his forgiveness.

"How long would it take him to come?" Nassim asked.

"Once he agrees, just a few hours."

He gave me a quick nod in response, reaching for his tea and downing the rest of it before speaking again. "All right, not that I don't enjoy this beautiful company, but I do have a wife to go back to," he said, pushing off his seat to stand.

The previous jealousy that had been slithering in my veins instantly evaporated when the knowledge that he was married registered in my brain.

I had no right to be jealous, but Amalia was and would always be mine.

Once up, he extended his hand in my direction. "Wish we'd met under different circumstances, but maybe after all of this, we can talk more," he suggested, a soft smile playing on his lips.

I grabbed his hand in mine and stood. I wasn't one to let people in, but something about him being Reda's son was making me reconsider my stance. I didn't have much of a family anymore and I still didn't know if the one I still had would be there for much longer, but I decided I wouldn't turn down his offer just yet.

"Yeah, let's talk once my father's a distant memory," I finally replied.

He turned his body toward Amalia, who was still sitting. "Care to walk me to the door?" he told her, a tentative smile on his face, one of his dimples showing.

She rolled her eyes at him and motioned for him to lead the way. They strolled down the hallway, and I heard her fire a plethora of curses at him in Spanish as she harshly smacked the back of his head.

I stifled a laugh, covering it with a cough. She was already pissed at me and I didn't need more things working against me.

In response, Nassim simply rubbed the back of his head and shrugged, a hint of guilt crossing his face. His expression didn't seem to have anything to do with the fact that he'd agreed to my proposal and more because he didn't like overruling her decisions.

After a few more hushed words, he lifted two of his fingers to his forehead, saying goodbye with a swift motion before opening the door and leaving. Once the door clicked shut, the palpable tension that had been present in the car reemerged in the air between us.

She locked the door with a key and fastened the bolt underneath it before walking back down the hallway.

"Amalia," I called out to her when she stepped into the living area without a glance in my direction.

We were well into the night and dawn would break the horizon in just a few hours, but I wanted to talk to her. She'd ignored me earlier and I hadn't pressed her, but I was done waiting.

She made her way into the kitchen, grabbed a bottle of water from the refrigerator, then moved toward the closed door in the living room where I assumed the bedroom lay.

"Amalia," I tried again.

Please, baby, look at me.

She didn't and grabbed the handle, pushing the door open.

I stepped in her direction and was about to call her name out again when she turned around, meeting my gaze head-on. A myriad of emotions crossed her face—anger, betrayal... hurt.

"I already told you in the car earlier, I have nothing to say to you." I took another step in her direction, but she held her hand up. "It's late, Noah. I don't have the energy to keep telling you no, so just let me go."

I can't.

I opened my mouth to protest, but she interrupted me again. "*Please*, Noah." She gestured toward the door leading to the courtyard. "There's a faucet and a bucket outside you can use to shower. Bathroom's over there." She pointed to a small door in the corner opposite the kitchen. "You can sleep on the cushions or I think there's an old mattress in the courtyard you can use, although I don't know how long it's been outside if it's still even there."

Once she was done, she walked inside the bedroom and shut the door behind her, not leaving me room to say anything back.

I stood still in the middle of the living room, hesitating on what to do next. On one hand, I wanted to barge into the room and make her talk to me, but on the other, I knew that if I pushed her too hard, too fast, she would close me off forever and I'd lose the opportunity to have her give me a chance to explain myself.

So I decided to respect her wishes for now and instead retreated to the courtyard. Once outside, my eyes scanned the area. It was relatively small, but for the size of the house we were in, I wasn't surprised.

Patterned tiles lined the ground while tall stucco walls shielded us from peering eyes. I spotted the mattress Amalia had been referring to was propped against the back wall, but it was a mess.

The stitching on the sides was frayed, the surface had various dark spots, and the glint of a spring piercing the surface showed how much this bed had been worn down with time. I'd slept on concrete floors for the last three weeks. The living room cushions would do just fine.

I found the small brass tap mounted on the wall and made my way over. There was a large blue bucket with a small pink cup inside underneath it. I opened the tap and rinsed both items before filling the bucket. The water was cold, but I didn't have the patience to sit and wait for water to boil so I could add it to it.

While it was filling, I opened the small bin a few steps away and found towels, a bar of soap, and a few small washcloths. Walking back, I shut the water off, removed all my clothes, discarding them to the side to wash later, and grabbed a handful of water with the pink cup.

I poured the water over my head and the icy temperature sent a shockwave of shivers down my spine, amplified by the whipping wind of the night air.

Fuck, this is cold.

I kept going, focusing my attention on relishing the feel of the water on my skin after weeks without and not how cold it was. I quickly showered, using the bar of soap to wash both my hair and my skin.

Once I'd finished, I tied a towel around my waist and proceeded to wash my clothes before hanging them on one of the chairs around the table.

I doubted there was a change of clothes inside, so I just had to hope that the morning heat would dry them up by the time I woke up. I grabbed another towel from the bin and walked back inside, dried my upper body with it and locked the door behind me.

The lights were now turned off and Amalia had shut the bedroom door. I ran the towel over my head as I padded over to it. I stood in front of it and contemplated whether I should knock. She might be asleep, but I had to try again.

So after softly knocking on the door, I quietly called out her name, "Amalia? Are you up?"

No answers.

I rapped my knuckles on the wooden door again and listened for movement on the other side, with no luck. With a resigned sigh, I walked back to the living room to find that she'd left a flat bed sheet on one of the cushions.

The gesture added an ounce of hope into the well I'd been cultivating since the day I'd left.

After I finished drying myself off, I placed a towel over one of the pillows and wrapped myself into the plaid orange sheet, the other towel still wrapped around my waist.

Then I closed my eyes, hoping the accumulated exhaustion of the past few weeks would take over and lull me into a deep sleep.

But all I kept thinking about was Amalia.

Amalia

CHAPTER 16

PRESENT

GOD, HE'S RELENTLESS.

One thing about him definitely hadn't changed over the years and it was his sheer determination to get what he wanted once he'd set his mind to it.

I'd used to love that about him, but now I resented it.

I'd been trying to sleep, but every time I closed my eyes, Noah's face flashed in my mind, torturing me just a little more. And it didn't help when his voice drifted to my ears again as he stood on the other side of the closed door.

After a fleeting pause, he finally relented, his steps drifting farther away from the door. The sound of fabric rustling briefly filled the air until it was quiet again.

I waited with bated breath, listening for signs of him coming back, but he didn't.

A wave of conflicting emotions washed over me as a burning fire lanced my chest. I closed my eyes, breathing deeply. I'd done my best not to react when the words "Omar Barrera's my father" left his lips, but his earlier confession still made my stomach churn and my head feel light.

At first, I'd thought I must have misheard for a second time in one night because surely the man I'd fallen in love with all those years ago didn't lie to me.

Surely the man I loved—*had* loved, I reminded myself —didn't hide from me who he was even after he'd spent weeks learning everything about me, after I'd revealed all my scars to him, something I'd never done before.

I had shattered the walls I'd built around me my entire life to let him in and in return I'd been a fool and fallen head over heels with a lie, not even seeing it when I'd literally been trained to detect them.

With the truth now displayed in front of me, pieces of past conversations we'd had about his family were finally falling into place.

He'd been guarded when topics of our families were brought up, but he'd always spoken freely of his mother and how close they were. But I did remember how he'd immediately grown quieter at the mention of his father.

I'd never thought much of it because I'd had my own fair share of terrible parents. I might speak freely about how much I'd considered mine's existence irrelevant after they'd abandoned us, but not everyone was ready to share their story.

The only time he'd ever given me insights into his relationship with his father had been when I'd asked him about the large scar nestled at the base of his neck. When he'd told me that it had been a birthday gift from his father, I hadn't pried and knew he'd share about his past when *or* if he was ever ready to do so.

The funny thing was, I didn't care about him being Barrera's son. No one chose the family they were born into. *I* knew that better than anyone.

I would have never cared about that.

What I was furious about was the fact that he'd hid it from me, lied to me about it, and then left me behind like a discarded piece of clothing you forget under your bed instead of trusting me to stay.

To be there for him and accept all of him.

Was I that untrustworthy that he'd thought he couldn't be honest?

I wanted to be indifferent to him. I *wanted* to keep living in the world I'd built where he didn't exist, but it never had been that simple. He was my first everything. My first true love, my first taste of true and intoxicating happiness.

I'd been content with my life before him. I'd known what I wanted to do with my career, loved being by myself, and had a pretty great relationship with my siblings. But I'd be lying if I said life hadn't felt lonely.

I'd thought I was happy, but when I met him, happiness gained a new definition. I didn't just fall in love *with* him. I fell in love with the person I'd become when I was with him.

I had been *happy.*

And all of it had been taken from me when he'd left.

I'd felt betrayed. I *still* felt that way.

And to learn that the betrayal ran even deeper made the wounds I'd worked so hard to conceal resurface like they'd been freshly inflicted. Especially when after being silent for ten years, he had the nerve not to let me out of his sight, like I couldn't take care of myself.

That made the anger burn even brighter.

But despite it, I kept facing one problem.

No matter how much I hated him, and God was I so angry with him,

I still fucking loved him. I felt so stupid for letting the hollow look in his eyes get to me. The one that told me something was off, that he wasn't the same man I'd spent time discovering ten years ago. I felt like a fool for letting it affect me as much as it did.

My emotions felt at an impasse because they constantly tugged in different directions. A part of me wanted to cling to the anger and resentment and wished he'd never bull-dozed his way into my life while another part wanted to have him back.

¡Vaya tontería[1]!

I needed to keep my focus on the task at hand, not sift through how my emotions were at odds.

The moment Nassim told me I had to leave, I knew things were bad, but I didn't expect them to be this bad. I'd been undercover for the last five years and I was *good*. My mask had never faltered, no matter how hard it was and how many times I'd wanted to give up at the beginning.

I'd learned to compartmentalize *except* when it came to the kids Barrera stole from their parents. I'd helped a few escape, but I'd always been more than prudent.

I knew no one had ever suspected my real identity and I'd always been careful of my surroundings, but I hadn't noticed my picture being taken last month.

At first sight, the conversation depicted in that photograph wasn't incriminating. The picture showed me with one of the cartel's distributors, but Barrera had never been made aware of the meeting.

He might not suspect that I was undercover, but if he'd sent a request for a hit on the dark web instead of asking me to do it, it meant he at least suspected I might be double-crossing him, putting me in a much worse position than if I'd been compromised.

Nassim's and my original plan was to overthrow Barrera right from under him instead of staging a coup

---

1. This is such nonsense.

because we knew it would be difficult since we'd never be able to gather enough people to go against all of his.

So instead, over the past year, I'd met with key figures in the cartel and worked out deals to sway them on our side. Some were much easier to convince than others, but after some long *and* pricey negotiations, I'd been able to get most of them on board.

What I'd been doing was risky and put me in a precarious position because any of them could easily turn around and expose me to Barrera, but everyone I'd spoken to came to the same conclusion.

Change in power was needed.

Barrera had grown more reckless over the years and started taking a bigger cut than he'd used to. In this world, money talked and if you could offer a better deal, one would be stupid not to take it.

We were offering them a better profit margin, protection, and respect.

Something only a fool would say no to.

And I had enough blackmail against each and every one of them if needed.

I'd still had a few more people to meet with, but with the short time frame we were put up against, we wouldn't be able to turn everyone before Nassim took over.

We still had to discuss what the next steps were, but I decided to push the thought to the back of my brain and try to get some sleep before the long days we were about to face.

It felt like I'd barely just closed my eyes to get some sleep when a loud voice roused me awake. I pinched the bridge of my nose as the merchant outside yelled about carrots and zucchinis being discounted over and over again as he passed under the window above the bed where I was lying.

With my eyes still closed, I patted the sheets next to me for my burner to look at the time. Once my palm closed around the phone, I barely peeled one eye open and flipped it open, noting that it was just a little past 8:00 a.m.

I let out a groan and dropped the phone back on the bed. I tried to fall back asleep but after a few tosses and turns, I placed my palms over my face and let out another frustrated groan.

I was fucking exhausted and wanted to sleep, but it was too late. I wouldn't be able to fall back asleep. I ran my hands over my face and sat up in bed, throwing my legs over the edge of the bed.

My stomach grumbled, reminding me I hadn't eaten in almost twenty-four hours. I retrieved my pants from where I'd discarded them on the floor and swiftly tugged them back on.

I reached back for the burner and quickly fired a nondescript text message to Nassim to arrange a meeting time. Once he replied he would meet us at the large market in town around ten, I rose to my feet and made my way out of the bedroom, stopping by the bedroom closet to grab a *djellaba*[2] and a pair of *belgha*[3] from it.

Pausing before opening it, I listened for signs of Noah being awake. My own self seemed to be conspiring against me, so the more I avoided him, the better.

When I didn't hear any movement on the other side, I cautiously turned the door handle and slipped out of the bedroom, doing my best to keep quiet. I turned and glanced in Noah's direction, stopping short.

My breath hitched in my throat because for the first time in almost a decade, I had a full—almost—view of his body. Noah was sprawled shirtless on one of the low sofas, the strong planes of his body on full display.

He had one arm shielding his face while the other rested where the plaid orange sheet I'd left for him earlier this morning, the fabric pooling dangerously low around his waist.

Despite my efforts to tear my gaze away, he was hard to ignore. My gaze unwarrantedly traced over his golden-brown skin, lingering on the chain necklace that I hadn't noticed before, one that he used to always wear. It rested low on his neck, the bottom brushing against his collarbone.

Unbidden flashbacks of how his skin used to feel under my fingertips and how much I'd loved looping my finger

---

2. Long, loose-fitting unisex outer garment with full-sleeves.
3. Heeless slippers made from leather.

around the chain to bring him closer suddenly assaulted my mind.

I felt the sound of my heartbeat in my ears, the cadence increasing with each passing second.

"Not that I mind, pretty girl," a hoarse voice said, immediately snapping me out of the trance. "But are you gonna keep staring at me like that or is there something I can help you with?"

My skin blazed from the fact that he'd caught me, but I quickly gathered myself. I jerked my head up to find he was still in the same position, unmoving.

I scoffed. "I wasn't. Don't flatter yourself," I countered, obviously lying.

He suddenly sat up and leaned back, propping himself on one of his hands. The movement sent the linen pooling even lower around his waist, revealing the deep cut leading underneath what I could still, to my disgruntlement, vividly picture.

Joder[4], I cursed silently in my mind as his eyes met mine.

He let out a knowing laugh and stood, stepping around the low table to walk toward me, grasping the linen with one hand so that it wouldn't drag on the floor. It did nothing to hide what it was attempting to conceal, but I didn't let my gaze falter from his.

---

4. Fuck.

I knew he was taunting me, but I wouldn't give him the satisfaction.

"Where are your clothes?" I asked as he stood closer, slightly craning my neck as he towered over me.

"Outside, drying," he replied, further closing the distance between us with another step. "Though there isn't much left to wear."

I didn't move. "There should be spare clothes your size in the bedroom closet. Make sure you're wearing something by the time I get back," I told him, turning away and heading toward the front door.

Before I could take more than a few steps, his free hand wrapped around my wrist to stop me. "Where are you going?" he asked, his voice tinged with concern.

I jerked my hand away from his grasp, meeting his alarmed expression with a roll of my eyes. "Relax, I'm just grabbing breakfast from the *hanout*[5] right around the corner."

"I'm coming with you," he announced, striding over to the bedroom and disappearing inside.

"No need, it's not far," I insisted and walked toward the front door, slipping the loose-fitting outer robe and shoes on. I then grabbed the keys hanging on a small hook next to the front door.

"I don't care," he countered firmly as I turned the keys

---

5. Name for small corner stores in Morocco.

inside the lock and unfastened the latch underneath to unlock the door.

I heard him call out my name as I pulled the door open, but I was already out the door before he could follow behind.

Noah

CHAPTER 17

PRESENT

Frustrated with myself, I closed my eyes and drew in a deep breath.

I should have known she'd leave the moment I stepped out of her sight. I'd barely slipped on a fresh pair of boxers when she left. I'd never met a woman so fascinating yet equally frustrating.

I debated rushing after her before deciding against it. But if she wasn't back in the next fifteen minutes, then I would. Sighing, I finished getting dressed, opting for linen shorts and a loose white T-shirt, and headed to the kitchen.

After looking through the few cupboards, I found a box of loose gunpowder tea, grounded coffee, and sugar. While the coffee brewed and water boiled in a kettle, I grabbed a knife and walked outside. Finding the small pot of mint I'd noticed yesterday, I cut a few pieces and walked back inside.

I turned on the gas stove, firing it up with the small lighter that was on the counter, and let the teapot I'd prepared simmer.

Both the coffee pot and tea were ready when the front door opened again. "I'm back," she called out before appearing in the living area a few seconds later with a clear plastic bag filled with items.

She walked into the kitchen and set the bag on the counter before pulling her *djellaba* over her head. In the process of removing it, her tank top rode up, revealing her toned stomach and giving me a peek of the dainty butterflies I knew she had tattooed on her left hip.

My grip on the handle of the mug I was holding tightened as I remembered what it was like to trace my tongue there as she writhed under my touch.

What I wouldn't give to get to do that again.

She threw the garment to the side, the fabric landing onto one of the cushions in the living room. She faced me again, only to find me looking at her. She quickly tugged her top back down and propped her hip against the side of the counter.

"Now, look who's staring."

Her comment pulled a small smile on my face because it gave me a glimpse of my Amalia. The one I knew was still there.

I met her gaze. "Never said I wasn't. I'm always looking at you."

Something familiar washed over her gaze, but it was gone in the same breath. Amalia tore her eyes away from me and pulled the items she'd bought out of the bag—a fresh baguette, two individual Kiri cheese blocks, and two eggs.

She walked past me and grabbed a knife. While she assembled the breakfast sandwich, I poured a cup of coffee for her, knowing she preferred it over tea.

After making it the way she liked it, I walked over to her. "Here," I said, handing her the cup with the spoon still inside.

She glanced at me over her shoulder as she cut the now filled baguette in half.

When she just kept looking at my outstretched hand, my lips pulled down into a frown. "Do you not like coffee anymore?" I questioned, thinking I might have been wrong.

"No, I still do," she answered, still not taking the mug from me.

When she looked up at me with a puzzled look on her face, I asked, "Then what is it?" It was quiet between us for a moment as we both looked at each other, my eyes roaming her face, trying to read her.

She shook her head and finally grabbed it from my hand, her fingers brushing against mine in the process. She took a sip before muttering, "Thanks."

After that, she grabbed a half of the breakfast sandwich

she'd made and with her mug in hand, she headed for the courtyard. "Eat, we have to leave soon to meet with Nassim," she instructed before pushing the iron door open and walking outside.

I hesitated on following her but knew that she'd most likely just walk back inside if I did. So instead, I poured myself some tea and rested against the edge of the counter to eat.

As I did, I caught a glimpse of her through the small window over the fridge. Amalia sat in one of the chairs around the mosaic outdoor table there, propping her foot onto the seat, something she always did when she ate. She took bite after bite of her sandwich, sipping her coffee every once in a while.

Watching her do something so mundane reminded me of the week we'd spent together at my apartment before everything changed and I ended up ruining the best thing in my life.

Recruits always got a week off in the middle of their training to rest before the more intense second part of their year. So a few days before they were set to leave, I'd pulled Amalia into my office to both steal a kiss and ask her if she'd want to stay behind with me.

I'd been contemplating asking her for a few weeks, but I'd been too nervous to—something that had never happened to me before. I'd kept telling myself that she might have a family she'd want to spend time with instead of me and I could've used the time off to see my mother who'd been asking me to visit every time we spoke on the phone.

But I'd wanted to be selfish for once and have Amalia all to myself.

I'd been tired of the stolen kisses and lingering glances across crowded rooms. I'd wanted more. Wanted her in my space, in my bed, and just with me for longer than a few fleeting minutes before someone noticed we were both gone.

When she'd agreed, I'd never felt more relieved to hear a "yes" coming from someone's lips.

She'd shown up on my doorstep on Sunday night and for the rest of our time together, I'd discover her, what she did and didn't like, what made her tick, what made her laugh. I'd spent hours exploring every inch of her body and she'd done the same with mine.

It had been the most blissful week of my life and in that time, I'd realized I'd never really known what true happiness felt like until Amalia had come into my life.

I'd always felt like my heart couldn't welcome the feeling, that it'd been wired in a way that all it could harbor was hollowness and occasional fleeting moments where I thought I should be happy but couldn't feel it.

All of that had changed the moment she landed herself there and reengineered it in a way where I *could* experience it.

When she smiled at me, I felt the warm embrace enveloping my skin. And with her laughter came the fluttering feeling in your chest when everything just seemed to fall into place.

Amalia had made me feel seen. She'd made me feel alive.

But it had been beyond just how she'd made me feel. I'd also started to be happy with who I was, despite my past. My mother had always told me that who I was wasn't tied to my father and what he'd done to me, but I'd never truly believed it.

I'd always told myself that she was my mother, so of course she had to say that.

But the way Amalia had seen me, truly seen me, had made me realize what my mother had been trying to make me understand.

When Amalia had fallen asleep in my arms before that pivotal Saturday, the night where everything had completely changed, I'd stayed awake, my mind wandering about what-ifs.

The secrecy and sneaking around had been fun at first, but as I'd stared down at her in my arms, noting how peaceful she looked there and how at peace *I'd* felt having her against me, I'd known that Amalia wasn't someone I was willing to live without.

Over the weeks, I'd fallen in love with her completely and intoxicatingly. She'd become my favorite person and place to be next to all wrapped into one. She left me breathless while simultaneously breathing life back into me.

I'd gone to sleep that night, dreaming of a future and

hoping she'd wanted the same. Until a call woke me up the next morning and flipped my world upside down.

I never wanted what we had to end, but when the words mother, cancer, and dead kept ringing over and over in your ears, the only thing you wanted to do was find a way to make them stop.

I'd thought I'd get over it, that after a few days, the grief wouldn't be so poignant and I'd be able to go back and tell her why I never came back with breakfast like I'd told her I would.

But the grief had swallowed me whole and drowned me until I found myself facing the edge of a cliff, wondering if having everything stop altogether would be easier than having to swim against the treacherous waters with no guarantee of making it to the other side.

It took me a long time to realize that I *could* do this, that losing my safe haven wouldn't be the end of me and that I *would* be able to see the other end, despite how hard it would be.

I'd done the work, I'd been ready to come back, but it had been too late. Amalia had already been gone and no matter how many times I'd tried to find her and reach out, I'd never been able to.

Now, I was faced with an opportunity to right my wrongs. The odds may be stacked against us, but I'd make her mine again. I'd lied and betrayed her trust, but I'd do anything to earn it again. No matter how long it took.

I knew a simple conversation wouldn't fix everything, but it was a start that I'd never gotten years ago.

I was tired of living in this constant state of hollowness, of having a darkness looming over my head that only Amalia could chase away.

I looked over at where she'd been sitting, only to find her no longer there. Panic sank in my gut at the thought that something happened to her and I was about to rush outside when she walked into the kitchen in the next moment, with an empty cup in her hand.

I let out a breath of relief and stared at her as she brushed past me to rinse her cup and leave it in the sink.

She faced me again. "What's wrong with you?"

I cleared my throat. "Nothing?"

"Is that a statement or a question?"

"I—"

"It doesn't matter. We have to get going," she ordered before heading for the door.

"Wait," I called out.

She halted in her steps and pinched the bridge of her nose. "We don't have time, Noah."

"I need to make a phone call."

"Then make it."

"I'd love to, but my phone was unfortunately lost in transit to my cell," I deadpanned.

She immediately realized her mistake and muttered something under her breath as she reached for her back pocket. Then she tossed an object in my direction and I caught it before it hit my face.

"Make it quick," she said before turning around and walking out the front door, leaving it ajar. I followed behind and locked the door with the keys she'd left inside the lock.

While Amalia got the car started, I stood by the front door, flipping open the burner phone she'd handed me. I hesitated for a moment before finally dialing his number.

He picked up on the first ring. "Who's this?" he demanded harshly.

"Hey, Jamal. It's me," I replied, careful not to let my tone reflect how I felt.

I planned to tell him everything once we were face to face, but the anticipation of his reaction to my confession terrified me.

Amalia hadn't taken it well and I could only imagine how he would react to knowing that my own blood robbed him of his.

"Uncle Noah?" he asked, his voice softer now. "What happened? Why are you calling me from a burner phone?"

I closed my eyes, inhaling deeply before saying, "I'll be texting you an address and time in the next hour and need you to meet me there. You'll need to be discreet."

"Okay." I could hear the apprehension in his voice, but he knew I wouldn't ask if it wasn't important.

"Bring Valentina and Kai with you," I tell him.

Jamal wasn't aware that I knew what he and his friends actually did and I'd intended to keep it that way, but based on Nassim's comment last night, we'd need all the extra hands we could get.

"I will. How do I contact you when I get there?"

"You won't. I'll be in contact."

There was a pause before he spoke again, "Do I need to be concerned?"

"Just get here. I'll explain everything then," I replied and hung up.

When I looked up, I found Amalia leaning against the hood of the car, watching me with an unreadable expression on her face.

She pushed herself off without a word and rounded the car, then slid into the driver's seat. I opened the passenger door and settled into the seat beside her, then handed the phone back to her.

She grabbed it from me, our fingers brushing in the process, and dropped it into the door pocket. She started the car, cranking the A/C up to counter the fact that some of the windows were now incapacitated, and put her hand on the stick shift.

I waited for her to reverse the car, but instead, she surprised me—and her—by asking, "Everything okay?"

I turned my face toward her. "Yeah," I started, feeling the burden of the impending conversation weighing heavily on my shoulders. "At least I hope it will be."

She looked at me for another beat before nodding and reversing the car into the small alley behind.

We drove through the bustling streets of the city, Amalia maneuvering through the street vendors' carts piled high with goods and weaving through the throngs of pedestrians.

We were nearing the end of August and tomorrow was one of the main holidays in the country, so everyone was out to get their last-minute items for the celebration that would last the next four days.

After a few miles, Amalia turned onto a quieter side street and drove down the road until she turned into an alley and parked behind an older building near the entrance to the old city's marketplace.

Turning the engine off, she grabbed the black cell phone on her way out of the car, her fingers flying over the small keyboard. Then she broke the phone in half and threw it into the dumpster she'd parked in front of.

She reached for a bag I hadn't noticed before in the back seat and pulled clothes from it. She tossed a short-sleeved thobe and a baseball cap my way, ordering me to put them on.

I did as told, slipping the chocolate brown thobe over my clothes. Then I brushed my hair back, secured the hat over my head, and walked over to her as she pulled a lighter *djellaba* over her own clothes and closed the back door.

Suddenly, she grabbed my hand, intertwined our fingers together, and simply said, "Let's go. We don't have all day."

I didn't question it, reveling in her skin against mine, and followed as she guided us into the maze of alleyways.

Noah

CHAPTER 18

PRESENT

WE WEAVED THROUGH THE BUSTLING CHAOS, DODGING locals and tourists alike left and right. The hot and humid air was thick around us, mixed with the aroma of sizzling meat and fragrant spices at every turn.

I hadn't gone to a market like this since I was a child and the sudden nostalgia of coming to a place like this with my mother washed over me.

I didn't have time to dwell on the feeling when Amalia stopped short in front of a store nestled in the far corner of an alley, her grip on my hand suddenly gone.

Startled, I looked over at Amalia, only to find her already pushing the curtains of the store apart and disappearing into its depth.

With a heavy sigh, I shook off the feeling of the loss of her hand in mine and followed right after her.

Once inside, a strong wool scent and the faint hint of incense greeted me, soft notes of Arabic music drifting in the space. Colorful and patterned rugs covered every inch of the store.

At first sight, you'd think the place was tiny, but it seemed endless as I kept walking the long corridor. I moved farther into the store until I noticed the back of Amalia's head.

She was standing in front of Nassim and another woman, who I assumed to be his wife. She was about the same build as Amalia but slightly shorter than her, with long, curly brown hair that was pulled back into a ponytail.

The three of them were exchanging greetings as I made my way over to them. Nassim glanced at me over Amalia's head with a smile on his face. "Glad to see she hasn't murdered you in your sleep," he said, winking at Amalia.

I huffed out a laugh and returned his smile with a small one of my own. "I wouldn't speak too soon," I replied as I reached them and stood right behind Amalia.

I heard her groan at my comment and the woman next to Nassim looked between him and me, shaking her head.

"Hey," I said, brandishing my hand forward to shake Nassim's. My front brushed against Amalia's back in the process, but she didn't move despite her stiff posture. It probably didn't mean anything, but I'd be delusional and take it as a win.

"Hello to you too," Nassim began, shaking my hand once before letting it go. He looked at the woman next to him with a soft expression on his face as he put his hand on the small of her back. "This is my beautiful wife, Daniela. Daniela, this is Noah, my cousin I told you about last night."

Cousin? I didn't bother correcting him and looked over at his wife with a courteous smile, giving her a small nod. "It's nice to meet you, Daniela."

"Same to you too," she replied, reaching for her husband's hand behind her and letting her hand rest over his. The small gesture sent a pang straight into my chest, wishing I could reach for Amalia that effortlessly. "Nassim told me you knew Reda." An appreciative look washed over her features at the mention of my uncle's name.

"Yeah, I did a long time ago," I responded, my voice growing tight.

"He was a good man," Daniela added, glancing up at her husband. Nassim placed a kiss on top of her head.

"He was," I managed to get out despite the feeling of my throat swelling up from him being gone.

Amalia's body grew closer to mine as if she was subconsciously trying to comfort me with her proximity, but I must have imagined it because the feel of her body against mine disappeared in the same instant.

"All right, let's get to work," Amalia said, breaking the growing silence.

Nassim gave a nod of agreement and led us farther back

to a small table with leather poufs surrounding it. An older man, the merchant I presume, was sat there, cross-legged, amidst a sea of his products, working on them.

Nassim slipped a stack of bills in his hand and without another word, the man swiftly got up and left his store.

Without wasting any other time, we all settled around the table and got started.

The sun was setting by the time we were heading back to the safe house.

We'd spent the last few hours going over the layout of my father's property while I added details about the surrounding grounds we could use to our advantage.

I hadn't visited the place in a little over thirty years, but based on both what little I'd seen when we left the premises yesterday and Amalia's recollections of the house, I knew my father hadn't changed much except for expanding the garage to host more cars and make his bedroom bigger at the request of his new wife.

I'd learned a few years ago that while he'd still been married to my mother, he'd had a whole other illegitimate family that we'd known nothing about.

Matheo had been born a few years after me, and when my mother and I had left, he'd moved them in like we'd never been there in the first place.

Amalia's grip tightened around my middle as I turned

the corner street that led to where we were staying. We'd abandoned her car behind to avoid being traceable and instead used Nassim's motorcycle to get back home while his men took care of getting rid of the car we'd left behind.

Daniela had driven a separate motorcycle on their way to the market this morning, so they'd used that one to get back to their place where some of Nassim's men were staying with them.

Amalia had initially refused to climb behind me, saying she'd rather walk, but eventually, she'd relented, knowing there were no other options.

The second her arms had wrapped around my waist, the oxygen in my lungs had stammered and for the rest of the ride, all I could focus on was memorizing the feeling of her against me because it might be the last time I'd have her this close no matter how hard I tried to win her back.

I'd never relent from trying, but in the very far back of my mind, there were whispers of there being a chance she wouldn't take me back, but I didn't want to think about the possibility.

I turned the corner of the alley that housed the place we were staying at and parked the motorbike in front of the building. I expected her to jump off the moment my feet landed on the pavement, but neither of us moved.

I closed my eyes and felt her chest rise up and down against my back. One of my hands traveled to rest against her thigh and I heard her breath hitch behind me at the gesture.

But the sound of a kid screaming as they ran out of the house in front of us had us breaking apart.

With the moment broken, she swung her leg over the seat and headed for the front door without sparing me another look.

With a sigh, I turned off the ignition and went to stand behind her as she unlocked the front door. She pushed it open and I braced my hands over the frame, watching her retreat inside.

I was trying to tell myself that I needed to leave her alone, to give her some time to adjust, but I was failing at it.

I was tired of having her walk away from me. Tired of her not talking to me. I was losing my fucking mind over the fact—albeit I'd deserved it.

"Amalia," I called out, stepping under the mantle and into the house and closing the door behind me. To no one's surprise, she didn't give me her attention.

"Amalia," I said louder this time, walking toward the living room to find her heading for the kitchen.

She peered at me over her shoulder, her hand on the refrigerator's door handle. "What is it?" she asked, irritation flashing in her eyes. "What do you want?"

I stared at her and said what I'd been holding in without hesitation. "You."

A hoarse laugh left her lips as if my previous statement was a mere joke. She sighed a frustrated breath and opened the refrigerator to grab a water bottle.

I stood rooted at the outskirts of the entry hallway, her back to me. "Amalia, come here."

Her fingers tightened around the bottle. "No," she replied sharply, still not looking at me as she walked toward the back door.

"I *said* come here, Amalia."

She whipped around, the anger that I knew was brewing deeper inside finally coming out. She dropped the plastic bottle on the counter and took a step toward me, pointing an accusing finger in my direction.

"You do *not* get to tell me what to do," she snapped.

There's my girl.

My gaze didn't falter from hers. "We have to talk."

She laughed, but there was no humor in her tone. "Talk? About what? More lies? You know, every time I learn something new about you, I think to myself, "That's it, there can't be any more secrets between us." And then something else pops up and I'm reminded that I don't know you at all. That all the time we spent together was just a lie."

I winced at her words but didn't back away. I deserved it and I would face every ounce of her anger if it meant she talked to me.

I ran a hand through my hair. "I never lied to you about *who* I was or how I felt about you. How I *still* feel about you."

Her fists tightened at her sides, her knuckles turning

white. "Don't you dare do that. Don't you dare fucking pretend you felt anything for me," she snarled.

How could she ever think that? I'd messed up, *badly*, but never did I think she thought I'd never cared for her, never loved her. I hadn't said the words, but she must have known.

My brows furrowed. "Do you really believe that?"

She crossed her arms on her chest. "Why would I believe anything else you say when you left without so much as a goodbye? No warning, no note… *nothing.*"

"I didn't—"

"You didn't what?" she said, her words low and bitter. "Please just spare both of us from more of your lies."

She moved in my direction and brushed past me, heading for the front door.

I wrapped my fingers around her forearm. My grasp was gentle, but it didn't stop the feel of her skin from burning through mine. "Do not walk away from me," I warned.

She jerked her head up to look at me and tugged her arm out of my grip, putting distance between us. "No," she hissed. "You do not get to tell me that. *You* walked away from me."

She shook her head, huffing out in disbelief. "You know I waited for hours all alone in your apartment for you to return with 'breakfast.' I waited as long as I could before I had to leave and return to the dorms before anyone grew suspicious. Then on Monday morning, I walked into the training room to learn from a complete fucking stranger that you took an unexpected leave of absence with no known date for your return and that they would be replacing you until further notice."

"I'm sorry," I started, taking a tentative step toward her.

She took a step back. "I don't care. Your apology doesn't matter to me. Not anymore." She headed for the front door again.

My heart pounded furiously in my chest, my mind a chaotic whirlwind of emotions. Watching her walk away from me felt as if everything I cared about was slipping through my fingers again.

But this time, I wouldn't let it happen.

It'd been almost ten years and I still felt like I was fucking things up despite carefully trying to find the right words to say. So fuck it, no more thinking. I needed to lay it all out on the table and stop walking on eggshells, trying to find a balance between telling her everything while trying not to further enrage her.

"You changed things for me, Amalia."

She turned to face me again. "Oh, spare me with your bullshit. You left me. I fell in love with you and you skipped town without a goodbye."

"I couldn't stay. I wanted to, but I just... I couldn't. I needed to leave."

"And somehow you couldn't say goodbye or give me the decency of an explanation."

I took a deep breath, ignoring the ache in my chest. "When my mother died, I was lost and I just…"

"You just what? You could sleep with me, make me fall in love with you, but you couldn't tell me you lost the most important person in your life and needed some time to process."

"I didn't know how," I said truthfully. "I loved you. I still—"

She cut me off, her eyes blazing. "Don't you dare say you love me. When you love someone, you stay. You *talk*. You don't just vanish into thin air and break them, leaving them to pick up the pieces of a mess *you* left behind. You know what, I'd thought so long about what I would say to you if I ever saw you again, and now I realize I don't want to talk."

"Amalia, please," I said, pleading. My fingers reached to grasp her wrist again.

"Just let me go, Noah," she said in a near whisper, her voice trembling with emotion she was trying to conceal as she pulled her hand away. She shook her head, her features morphing into anguish as if the more I spoke, the more hurt I was causing her. "We're over. We've been over for the last ten years."

Her words lit a fire inside me, making it burn even brighter in my resolve. "I fucked up, but we are not over. We were *never* over. How could I ever get over you?"

She opened her mouth, but I held up a hand, silently asking her to let me finish.

"I never thought I was worthy of love." My words were barely audible as if they'd been dragged from my throat, but I pushed against the ache in my chest and continued.

"My mom always tried her best to show me that she loved me, but deep inside, there was this voice, this nagging feeling that she only did it because she was trying to undo everything my father did to me, to erase in her own way how he made me feel and the stain he left on my heart."

I paused for a moment, my heart thundering as I realized how close we were now standing. Her back was now to the wall, her eyes flickering between mine, a conflicting ocean of emotions swarming in hers.

But she didn't move, which meant there was a chance she'd let me back in. If she was over me, if she truly believed we were over, she wouldn't let me stop her from leaving.

I leaned my head down, slowly enough so as to not startle her, and pressed my forehead against hers. Her breath hitched as I stared into her eyes, noting that buried deep under her hard exterior, what I'd done weighed on her.

"You breathed life back into me, Amalia. *You* showed me that I don't have to be or do anything to be loved. That I can just exist and be loved. That's what you did for me, what you've shown me, what you've *always* shown me. I was just too fucking stupid, too hurt to see it before, so I ran away.

"I ran because that's all I knew how to do, but I don't want to run anymore. I want to stay and love you." My fingertips grazed her wrist. "I made mistakes and I regret hurting you, but I would go through it all again if it means me ending up here telling you that I love you."

"Noah," she whispered, her eyes drifting closed.

The air between us grew heavy, time passing at a snail's speed as I waited.

Fuck waiting.

I hovered my lips a mere inch away from her mouth. "I love you, Amalia," I murmured before dropping my lips in a whispered kiss over her jaw. Her throat bobbed down with a swallow, but she kept her eyes closed.

I moved down to her neck. "Baby, I always have," I mumbled against the skin right below her ear before pressing my lips there too.

Her arm rose to settle on my stomach and I held my breath, afraid she'd push me away. But she merely just left it there as if to brace herself.

"And always will." My mouth hovered down to her collarbone. "Come back to me," I muttered against her now blazing skin before dropping another featherlight kiss there.

Her breath quickened when I bent my legs and pressed another one at the top of her breasts. Then I placed my mouth on the skin between her breasts. I kept my eyes on her to study her reactions as my fingers lightly touched her on her waist to steady myself as I kept making my way down.

I dragged my lips down the front of her top until I reached the hem of her shirt that had slightly ridden up. I held her hips more firmly this time and her hand dropped to my shoulder.

I looked up at her just as her eyes fluttered open to find me on my knees. My breath fanned across the skin right below her navel.

"Forgive me," I said against her skin before moving slightly down and hovering over her front.

"Amalia," I whispered against the fabric of her pants. "Please let me earn your forgiveness."

Every part of me screamed to move, to grab her and kiss her and remind her of who we were together. But this was her call and I'd take her however she wanted. I just needed her to say yes, to let me absolve myself from the hurt I'd caused her.

Please, I said over and over again in my head, hoping the message was being conveyed in the way I looked at her.

Amalia

CHAPTER 19

A RIOT OF EMOTIONS BLASTED OVER ME AND HIT ME SO fast I could barely identify how his confessions made me feel. I hadn't *felt* this much or quite frankly anything aside from numbness, annoyance, or anger in a very long time.

I didn't know what to do with this resurgence of emotions, whatever *they* were.

His proximity and the determination in his eyes made my breath falter as I stared at him. I found myself internally battling between pushing him away and telling him I wanted nothing to do with him and just giving him a chance to redeem himself.

I'd spent the major part of the last decade building walls around my heart, creating a refuge within myself to never be hurt again.

I'd buried my feelings and convinced myself that they were no longer there because it was easier to deceive myself that they'd never existed than deal with the pain.

Can't feel something you convinced your brain didn't happen.

Only the pain was never expunged. I'd just grown to sort it as an inconvenience.

My heart raced at higher speeds the longer I looked at him on his knees. I could hear the remorse in his words, see the vulnerability in his position. I could *feel* the sincerity in his pleading eyes.

He made my skin flame ablaze, but him being on his knees was about him letting me know that he was surrendering control, something neither of us was very good at.

I was still so mad at him, but I was just as tired of fighting him. Tired of telling myself that I didn't miss him, that I didn't *crave* him.

I knew that if I told him I wanted nothing to do with him, he would respect my wishes no matter how gutting my decision would render him.

But I couldn't bring myself to say the words. I'd be lying to both of us if I did. Because truthfully, I still loved him. As livid as I was with him for leaving and not trusting me, my heart still belonged to him.

I loved this man and I was so fucking tired of convincing myself otherwise.

I lowered to my knees and cupped his face in my hands.

"Okay," I said, the word so low I was surprised he'd heard me.

"Okay?" he said, his voice thick with emotions, but despite the hesitation in his tone, he leaned into my touch.

I brought my forehead to his and whispered what we both needed to hear. "This is far from me forgiving you, but I'm tired of pretending I don't love you."

He met my gaze hesitantly, his eyes glistening with unshed tears. He reached up and placed his palms over mine as if to confirm that mine were truly there. "You do?" he questioned tentatively.

I'd known Noah was different the moment I'd laid eyes on him in that bar. But over the weeks that followed, he'd turned into something more.

From the fleeting glances, to the stolen kisses and touches and the week we'd spent at his place, I'd grown to know that he was it for me.

That despite the frustration he'd always seemed to rile up in me, I knew I'd fallen in love with him.

Completely and irrevocably.

I gave him a small nod. "I love you, Noah," I told him, my voice a mere whisper.

The words had barely left my lips when I realized I'd never said them to anyone before. Sure, I'd told my sister and brother that I loved them, but the weight they carried as I confessed them to Noah felt… heavier.

I wasn't the greatest with words and there was a lot

more I'd wanted to tell him, but those three little words were the most I could manage right now.

I slid my fingers into his hair and closed the remaining gap between us, pressing my lips to his, the single contact seeming to alter everything in a heartbeat.

Our kisses had always felt different, but this one ignited something I'd kept buried deep inside me for far too long.

This kiss felt all-consuming.

My fingers gripped at the strands at his nape while his arms circled around my waist, his hands tightly gripping my hips.

I gasped as he lifted me off the ground and pulled me onto his lap without ever breaking the kiss. His back was now pressed against the wall and he hugged me closer to his body, pulling me as close to him as possible until not even an inch separated us.

I suddenly became hyper aware of every part of his body pressed against mine. My soft thighs hugging his firm ones on either side, my aching breasts pressing against his hard chest. The length of his thick cock brushing against my craving pussy, just a few unfortunate layers separating us.

Even with us both fully clothed, I felt him everywhere.

Arousal flooded my body, slowly growing desperate for more as his lips moved against mine, teasing, tasting, *taking*.

I sighed into his mouth as he curled his hand around the back of my neck to deepen the kiss. His tongue teased the seam of my lips, silently asking for permission, and I granted it without hesitation.

The second he slipped his tongue into my mouth, tangling it with my own, I moaned into his mouth as I widened my stance to rub myself along his growing erection, the thin fabric of his linen shorts doing nothing to hide it.

"God, how I've missed the way you sound when you're writhing under my touch," he panted against my lips as he pulled back to look at me. He only broke our kiss for a brief moment before he returned to devouring my mouth with an ardent fervor, making my entire body erupt in flames.

"And I've missed the way you taste," I moaned, biting down on his bottom lip as his hands roamed over my body, gripping.

I worked my hips faster and Noah grunted in approval, the slight thrust of his hips providing me with the perfect amount of friction and urging me on.

My chest rose and fell with heavy breaths as his lips moved from my mouth, down to my jaw until their path ended at the swell of my breasts. The feel of his stubble rasped against my skin, sending tiny jolts of pleasure down my spine.

His teeth grazed my skin there before he nipped and sucked at it. Then he worked the neck of my top and bra under my breasts to free them.

One of his hands moved to cup one breast, pinching my

nipple while his mouth latched onto the other, sucking and twirling his tongue around the hardened peak.

Fuck, I missed this.

I missed *him*.

"Noah," I whimpered as he moved his attention to my other breast. My hands gripped tighter on his hair, pulling his face closer and I felt him smile against my skin at the gesture.

Pleasure and need continued sweeping through me as he kept licking and sucking. Then he bit down, *hard*, my lips parting as I screamed out his name.

"That's my girl," he groaned against my skin.

I dragged his head back up and hovered my lips over his mouth. "Your girl needs you," I whispered with urgency.

The moment the words fell from my lips, he fastened my legs around his waist and stood, holding me in his arms before slamming my back against the wall. His body engulfed mine as he grinded up his erection into me.

I let out a soft whimper and brought my hips forward, wanting more.

We were both breathing hard, my hands fisting the fabric of his shirt, needing for it to be off him.

Shifting, he brought my feet back down to the floor and reached over his head to grab the back collar of his T-shirt, helping me remove it in one fell swoop and throwing it somewhere to the side.

I brushed my lips over his as my hands slid from his

shoulders down the expanse of his chest, my nails gliding across his perfectly toned abdomen, marveling at how his muscles tensed and tightened as I moved lower.

I hooked a finger into his shorts and underwear, teasing and reveling in the shudder that traveled down his body. I then slid my hand inside and wrapped it around his cock, squeezing and tugging at it the way I remembered he liked it.

He braced a hand above my head, his other one gripping my waist as he jerked forward. "*Amalia*," he choked out.

I basked in the sound of him being at the mercy of my touch. "I love when you call out my name like that," I said against his lips, toying with him.

His head fell onto my shoulder and he whimpered, the vibration reverberating against my skin and sending another wave of pleasure pooling down to my core.

I ghosted my lips to his ear. "I love the feel of you in my hands," I whispered before biting and tugging at his earlobe.

My words were barely out when I felt the hand at my waist suddenly gone. I barely had time to register what he was doing when he swiftly unfastened the button of my pants and pushed his hand between my thighs.

I sucked in a sharp breath, my hand on his cock halting in its movements.

"Oh, my—" My head fell backward against the wall as

he effortlessly slipped two fingers down my drenched pussy slowly, teasingly.

He let out a satisfied sound and his cock twitched in my hand. "Look at you being so wet and I've barely touched you," he praised, resting his forehead against mine, his fingers teasing my entrance and drawing a moan from me.

He pressed a brief kiss to my lips at the sound, like a reward for still reacting to his touch like no time had passed.

"Look at me, pretty girl," he ordered and the moment I met his gaze, he stopped his teasing touches and pushed his two fingers hard into my cunt.

"*Fuck me*," I gasped, my hand growing lax around his cock and slipping out of his shorts.

"Patience, Amalia. That'll come soon enough." He chuckled, pleased with himself as he drove his fingers in and out of me, his thumb joining and pressing against my clit.

I would usually be annoyed with his taunting, but with the feel of his fingers inside me, I barely could think straight to remember to breathe, let alone try to retaliate.

Instead, I gripped his shoulder with one hand, wrapping the other around his wrist, and started rocking against his hand. "Noah, *please*," I moaned.

He hummed in approval as he drove his fingers into me even harder, his thumb firmly stroking my clit. "Now, take my fingers like the good fucking girl you are and drench my hand. Understood?"

I nodded and rode his hand faster, my orgasm creeping up my body. He must have known because he slammed his lips to mine and crooked his fingers inside of me, sending me over the edge.

My eyes fluttered closed to relish in the release of years of pent-up need as my cunt clamped down on him.

My lips parted on a moan and he slid his tongue inside, kissing me softly as he still pumped his fingers inside me, matching the way his tongue tangled with mine.

His fingers were still inside me when I opened my eyes and settled my dazed expression on him. For a moment, we both stood still and stared at each other.

Him watching me come down from my high while I let myself drown in the desire in his eyes.

Still holding my gaze, he moved his fingers out of me and lifted them between us. "What a pretty fucking sight," he growled before smearing my wetness against my bottom lip.

Then he leaned forward and sucked it into his mouth. His eyes slid shut as a groan tore through his chest before he let my bottom lip go and straightened himself, his gaze meeting mine again.

His irises turned black. A dark hunger I'd never seen before had taken over.

"Bedroom. Now."

Noah

CHAPTER 20

PRESENT

SHE STOOD THERE FROZEN FOR A MOMENT, SO I SPOKE UP again. "I said now, Amalia," I rasped, my own voice almost unrecognizable.

The taste of her still buzzed across my tongue and all I could think about was drowning in her scent, but this time right from the source. Ten years of being deprived of it sent my mind into a tailspin.

Finally, she did as told and I was right on her heels.

"Take off your clothes," I demanded as I stepped into the bedroom.

My heart drummed against my chest as I watched her do exactly that, discarding the pieces on the floor next to her until she was completely bare for me.

I stepped closer as my eyes roamed all over her body,

memorizing all the changes the years had brought, a primal need rushing through my veins.

I was *so* desperate for her and was driving myself crazy the longer I waited to be inside her, but I wanted to take my time. I hadn't been with her in almost a decade and needed to brand every moment to memory.

I leaned down, cupping the back of her head, and kissed her slowly and deliberately. The faint remnant of her arousal still tangled in *her* taste and I reveled in it.

She skated her hands up my bare chest and pushed on her tiptoes to tangle her fingers at the back of my head— where she loved to grip my hair—and pulled me closer, deepening our kiss.

My own hands glided down her body, my fingertips soaking to memory the feel of her skin and the curves of her body. She was feverish, yet goose bumps prickled across her skin.

Eventually, my hands moved over her hips to her ass, and I slid my hands under and gripped the flesh there, bringing her flush to my front.

"I need you," she said against my mouth.

"I do too, baby, but I need to do something else first," I replied, breaking the kiss and moving to lower her onto the bed behind her.

I fought the urge to dive right in and stepped back a bit, just to look at her. Time felt like it stopped as my gaze traveled over her.

Beautiful. Just fucking beautiful.

She watched me curiously as I came closer and kneeled in front of her. Grabbing her legs, I placed her foot flat on the bed and opened her wider for me.

She let out a surprised "Oh," but my eyes were solely focused on moving two of my fingers down her cunt, then moving them on either side to spread her open.

My breath stuttered as I looked at her.

"Just like I remembered," I breathed against her aroused center before swinging her legs over my shoulder and pulling her toward me.

Then I took a long, awaited, languid lick up her perfect pussy.

The need that had been coursing through my veins before flushed all over my body and shot straight up to my brain, altering a part of it to remember this forever. I was already painfully hard before, but her taste exploding onto my tongue just... *fuck me.*

Something inside me snapped and I held her tightly against my mouth, burying my face in between her legs and devouring her as if I'd been trying to quench the starving thirst I'd been holding onto for the last decade.

I was desperate for her taste. I was desperate for *her.*

I could suffocate myself between her thighs and it would never be enough.

"Oh God, *Noah,*" she moaned, her hand sliding into my hair and her thighs tightening around my head.

I used my hands to force them open so I could get better

access. I then blew across her swollen clit before sucking it into my mouth.

Her hips rolled onto my mouth as she rode it, chasing her pleasure.

I looked up at her, only to find her eyes already glued on me. I groaned and smiled against her before sucking on her clit harder. Her mouth fell open and her head fell back at that, her breaths coming in quicker now.

I knew she was close, so while one of my hands firmly gripped her thigh, the other snaked its way up to grip her throat, squeezing gently. She bucked her hips faster against my mouth and her grip on my hair tightened.

I moved my mouth down to her entrance and plunged my tongue inside, fucking her with it. Her pussy tightened around my tongue and her back arched off the bed, her arousal spilling inside my mouth.

Chants of my name followed by a string of moans and sighs fell off her lips as I continued wringing her second orgasm out of her.

Perfection, I thought to myself. Fucking perfection.

I was still licking her when she tugged on my strands, bringing my head up and onto her mouth, pulling me so fast on top of her body for a kiss.

I brought my hands on each side of her head so as not to crush her as she drove her tongue inside my mouth to meet mine, sucking her taste off with a satisfied moan.

"You taste like me," she groaned into my mouth, writhing underneath my body. She pulled from the kiss.

"Noah, I want you inside me," she said against my mouth as her eager hands reached behind my back and fumbled to push my shorts and briefs down, her hands cupping my backside and bringing me closer between her legs.

I pulled my mouth away from hers and she whined in protest when I moved off the bed to stand at its edge.

"So impatient for my cock, aren't you, Amalia?" I teased, my eyes never leaving her as I pulled the remaining piece of clothing I had on and stepped out of it.

I grabbed my length and pumped my cock a few times as I came back to stand at the edge of the bed, looking at her before me. "Is this what you want?"

My last question ended with a deep growl torn from my soul as my head rolled backward.

My hands landed on the back of her head, my fingers knotting into her dark waves, as I tried to ground myself from the sudden and shocking sensation of having Amalia's wet mouth wrapped around me.

I watched her from under hooded eyes to find her looking back at me and it took everything in me not to fuck her mouth harder.

She moved to lick the underside of my length, swirling her tongue around the head at a torturous pace before wrapping her pretty mouth around it.

My fingers tangled into her hair further and I kept my eyes on her as my cock further disappeared into her mouth, her humming and moaning around it.

My entire body felt like it was about to combust.

She was going to kill me.

"Amalia, I—" I choked on my words as she coaxed more of me between her lips, her hands gripping my backside to bring me closer. "*Fuck*," I groaned as she moved up and down.

"You look exquisite like this, pretty girl," I murmured in a haze. Watching her work more of my length into her mouth, so hungry for me…

Obsessed didn't even begin to cover it.

My hips slowly moved and my muscles shook as I fought the urge to ram them forward and shove my cock to the back of her throat.

My eyes drifted closed and pleasure trickled down my spine, pooling low at the base.

Fuck.

"No," I rasped, tugging her head back, and leaned down to press a hard kiss to her lips. "I want to come inside your cunt," I moaned into her mouth.

"I want that too," she mumbled between kisses. "I want to feel you, all of you."

The mattress dipped as I pushed her back and crawled over her, placing my knees between her legs. I sat on my heels and ran my hands up the sides of her thighs, over the curves of her body and feathering over her breast before cupping the back of her head and bringing her lips to me.

I kissed her, hard and hot. Then I set her head back down on one of the pillows behind her and wrapped a hand around my throbbing cock, the briefest touch almost making me come.

I needed a medal at this point for not coming all over her skin yet.

"Do you have any idea what you do to me?" I whispered as I brought it a whisper away from her pussy. "I want to drive so deep inside you that my cum stays inside forever when I paint your cunt."

"Stop talking so much and show me," she said, her eyes dark and dazed with lust.

With that, I ran the tip of my cock along her pussy and we both moaned at the sensation.

God, it's been so long.

I crawled over her body and held myself up with one elbow, my free hand resting next to her head. Tired of prolonging this for any longer, I lined myself with her entrance and rested my forehead against hers, snaking the hand next to her head under her neck, my fingers lightly grabbing the back of it.

Her hands traveled to the back of my head and when she nodded for me to go ahead, I slid the head of my cock inside her.

My eyes fluttered shut, my bones liquefying at the feel of her tight cunt squeezing me so perfectly. "Amalia," I whispered as I slowly worked myself into her. "You were fucking made for me."

I worked myself inside her slowly, pulling out and then sliding back a little farther each time, but I must have been going too slow for her because she wrapped her legs around my waist, her heels moving to rest on top of my backside before she pushed down until I was all the way in.

My eyes practically rolled to the back of my head with how good she felt. I collapsed against her neck as her nails dug into my skin, her shuddering moan drowned out by my own muttered curse.

"Fuck," I mumbled against her skin before pressing a kiss there.

My heart was thundering so hard inside my chest, I thought it might break through my ribcage. It was taking everything in me to stay still instead of thrusting into her because I knew that I needed a moment to gather myself before I came from the ecstasy of her walls gripping me so tight.

I moved to rest my forehead to meet her dazed expression. "You feel even better than I fucking remembered," I whispered in the small space between us.

"And you feel just as good," she panted. "But I need you to move. *Please*."

I huffed out a small laugh and pressed a small kiss to her lips. Only she could make me laugh while I was buried so deep inside her that I couldn't even tell you where she began and I ended.

Finally, I started to move and everything around us seemed to come to a stop.

I thrust inside her, slowly at first, then picked up the pace. I moved a hand on her hip and pulled all the way back before tilting my hips and immediately driving back into her with a hard thrust, making sure to grind against her clit.

"*Noah*," she moaned, clutching at me anywhere she could get her hands on. Her nails dug so hard at my skin with every thrust that I wouldn't be surprised if I had permanent marks from now on. Not that I minded.

"I love the way you say my name," I groaned. I looked down at the perfect view of my cock disappearing inside her every time. "I love how I fit so well inside you."

She let out a strangled noise and I gripped her jaw before lowering myself to kiss her. Her moans against my lips grew louder and I sensed both of our orgasms looming, so I drove my hips against her, faster and harder.

Her breathing was erratic—not that mine was any better —and I kept my punishing pace, both of us careening toward the edge.

"You're doing so good, pretty girl." I panted against her lips. "But I need you to come for me, Amalia, so I can fill you with my cum. Can you do that for me, baby?"

"Yes," she cried out, her cunt tightening around me.

I kissed her sloppily and roughly and when I bit down on her lower lip, she came on an aching cry, her back arching and her walls constricting around me as her orgasm took over her.

Her moans turned into screams and the euphoria of her around me and the sound of my name being chanted over and over again from her exquisite lips ringing in my ears sent me over the edge barely a second later.

I kept riding her through both of our orgasms until I finally slowed my pace and collapsed on top of her, breathless. I knew I should move but couldn't bring myself to just yet.

I wanted to bask in the feel of her skin against mine for just a little longer.

"That was," she started, stopping to catch her breath.

I pressed my lips against her neck in a soft kiss and lifted my head to look down at her, finding her smiling and sated. I hadn't seen that expression in a long time and my heart felt like it could burst at the sight. "It always is with you," I whispered.

Reluctantly, I pulled myself out of her and stood on my knees, watching myself leak out of her. On instinct, I reached with two fingers and slowly worked it back inside, wanting my cum to stay imprinted inside her walls.

"Wh-what are you doing?" Amalia half-asked, half-moaned, looking down at where my fingers were.

With a small smile on my face, I pushed more of us back inside her. "Just putting my cum back where it belongs," I noted before leaning down and pressing a slow kiss to her lips.

It only took a few minutes of me fucking my cum back into her before she squeezed around my fingers and came again so effortlessly, my mouth catching her sighs of pleasure.

I eventually withdrew my fingers and reached up to push them past Amalia's swollen lips and into her mouth, surprising her.

She lapped up our taste with a feral look in her green eyes and I groaned at the feeling. She eventually let them go with a pop and looped her finger through my necklace, pulling me down for a kiss.

I loved fucking her, but her kisses were my favorites.

I could never tire of them.

I plunged my tongue past the seam of her lips to taste us inside her mouth and a moan roared inside my chest.

I eventually pulled away and rolled out of bed, walking to the old wooden wall wardrobe to the right of the room. I opened a few doors, trying to find a small towel to use to help clean her instead of going outside to grab one.

"What are you doing?" she yawned, propping herself up onto her elbows.

"Just looking for towels so I can clean us up since there's only an outside shower and I'm not about to have you freeze outside."

I didn't know how long had passed since we'd come home, but by the moonlight filtering from the small tempered glass window above the bed, it was most likely the middle of the night.

She let out a small laugh and I peered at her over my shoulder. "What's so funny?"

"So..." she drawled, a guilty smile on her face.

"There's actually another bathroom with a shower right there," she confessed, pointing at something.

I turned around and realized what she was pointing at. A closed door that I hadn't paid attention to before—quite preoccupied with more important things—was tucked in the far right corner of the bedroom.

My head cocked to the side as I looked back at her, her smile widening at the look on my face. "So you had me shower outside when there was a perfectly functioning one, with hot water, right here?" I said, stalking toward her.

She playfully shrugged. "I would say I'm sorry, but I'm not really." She yelped when I grabbed her foot and tugged her toward me.

"*Noah*," she yelled as I bent down and threw her over my shoulder.

I slapped her ass. "Let's get you cleaned up," I told her as I carried her over to the bathroom.

Her laughter boomed around us and God, did I miss that sound too.

Noah

CHAPTER 21

PRESENT

I HADN'T BEEN ABLE TO HELP MYSELF AND HAD HER ONE more time before we thoroughly cleaned ourselves in the shower.

We were currently in bed, sitting in a perfectly peaceful quiet as Amalia half lay on top of me with my arm around her waist and resting against her lower back under her shirt. She had one arm folded over my chest, her cheek resting on top. Her eyes were watching her other hand as it traced idle circles along my front.

If I could stop time and stay in this snapshot of a moment for the rest of my life, I would do it in a heartbeat.

I reached and tucked a wet strand of her hair that had fallen over her forehead behind her ear. Then my hands

281

skimmed behind her body, my palms splaying on her back to bring her closer.

"I never stopped thinking about you," I confessed in the quiet air.

She let out a breathy laugh. "I wish I could say I didn't think about you, but I'd be lying. No matter how many times I tried, you were always there at the back of my mind."

I knew her words weren't meant to hurt me, but guilt instantly washed over me at the fact that I'd played a major part in us being apart for so long.

I'd always regretted not having been able to do something before it felt too late to try. I'd then ended up falling into complacency because I'd thought it'd be easier for her to live without me and be angry than be with me and all my scars.

Realistically, I knew being perfect wasn't an achievable goal, no matter how many times my father had tried to beat it into me. But when I'd been faced with my demons after the loss of my mother, coming out on the other side had appeared to be a lot more difficult than I'd imagined.

I'd always felt like my brain wasn't my own, but after my grief dragged on for months, I'd sought help for the first time in my life and was diagnosed with major depressive disorder and complex post-traumatic disorder.

I'd masked my pain for so long because mental health simply wasn't something we talked about where I was from and the environment I'd grown up in.

I'd been taught to hide any of my feelings but especially the negative ones. It'd been ingrained in me to push them aside and keep going because doing otherwise made me inadequate.

Being sad or losing interest in things wasn't normal. It was shelved as me being lazy. Feeling wasn't seen as a strength. It was a weakness. Barreras didn't have weaknesses as my father had always loved to remind me.

And I'd unfortunately found a way to be the best at keeping my feelings in to avoid his wrath. But the moment the news of my mother's death broke, it acted as a dam over years of repressed emotions and worsened my condition.

I'd eventually learned to live with both and found a regimen that worked for me, which meant that the darkness that used to constantly loom over my head wasn't as frightening anymore.

But finding something that worked didn't mean I'd magically been healed and was fine to go on with life like nothing had ever happened. It just felt like when I was faced with it, I could handle it and not retreat into old habits of pushing it away and acting like everything was fine.

Because I'd realized after several sessions with my therapist that I hadn't been okay for a very long time.

"Hey, where did you go?" she whispered, her fingers brushing against my stubble.

My gaze met hers and hesitated for a moment. I

brushed a thumb over her cheek and finally readied myself to finally tell her what I'd wanted to all these years ago when I came back looking for her.

"I'm sorry I left. I just… When my mother died, I felt like I was drowning and I didn't know how to… survive." The last word came out barely above a whisper.

I thought back to the time when I'd been at my lowest. Despite everything I'd been through during my childhood, my mother had always been a constant, there to guide me through it all. But when she died, so did the balance that kept me from faltering.

Her loss had made me unsteady.

My father's voice had always been at the back of my mind, reminding me that I wasn't worthy. That I wouldn't amount to anything because I was weak.

The list went on and on, but my mother's presence had always dulled the voices to a quiet hum instead of the constant blare they'd used to be.

She'd shaped how I saw myself and with her gone, I'd been left with endless questions of whether I was truly my own or that I'd tricked myself into thinking I was because my mother had constantly told me so.

"I didn't know how to navigate her loss. She meant a lot to me, more than I could even put into words and losing her *so*… unexpectedly sent me into a really bad place. She'd never even told me about her cancer or given me a chance to be there for her or say goodbye."

I paused, taking a deep breath before I continued.

"I wanted to talk to you, I really did, but I thought it'd just be easier not to burden you with what I was going through, what I was about to go through."

Amalia brushed her fingertips over my cheeks before reaching for my locks and brushing them back. Her gaze hadn't left mine the entire time, and she looked at me with so much... I didn't even know how to describe it except that it made me feel listened to and not pitied.

"That's why you left," she mused, but her tone wasn't accusatory. Instead, it felt filled with understanding of why I had, but I didn't want to get my hopes up. Her fingertips grazed the contours of my face as if she knew I needed the physical comfort of her touch. "It doesn't erase the anger and hurt I felt for years toward you for leaving, but I understand it a bit better now. I see *you* better now."

I took a shuddering breath.

I'd never allowed myself to dream much growing up, but deep down, I'd always wished to find someone with whom I could be there and just... be. I didn't have to provide them with something or be someone.

I'd found exactly that the moment Amalia had stepped into my life. I might have realized it too late and after I'd fucked things up, but having her in my arms right now felt overwhelming.

What did I ever do to deserve her?

Emotions I'd buried deep surfaced and my throat grew tight.

She must have seen the change in my expression because her fingers trailed to my chin.

"Come here," she said gently before pulling me to her and pressing a gentle kiss to my lips. She pulled away after a few seconds before giving three more chaste kisses, each one a direct line to my heart, making it stutter every time her soft lips brushed mine.

I fucking loved this girl.

I see you better now.

Her earlier words slowly loosened the vice grip that had been squeezing around my chest for the last decade.

I'd never told her about my father because it terrified me that she might look at me differently, that she might think I was too much and abandon me, which had been another reason why, despite how much it pained me to leave her, it was a little easier to do the leaving than to be left.

But her understanding made me confess the rest of my story because I wanted her to truly see everything about me.

I just had to hope I was still enough.

Her eyes were still on me, her fingertips having resumed randomly tracing lines and shapes on my chest.

I pulled my gaze away from hers, focusing my attention on what she was doing because nerves rattled my heart, making its beat hitch up to a dangerous zone.

Silence stretched between us, but she wasn't forcing me

to speak up. She just let me take my time, however long that was.

Finally, I swallowed and started to explain everything I hadn't felt ready to tell her before.

"My father didn't like me very much growing up. He…" I paused, clearing my throat. "He didn't think I was worthy to be his heir. He felt like I had too many emotions for a job that required you to have none. He used to tell me that he would have preferred my mother to never have had me because at least that would have been better than having to raise someone like me."

Amalia stopped her movements and I could feel her gaze boring into me, but I couldn't look at her just yet or I would never finish telling her everything.

"My father would have undoubtedly preferred me succumbing to one of his beatings or weeks-long stays in the basement cell than be associated with him. I mean, he did eventually try to have me killed because I'd survived everything else he'd put me through despite his best efforts."

Amalia's body stiffened against mine at my last words.

"Good thing my mom came in just as one of my father's henchmen was about to slice my throat open." A self-pitying laugh escaped me as I shook my head. "If she'd arrived a second later, my father's wishes would have come true."

In the past, I used to wonder if it would have been easier if his wish *had* come true. I'd used to think that maybe the wretched memories that coated my soul like a second skin wouldn't be painful anymore and I'd be granted some peace.

No one ever prepared you to receive the hate of another person, especially when that person was your own flesh and blood. I'd never understood what I'd done to garner such hatred from him, from my own father.

But then I learned that I wasn't the problem.

He was.

His anger wasn't rooted in something I'd done or who I was, but was a reflection of sick demons he harbored and I wasn't responsible for that.

It took me a long time to recognize it, but just because you realized something, didn't mean you believed it. It would take a lot more than therapy sessions for me to eventually heal, but everything needed a start.

"My mom got us away the night he tried to have me killed, with my uncle Reda's help. They kept me hidden for years until we moved back to the country under the Bureau's protection. The rest is history."

I sighed, feeling slightly relieved. Telling someone, telling *her*, alleviated a little of the weight I'd always carried.

Sharing my past with someone I loved felt… freeing in some way.

Amalia's right hand moved to rest against my heart. I brought my own hand up and placed it above hers. My thumb brushed over her knuckles, briefly bringing our joined hands to my lips to kiss her fingers before placing it back where it was, right where it belonged.

I hope she knows it's all hers.

I could sense her eyes were on me, but I still couldn't bring myself to look at her and she didn't push me to. I already was in love with her and didn't think it would be possible to love her more, but the space she was giving me to do whatever I felt comfortable with made me fall for her just a little harder.

My stomach was in knots, waiting for what she'd say, and when I finally mustered the courage to look at her, she wasn't looking at me.

Instead, her gaze was fixed on my neck.

My heart was beating out of my chest when one of her fingers traveled toward the base of my neck. I shuddered when the pads of her fingertips briefly grazed against the large scar there before she pressed her lips to it in a gentle kiss.

"You're beautiful," she whispered against my skin and I closed my eyes briefly before opening them again, letting out a deep breath.

She pulled herself higher onto my chest and took my face in her hands with such gentleness, my heart tightened at the gesture. She simply gazed at me for a moment, with so much adoration despite the anguish she was hiding underneath from my revelations.

"Just because your father didn't believe it, doesn't mean you weren't worthy of love because you needed to be without fault. He was wrong. Being loved isn't about being perfect or should ever be conditional. Being loved is about accepting the other person in their entirety and loving every piece of them."

She brought my forehead to hers and briefly kissed me before continuing. "I love you, Noah. I love you because of you. I love every part, no matter how much you may think it's too damaged or too broken."

The way she looked at me was almost too painful. This beautiful human was all mine.

I leaned in to kiss her and tell her I loved her just as equally, if not more, when she spoke again. "Besides, your dad's an asshole, so fuck his opinion."

For a moment, I looked at her wide-eyed at her unexpected remark before a sound I hadn't heard in a very long time boomed around us.

I laughed.

I laughed and this time it was genuine.

It came deep from within my chest and I felt a sudden rush of warmth spread across my limbs.

I was laughing and it felt freeing.

Amalia's laughter bubbled up, the sound of our laughter mingling in the room.

My laughter faded and when she leaned in to kiss me, I basked in the happiness I felt with her in my arms and the feeling that we'd be all right.

I had my girl back and no matter what obstacles we'd go through, I knew deep down we'd overcome them and make it work.

CHAPTER 22

PRESENT

AMALIA HAD FALLEN ASLEEP IN MY ARMS SHORTLY AFTER, her breathing now even as I continued drawing small circles against her bare back. She usually wasn't much of a cuddler—always preferring her space—but I loved that she hadn't moved from my side, her arms and legs clutched to my side.

Meanwhile, I couldn't bring myself to sleep despite it being well past midnight and knowing how trying tomorrow would be.

What if all of this was a dream and I woke up tomorrow, back in the same cell where I'd spent so much of my childhood and the memories of her telling me she loved me was simply that—a memory.

I gently pulled her tighter against me, trying not to

think about how empty my arms would feel without her in them.

On top of that, the thought of facing Jamal and telling him everything plagued my mind. Where did I even start? Would he understand why I'd kept everything a secret? Would he forgive me?

Or would he never speak to me again and cast me out of his life? Especially after what happened to his wife a few weeks ago.

Even if he excused me for keeping my connection to my father from him, would he forgive me for what happened to Sienna?

My brain imagined all the possible worst outcomes because they felt like the most plausible scenarios. And I didn't know if I'd be able to survive it.

When Ayoub's lawyers had initially informed me that I was meant to become his guardian, I'd almost run for the hills because I wasn't a paternal figure. I was barely a kid myself.

Besides, with the father I had, how could I even be put in a position to raise a kid?

Fun uncle I could do. But becoming a parental figure wasn't something I'd ever truly thought of. Maybe in a very far future, I'd come to terms with what had happened to me as a kid and would be willing to revisit the thought of having my own, but I wasn't there at the time.

But the moment I'd laid eyes on Jamal lying in a hospital bed, I knew I couldn't abandon him because of my own fears. And if I was being honest with myself, I also felt an immense amount of guilt because even if I hadn't set fire to the flame that ravaged their home, I was responsible for his parents' deaths.

My father had meant to send *me* a message—stop meddling in my affairs and with my empire.

Ayoub and I had been so close to finally unraveling my father's cartel until the informant I'd secured to testify against him turned up dead. Then a few hours later, my phone had rung with an anonymous text message to inform me that I'd regret ever coming after them.

Next thing I knew, I was racing through the streets of Sardenya toward Aguerd's house, only to find it crumbling under vivid flames.

I'd tried to get everyone out, but I'd barely gotten Jamal out of there when the roof collapsed, leaving me no chance to go back inside.

Looking after Jamal had been hard at first, especially with his recurrent night terrors from reliving the fire. I'd aimed to do my best to help him through his loss without crossing the line or taking over the place his parents had and would always have.

I hadn't known Ayoub and Nina for very long, but I'd always made sure to share everything I knew about them or the moments we'd share with Jamal so that he felt them even if they were gone.

And over the years, I'd grown very fond of him and considered him as if he were my own. He became family and was all I had for a long time, until I met the woman currently sleeping peacefully in my arms.

So the thought of losing him was unfathomable.

A heavy sigh left my chest and I pushed the thought aside, knowing that it would be to no avail, making my mind run a hundred miles an hour with countless scenarios when I'd know my answer soon enough.

Instead, I watched the mounted wall clock next to the wooden door tick the hours away until darkness gave away to light, a sliver illuminating the bedroom.

I felt Amalia stirring next to me and pulled her tighter against me, hunching down to press kisses all over her face. She kept her eyes closed, but I knew she was already awake and fighting a smile.

My hand that was on her back drifted down and over the curvature of her ass, brushing featherlight touches with my fingertips.

"I know you're awake," I said with a kiss to her lips.

She groaned against my lips.

I moved my hand farther down and brought her body further up against mine.

Her groan quickly turned into a low moan when my middle and index finger brushed against her entrance from the back, gliding inside ever so slightly and so easily with her being wet already.

"Are you sure you're not awake?" I whispered against Amalia's lips, still pressed to mine. I swirled some of her wetness already pooling there around my finger and ran it up to her back entrance.

I then pushed the tip of my finger through her tight rim and her eyes popped wide open.

"You don't—" A moan fell from her lips and cut her off as I pushed my finger inside farther. "You don't play fair," she managed to get out through a strained voice.

I softly nipped at her bottom lip. "I never claimed to play fair," I said, resting my forehead against hers.

With her leg already draped over my front, she grinded her wet pussy against the outer side of my thigh as I slowly worked my finger in and out of her. Her green eyes stared intently into mine, and my other hand wrapped around her waist, pulling her closer.

Her breath feathered against my lips and my cock throbbed at attention from the sound of her soft moans, the feel of her against me, the feel of her wrapped so tightly around my finger.

A groan escaped my lips when her hand skated over my chest and she gingerly wrapped her fingers around me, squeezing.

She swiped her thumb over the pre-cum already leaking at the tip and smeared it down my length.

I was about to roll on top of her, wanting to be inside her, when a loud knock on the iron door resounded in the house, breaking the moment.

We immediately both jolted at attention. Amalia swiftly

reached under the bed and came back with two guns in hand.

I looked at her, bewildered.

"What?" she questioned, handing me one.

I huffed out a laugh and grabbed it from her. "Did you have guns there all along?"

She raised a brow. "Do you think I'd come to a safe house unarmed?"

"No, but." I shook my head. "Never mind."

She quickly got up and pulled my shirt over her head and slipped her underwear and pants back on. She turned back to find me staring at her and smiling.

Her green eyes locked on mine, a confused look in them. "Noah, why are you smiling? Get up." She chucked a clean shirt at my head and I caught it.

Pulling the black T-shirt over my head, I said, "Nothing, I just like seeing you with my clothes on."

Another knock came on the front door.

She threw open another closet door, grabbing something from inside before facing me again and tossing another piece of clothing my way—this time linen pants. "We don't have time for this. The person outside might be trying to kill us."

I got out of bed and pulled the bottoms on. "Would someone trying to kill us knock on the door first?" I deadpanned, raising a brow.

She let out an annoyed breath and checked her gun before leaving the room without another word.

I laughed under my breath and followed her out. I hurried my steps and pushed her behind me, glaring at her above my shoulder before she could protest.

We neared the front door when another knock reverberated against the iron door.

"Who is it?" I shouted for the person behind the door to hear, my gun pointed at them. The nice thing about iron doors was that it didn't matter if the person behind was an intruder and armed. They couldn't shoot and actually hit us.

Amalia slapped my shoulder. "What are you doing?" she hissed under her breath. "Do you *want* to get us killed?"

I peered at her over my shoulder and narrowed my eyes at her. "Dramatic, much," I mouthed to her.

"It's me, open up," a voice yelled from behind the door. *Jamal.*

I lowered my gun and moved to unlock the door, when Amalia's fingers shot out to grip my upper arm.

"Who is it?" she asked.

I gently placed a hand on hers and faced her. "It's my nephew Jamal."

Her eyes softened at that and I saw a tinge of nervousness in them. I'd never seen her nervous about anything and it brought a half-smile to my face. It was the first time she was meeting someone important in my life.

I just wished it were under different circumstances.

After unlocking the door, I pulled it ajar to find Jamal,

Kai, and Valentina standing on the other side, all staring at me and Amalia.

Before I could usher them in, Valentina strode in with a large black bag over her shoulder, swiftly removing her shoes and giving me a curt nod before pushing past us.

Kai was next to step inside. He gave me a large smile and brandished his hand forward. "Nice to see you again, Noah. You've been a little MIA." He glanced at Amalia over my shoulder. "Guess maybe this is why."

I shook my head and let out a small laugh. "You too, Kai," I replied, taking his hand in mine, the other landing on his shoulder to give it a small squeeze.

Jamal didn't really have friends growing up since we'd spent the majority of his years after the accident in Blackwell at the Academy, so I'd always liked Kai especially because he seemed to bring a lighter side out of Jamal.

Finally, I came face to face with my nephew, a mix of concern and apprehension painting his features. But I ignored it for now—even if it was only for the next few seconds before everything changed—and wrapped my arm over his shoulders.

I grabbed the large black duffel he held in his right hand and pulled him into a side hug, tugging him farther inside. "It's good to see you, favorite nephew," I greeted him, squeezing the back of his head.

We never really were physically affectionate people—I'd even go as far as to say we avoided most of it—but I'd take any opportunity right now before the seemingly inevitable.

It took him a few seconds before he placed his free arm around my waist. He gently clapped my back a few times in response, rolling his eyes. "Yeah, you too *3ami*[1]," he huffed out, shaking his head.

Amalia moved to close the door while I guided Jamal into the living area where Kai and Valentina were standing, their bags at their feet and arguing in a hushed tone.

The moment we came into view, both of them snapped their heads up and Kai immediately plastered a smile on his face.

"Is everything all right?" Jamal asked them, raising a brow and pulling himself away from my side.

I instantly wished I could rewind the last few seconds and keep repeating in a loop to avoid the upcoming conversation. I'd evaded it over the last twenty years and I knew I had to tell him, but I felt overwhelmed.

Although I didn't regret telling Amalia everything—a part of me even felt relief after—it didn't stop the conversation from emotionally and mentally draining me, especially after being off my regimen for so long.

I wasn't one for communicating my feelings and most of the time I avoided them—even in therapy. It was just easier to do so than having to face them, despite knowing it was the better option.

---

1. Uncle.

But avoidance could only get you so far.

Kai cleared his throat. "Yes, everything is impeccably fine." He placed his attention on me. "Noah, will you finally tell us who that beautiful woman next to you is?"

Amalia was standing next to me, the side of her hand brushing against mine. I subtly interlocked my pinky finger with hers, knowing she wasn't a big fan of public displays of affection, and looked over at her while I said my next words.

"This is Amalia," I told them, introducing her because there wasn't an appropriate enough word to describe who she was or what she meant to me.

Girlfriend, partner, love of my life didn't feel good enough because she was so much more. But calling her my everything in front of practical strangers to her felt a tad too intimate.

Besides, she'd probably hit me if I did.

"It's a pleasure to meet you, Amalia," Kai said with a large smile on his face. He held out his hand and when she grabbed it, he raised it and brushed his mouth across her knuckles.

I might have been slightly jealous under different circumstances if I hadn't known this was just who Kai was and if he wasn't already completely enamored with the woman who was standing right next to him.

But it didn't mean his gesture didn't grate against my nerves. "All right, Kai. Pleasures have been had," I told him, a sharper edge to my tone.

Amalia lightly chuckled under her breath as she removed her hand from his grasp. She placed a hand on my bicep, glancing between Jamal and me. "I'll let you two talk," she said before squeezing my fingers once. She then gave Jamal a small nod and made her way to the courtyard.

"Yeah, we'll... we'll go get to know your girlfriend," Kai said, nudging Valentina to follow where Amalia was heading.

Once they were all outside, the door closing behind them, Jamal faced me and my stomach dropped at the expression on his face.

"Ready to tell me what's wrong?"

Guess this is the end of me trying to avoid this conversation.

I let out a heavy sigh, running a hand through my hair, and placed his bag, which I was still holding, against the wall in the entry hallway.

Dread crept up my spine as I headed for the living room. "I have to tell you something, and..." I blew out a breath. "Let's sit," I told him, settling on one of the couches.

The tension in the room climbed to a suffocating level and I kept my gaze fixed on the floor for a moment before eventually meeting Jamal's worried gaze, finding him sitting on the other sofa.

"You're scaring me, man. What is it?" Jamal urged me on.

I stared up at the ceiling before meeting his gaze again.

You can do this Noah, then he'll make his decision.

"I don't really know where to start or how to even tell you this. You might hate me after and I wouldn't blame you because I probably would feel the same way, but I need you to know one thing." I paused, taking a deep breath to try to dislodge the heaviness that weighed down my chest. "I'm sorry."

Jamal's eyebrows furrowed in confusion. "Noah, you're not making any sense."

"Can you promise me that despite anything I say, you'll let me tell you everything?" I asked, needing to hear him say the words. It was already taking every ounce of energy in me having to tell him. I'd never be able to get through a single sentence if he interrupted me in between.

"Wh—" he started, but I cut him off.

"Just promise me," I pleaded.

He stayed quiet for a moment, but the look on my face eventually made him relent in my favor. "Fine. I promise."

I took a final deep breath and told him everything. From being born a Barrera, to why I'd escaped. I told him about my father and my childhood, about my mother and Reda.

I didn't leave any details out. I unloaded everything I could think of because I was done keeping secrets.

Through it all, his face stayed impassive as he kept his promise and listened.

I didn't know if that was better or worse. When I'd told

Amalia, I'd wanted her anger, but with Jamal, I didn't know what would be easier.

His anger or his impassiveness, because in both instances, they weren't something I wanted to receive from him.

But his mask faltered when I revealed the truth about his parents, about what truly happened. He'd been aware that my father was responsible, but he hadn't known why.

A loaded silence fell upon us once I finished, a whirlwind of emotions displayed on Jamal's face.

I wanted to tell him how sorry I was over and over again, but my sorrys wouldn't erase the years of lies or the impact my legacy had on his past.

The only thing I could do right now was wait for him to make his decision, to react the way he deemed fit. I would like to say I was prepared for any outcome, but in reality, I wasn't.

After minutes that felt like they'd stretched into hours, a cloak of anger swarmed his irises and he stood up. Without a word or glance in my direction, he walked away and out into the courtyard, the iron door clicking shut behind him.

I wanted to stop him, but I stayed rooted in my spot. Jamal was rarely someone who lashed out when he was angry, although that might have been easier for me since then I'd know how he was actually feeling.

I'd normally force him to talk to me, but I knew he needed his space and I'd give it to him. My ease and need to know where his head was at wasn't a priority right now, no matter how gut-wrenching seeing him walk away was.

The stifling stillness that ensued after his exit sent sadness gripping me by the throat. I closed my eyes, soreness growing behind my eyelids.

I brought my hands up and gripped my hair, hoping to alleviate the ache in my chest. I wanted to scream, to break things, but I wasn't entitled to.

This wasn't about me.

Logically, I knew I wasn't responsible for my past. I didn't *make* my father do this to his family, but it didn't relieve my guilt. For some reason, it made it worse. I tried to control my breathing, but each lungful of air became harder to inhale.

This doesn't mean he's leaving you. He just needs time.

He's not abandoning you. He just needs time.

He's not...

No matter how much I was trying to convince myself otherwise, nothing guaranteed that he wouldn't. With my eyes still closed, I threw my head back against the wall behind me and brought my hands down to grip my thighs, hoping it might help ground me.

Yeah, that isn't working either.

I could feel the harsh sound of my breathing, but the constant echo of my voice inside my head drowned it.

I kept trying to breathe until a familiar touch graced both sides of my face and when I opened my eyes, I was met with the most beautiful shade of green.

Amalia

CHAPTER 23

PRESENT

The moment I saw Jamal walk out of the house with a quiet anger emanating from him, I knew I needed to rush to Noah's side. I could feel that he needed me, but I wasn't prepared for what I'd walked into when I stepped inside.

The door barely closed behind me when the sound of a ragged gasping breath filled the silence in the house, echoing off the walls.

My stomach dropped. "Noah?" I barely got out when my eyes landed on his figure seated in the living room.

He was panting heavily, sweat gleaming off his skin as his head rested against the tiled wall of the living room, his hands clutching the fabric of his pants where his thighs were.

His eyes were closed and his chest kept heaving up and

down in shallow breathing as I hurried to his side, my heart racing. I was no stranger to witnessing a panic attack—Ángel had them often after our mother left—but I'd never seen Noah like this.

I tentatively moved to cradle his face between my hands as I sat on the wooden table in front of him to level myself with him. When he didn't flinch at my touch, I kept my hands on him, holding the sides of his face more firmly.

"Baby, I'm right here," I said, but he didn't seem to hear me. So I repeated myself. "Noah, you're okay. You're not alone. I'm right here with you."

I repeated my last words over and over again, hoping my reassurances would help ground him. He eventually peeled his eyes open, his pupils dilated and unfocused.

"I... I c-c-can't breathe," he whispered through chattering teeth.

"Noah," I called a little harsher this time. "Look at me," I ordered him, hoping to pull him away from the panic he was tethering from, and he did, his brows furrowing lightly at my tone.

"You can breathe." When uncertainty wrestled in his eyes, I slowed my breathing down, intending for him to catch on and follow my lead. My thumbs brushed over his cheekbones. "You *can* breathe."

His eyes were still dilated, but this time, when he locked his glistening brown eyes to mine, he took me in, almost as if he wasn't sure I was real.

Then, slowly, ever so slowly, Noah's breathing began to

steady, his frantic gasp giving away to slower, deeper inhales that matched both of my own and the rhythm with which I was still brushing the pad of my finger against his skin.

"That's it, pretty boy," I said, infusing flirtation into my tone in the hopes that it would help slightly relax him. "You're okay," I said again, brushing my lips over his in a soft kiss.

His eyes fluttered closed at the contact before he opened them again. "I'm okay." He sighed after a shuddering breath with a nod.

"Yes, you're okay," I confirmed, giving him a small smile. "I'm right here with you and you're okay."

Noah's trembling gradually subsided and the harsh grasp he had on the fabric of his pants relaxed, a semblance of calm settling over his features. Eventually, Noah finally relaxed beneath my touch and brought his hands up to cup my own.

He brought his lips to mine in a featherlight kiss before he pulled away, his hands dropping down to rest on his upper thighs.

I moved my hands away from his face, brushing back a loose strand that had fallen on his forehead before placing my palms on his knees.

"Safe to say Jamal wasn't delighted with the news," I said lightheartedly,

A huffing laugh escaped him. "Yeah, you could say

that," he replied, but despite the small smile he gave me, I could see the torment in his gaze.

I hated seeing him like this. It broke my heart.

Despite never having met Jamal, I knew how important he was to Noah and I just hoped that in time, he would see past Noah's secrecy and forgive him. I didn't think Noah would ever be okay otherwise.

I knew firsthand how hard it was to be on the receiving end of Noah's confessions. But ever since last night, I was beginning to understand that Noah's actions had never been fueled by selfishness but were rather a mere consequence brought on after a little boy had grown up unwanted by someone who was supposed to care for him and had never been given a chance to heal from it.

He'd been embarrassed of his legacy and I couldn't blame him for what he'd chosen to do with it when I knew how he must have felt.

My own past had been tumultuous and I tried my hardest not to let it define me. But in comparison, my parents leaving me and my siblings behind was more a blessing than a curse.

I couldn't even begin to comprehend what it was like to be in Noah's position.

Hopefully, Jamal would see the same.

I pulled myself out of my thoughts and focused my attention back on Noah, a faraway look in his eyes. I gave his knee a light squeeze. "He'll understand," I said, trying to reassure him.

He brought his gaze back to me, letting out a heavy sigh. "What if he doesn't?" he whispered, uncertainty coating his tone.

No matter how much I wished I could guarantee him that Jamal would forgive him, how much I'd love to offer Noah the perfect reassuring words that would erase the doubts creeping up that beautiful mind of his, I wouldn't lie to him and offer false hope.

So I told him what I knew I could guarantee him. "Then we'll figure it out." I reached for his hands and intertwined our fingers together, squeezing once. "Together."

My words didn't dissipate the torment in his eyes completely, but it left room for a hint of relief to peek through.

He brought our joined hands to his lips, pressing a kiss to my palm. "I love you," he mouthed, pressing the words into the skin of my wrist, right above my pulse point.

I shook my head with a small laugh. "Yeah, yeah."

Noah cocked his head to the side as he narrowed his eyes at me. "No 'I love you too' or maybe a 'You're the love of my life, Noah, I love you dearly'."

I knew he was still hurting, but seeing him being playful tugged at my heartstrings. I'd missed this side of him.

I stayed quiet for a moment, pretending to muse over my response before saying, "I don't recall ever saying that."

"Oh yeah?" he taunted.

I fought a smile and playfully shrugged.

He tugged me forward until I fell onto his lap, scooping me up so that I was sitting sideways onto him. Before I could register what was happening, his fingers dug into my ribs.

My eyes widened as I let out a scream, not having expected the sudden pressure. "Noah," I yelled, squirming in his lap as I tried to get him to stop. He didn't, and a laugh so strong bubbled out of my lips, I struggled to breathe.

"Say it," he said next to my ear, playfully nipping at it as he continued to prod at my sides.

"Okay, okay, okay," I repeated between ragged breaths. "I love you," I yelled, hoping he could hear me through my fits of laughter.

The clearing of a throat sounded in the room and Noah's fingers stilled. He didn't move them as we turned our heads toward the source to find Kai, Valentina, and Jamal standing in the kitchen, looking at us.

Kai had an amused look on his face, Valentina's expression was impartial, while Jamal's features were torn with a mix of emotions.

An awkward silence cloaked the room until Kai broke it again, which seemed to be his role in the group—speaking for all of them.

"Sorry to interrupt, but perhaps we should get started on why we're here?" he questioned, his gaze bouncing between Noah and me.

"Yea—" I cleared my throat, turning my body forward. "Yes," I said, moving to stand, but Noah's hands kept me in place as if he were using me as a shield. I glared at him over my shoulder, but he just shrugged in response.

I shook my head and gently placed my hands above his, redirecting my attention back to our guests, who remained rooted in the kitchen.

Tension lingered in the air and I didn't really know how to dissipate it. In any other circumstances, I would simply take myself out of it and leave the room, but I didn't want to leave Noah alone.

Just as I opened my mouth to suggest grabbing something to eat since I was starving and I figured they might be too after traveling, a sharp knock echoed through the room.

Instantly, all of us went on high alert at the intrusion, each one instinctively reaching for a weapon.

Good to know everyone came prepared.

I swiftly made my way toward the front door, everyone trailing behind with their weapons drawn as it swung wide open.

I let out a sigh and lowered my gun when Nassim walked in, large brown bags in each arm, a sweet and savory smell wafting off it.

I had completely forgotten that I'd called him earlier both to get him to come and avoid more of Kai's relentless interrogation.

I'd barely had time to settle in my seat when he and Valentina had followed me outside, taking the seats opposite me around the outdoor tile table. While Valentina had remained silent and looking anywhere but at me, Kai had launched into asking me a series of questions.

The Academy's rigorous selection process paled in comparison to Kai's endless probing about who I was, where I came from, about my family, to which I gave vague answers. But he'd just kept going, no matter how much I'd tried to steer into not talking.

At one point, I hadn't known whether to laugh when he didn't get the hint or shoot him to get him to stop talking.

Who knew one person could talk this much?

So instead, I'd excused myself and had called Nassim to stall for a little while until Jamal walked out and I'd hung up on him without another word, knowing Noah needed me.

"Such a warm welcome," Nassim said, an amused smile playing on his lips.

"Sorry, I forgot you were coming," I said, clicking the safety back on my gun.

"Don't be, it turns me on being on the other end of a barrel," he teased, shooting a playful glance at his wife who was tucked behind him.

Daniela rolled her eyes and smacked his shoulder, a slight flush creeping up on her cheeks. "We're in company, stop saying shit like that," she muttered under her breath.

Nassim chuckled and blew her a kiss before turning his attention back on me and the others gathered behind me.

With a casual wave, he greeted them, "Hello, everyone

with their guns still pointed in my face, I'm Nassim, and the exquisite woman behind me is my wife, Daniela."

"I like him already," Kai said from behind me.

This should be interesting.

I shook my head, leading the way back into the living area. Everyone followed suit, exchanging handshakes and proper greetings before filing into the living room.

I plopped down on one of the sofas, Noah taking the seat on my left. Nassim and his wife squeezed onto the same one, while Jamal and Kai occupied the other sofa. Valentina, on the other hand, chose to remain standing, leaning against the wall.

Although she was mostly quiet, I liked her.

Her presence commanded attention, not in a way that she sought or demanded it, but because you couldn't help yourself but respect her.

Her expression remained mostly stoic, except for the rare softening when her gaze met Kai's, but I could tell she'd been through a lot beneath her unfazed facade.

Because she reminded me of myself.

She also didn't trust us, which I wouldn't either if I'd just met strangers asking me to overturn decades of a cartel.

We all dropped our guns onto the living room table, Nassim pushing some of them out of the way to clear a space for bags he was holding before placing them onto its wooden surface.

"There's sandwiches inside with *l7am bel ber9o9*[1] that I grabbed from a juice shop on the way here, some fruits and water bottles. Help yourselves," Nassim offered.

I didn't need to be told twice. Not only was I starving but *l7am bel ber9o9* was one of my favorite dishes I'd discovered when I'd moved to Morocco for work, so I immediately reached inside of the bags and grabbed a paper-wrapped sandwich, the scent making my mouth water.

As we ate, Nassim briefed Jamal and his friends, taking them through every step so that they'd be ready for tomorrow.

At one point, Kai and Valentina each had brought out a rugged laptop, typing away with every new information Nassim provided them.

Jamal mostly remained quiet, absorbing each detail and only interjecting when he needed clarifications or additional information on an aspect of the plan.

The hours passed in a blur, and after coordinating everything necessary and another food break, Nassim and Daniela left as the sun was setting with plans to meet tomorrow evening in Bab Al Mansour in another safe house he'd secured a few days ago.

Shortly after they'd left, Noah retreated outside while I moved to the kitchen to do the dishes. Kai and Valentina were still typing away on their computers and talking in

---

1. Beef tajine with prunes (Moroccan dish).

hushed tones while Jamal just sat next to them, his eyes far off like he was lost in another world.

I was rinsing the last plate when he abruptly stood and moved in my direction. Kai looked at him, worried, and I was about to ask if he needed anything when he breezed past me and opened the back door, closing it behind him as he stepped into the courtyard.

Through the small window that looked out into the back, I watched as Noah slowly turned around, his expression morphing when his eyes landed on Jamal.

Please let this be good.

Noah

CHAPTER 24

PRESENT

IT'D BEEN A DAY.

When Nassim showed up, I'd pushed this morning's conversation to the back of my mind and focused on the task at hand because I was good at that. Ignoring how I felt, putting on a façade, and keep going.

But now that the day was almost over, everything I'd buried was resurfacing.

I was standing outside in the courtyard, hoping the air would help clear my mind, but the quiet lull was just making the thoughts in my head spiral.

I closed my eyes and gripped the edge of the chair in front of me, trying to steady my breathing and calm my racing thoughts when a voice behind me cut through the air.

"Hey," he said tentatively.

I glanced over my shoulder to find Jamal lingering a few feet away from me, his hands tucked in his trousers. His expression was guarded, but beneath it all, I could see a subtle hint of vulnerability.

The realization weighed heavily on my conscience. I hated that I'd played a part in putting that expression on his face. My job had always been to protect him, to shield him from anything bad, but it felt like I'd failed him and had done the opposite.

A heavy silence stretched between us, uncertainty dancing in his gaze. Until he broke it. "Can we talk?"

Okay, I wasn't expecting that.

"Oh… yeah. Sure. Let's talk," I said awkwardly, stumbling backward as I gestured toward the table. "Want to sit?"

"Standing is fine," he replied quietly.

"Right, okay." I nodded, bringing a hand up and rubbing the back of my neck.

I'd raised this kid, and we'd had serious conversations before, but I'd never felt more nervous than I did in this moment.

Him wanting to talk should be a positive thing, *right?* Then why did it feel like I was standing on the edge of a cliff, waiting for the other shoe to drop?

Breathe, Noah. Stop jumping to the worst conclusion.

"So about earlier…" he trailed off, looking away.

A silent beat passed and I wanted to fill it, to make him

talk to me, but I fought the urge because Jamal had never initiated conversation, so I had to give him the space to do so.

Anything else would be selfish of me and I'd been selfish for long enough.

Taking a deep breath, he met my gaze again. "I'm sorry I stormed off earlier."

My eyes widened in surprise. "*You're* sorry? Jamal, I'm the one who should be sorry. I am sorry for not telling you sooner, for what my…" I paused, the word caught in my throat. I let out a deep sigh, but before I could continue, he interrupted me.

"Don't apologize for him," he protested. There was a hint of anger in his voice, but it wasn't aimed at me, at least I hoped it wasn't. But it quickly faded away with his next words. "You're not responsible for what he did."

I shook my head. "I know, but…" I began, but I wasn't sure what to say because in some way, I knew he was right.

I wasn't *technically* responsible for what happened, or for any of my father's actions, but deep down, everything always came back to one thing despite how hard I'd tried to ignore it over the years.

If I had been good enough, strong enough to withstand him, I would have completed my initiation, taken the role I'd been born for, and none of this would have happened.

My mother, Reda, and I wouldn't have had to hide for all these years. I wouldn't have worked for the Bureau. I wouldn't have met Ayoub or his wife. My father wouldn't have tried to teach me a lesson.

Jamal wouldn't have suffered for years from extensive injuries a fire *my* father had caused, wouldn't have lost the two most important people in his life.

Countless lives had been lost at the hands of my father. *What if I could have prevented all of it?*

A hand on my shoulder jolted me out of my rumination.

"Hey," Jamal said firmly and my eyes met his. "It isn't your fault. None of this was. I was angry earlier, but it wasn't at you."

I cocked my head to the side, raising a skeptical brow in response.

"Okay, okay, I was a little mad at you," Jamal admitted with a sheepish look, "but it was only because you didn't tell me sooner. The only person I—well, I don't even think 'hate' covers it—is Barrera."

There was a pause before Jamal added, "And I wouldn't be the man you raised me to be if I blamed you for what *he* did."

His words didn't erase years of guilt, but it eased the nozzle I'd had gripping tight around my chest from the moment I ran out of a house on fire, carrying a ten-year-old kid in my arms, only to watch his whole world crumble under the flames while I waited for the backup I'd called on the way there.

No matter how hard the aftermath of that day was, it

had brought Jamal into my life, who quickly became one of the biggest blessings of my life.

I learned so much about myself raising him and he taught me that all my fears about being a parent one day were unfounded.

That despite my missteps and mistakes, he'd still stand by me.

I wasn't my father and I'd never be. And there was something a little freeing about realizing that.

Tears welled at the back of my eyes as I reached up, gently cupping the back of his head like I always had when he was a kid. "Thank you," I murmured, my voice thick with emotion.

He placed a hand on my shoulders, squeezing once. "I don't know what you're thanking me for, but you're most welcome," he said, a teasing smile playing on his lips.

I shook my head and brought him into a hug, something we rarely did. He reluctantly wrapped his arms around my upper back, patting it once. He moved to pull away, but I tightened my hold on him, needing just another second.

He chuckled, giving me another pat on the back. "Okay, I think it's enough hugging to last a lifetime," he teased.

I released him from the embrace and wrapped an arm around his shoulders, bringing him to my side. "Guess I didn't do too bad of a job with you."

He glanced at me. "Well, don't give yourself all the credit," he countered with a grin.

I'd missed this side of him. He didn't show it very often or to most people, but whenever he did, you felt special because you knew every smile or laugh he gave you was genuine.

I smiled at him. "Fair enough," I conceded, ruffling my hand over the top of his head.

He jerked his head away but didn't move from my side. "You're messing up my hair, man."

I laughed, playfully flicking the back of his head. "Show some respect to your elders."

He furrowed his brows, a playful glint dancing in his eyes. "You're not even a decade older than I am."

"Doesn't matter. I'm still older," I retorted with a smile, giving his shoulder a final squeeze. "All right, let's head inside."

We made our way out of the courtyard, but Jamal paused once we reached the back door. He turned to me with a pensive expression on his face. "I know you were trying to protect me, but no more keeping secrets, okay?"

I gave him a solemn nod. "No more secrets, Jamal."

"Good," he said before reaching for the handle to open the door.

Once we stepped inside, my gaze landed on Amalia, who was still in the kitchen, a small rag in her hand. She offered a knowing smile as if she knew what had transpired between Jamal and me outside.

Knowing her, she'd probably watch our whole interaction through the window.

Valentina's eyes stayed glued to her screen, but Kai

glanced up from his computer, his eyes bouncing between Jamal and me.

"Finally," he exclaimed. "It was about time you two made up." He looked at Jamal. "You were getting even grumpier than you usually are."

Jamal rolled his eyes as he made his way to them. "Keep the commentary to yourself, Kai," he said, grabbing his own computer and taking the seat next to him.

Kai looked at him and held his hand up. "Apologies, sir. Just stating facts."

"Just get back to work," he told him, never looking away from his screen, his fingers tapping away on the keyboard.

I chuckled under my breath, amused by their back and forth. With one last glance at them, I turned my attention back to my girl, making my way over to where she leaned against the counter and placing my hands on either side of her.

She tossed the damp rag she'd been holding onto the side and rested her hands on my hips, the warmth of her skin seeping through the thin fabric of my shirt.

"I take it the conversation went well?" she asked, her gaze meeting mine.

I nodded, a sense of relief washing over me. "Thankfully," I responded, grateful that Jamal and I managed to have this conversation.

Leaning forward, she pressed a gentle kiss before

pulling away, a knowing smile playing on her lips. "I knew it would," she murmured.

I returned her smile. "Because you're always right?" I replied softly, brushing a stray strand of hair away from her face.

Amalia shrugged before leaning into my touch. "Well, someone has to be," she teased, her tone playful.

"So modest," I countered, shaking my head.

"I never claimed to be."

I wrapped an arm around her waist and pulled her closer. I huffed out a laugh. "I love you," I whispered, pressing a kiss to her forehead. Then I cupped the back of her head and brushed my lips to hers.

It was supposed to be a short kiss, but she gripped the front of my shirt and pulled me closer, deepening it. Her tongue slipped inside my mouth, tangling with mine and I groaned into the kiss.

I almost forgot where we had been when someone cleared their throat and Kai's voice called out, "Please remember you have company."

At the same time, Jamal said, "The last thing I want to see is my uncle making out with his girl."

I pulled away and Amalia rested her head against my chest.

Then we both burst out laughing.

We'd been driving for the past two hours, a mix of anticipation and fear racing through my veins with each passing mile. On one hand, I couldn't wait for today to be over and close a chapter that had been hanging over my head my entire life.

But on the other, what if it didn't?

What if getting rid of my father once and for all didn't free me of this constant gnawing I felt in my chest no matter how much I tried to tamp it down?

Not only that, but what if something went wrong? What if my father went after Amalia or Jamal?

I pushed the thought away and focused on getting Amalia and me to where we needed to be.

We were now only a few minutes from our destination. The drive back to Bab Al Mansour was normally only forty-five minutes, but Amalia and I had taken the back roads while Kai, Jamal, and Valentina took the main highway.

All of us yesterday had agreed to not only leave at different times but also take different routes to avoid landing on my father's radar.

Nassim had sent a text earlier, informing us that he and Daniela were already at the safe house. They'd left late last night and had met with their men this morning to brief them on the plan we'd devised yesterday.

The only variable we weren't able to account for was the number of men on the premises. Nassim's men had tried to do so, but since Amalia and I fled, my father had upped the security around the mansion and they couldn't get close enough without attracting attention.

This meant two things—Infiltrating the *riad* would be much harder than we'd anticipated and we'd be outnumbered.

At least Kai's drones and Valentina's skills as a sniper would give us a better chance at mapping out how many were on the grounds and where each one was.

It was almost sundown by the time we pulled over behind the apartment building, the descending sun casting long shadows across the alley. Amalia's burner phone buzzed against my back as I brought the motorcycle to a stop, cutting off the engine.

I waited for her to get down before throwing my leg over the seat and turning to face her. She removed her helmet, raking her fingers through her hair.

I pulled off my own and grabbed hers as she reached into her leather jacket pocket, retrieving the new burner phone. She'd bought it when we'd stopped for gas earlier because she'd wanted to leave anything that had the potential to be traceable behind.

Flipping it open, she read the new message before showing it to me. It was a message from Nassim, giving us the information on which building, the apartment number, and the code for the door.

She slipped the phone back into her pocket. "Ready?" she asked, her features betraying her worry as she glanced back at me.

I gave her a small nod. "Yeah, I am," I replied, despite the apprehension now coursing through my veins. A million thoughts spiraled through my brain because I needed this to work, but what if it didn't?

What if everything we'd planned wasn't enough?

Focus, Noah. Feelings are for later.

"Hey," Amalia's voice softened as she reached up to cup my cheek reassuringly.

I grasped her wrist and leaned into her touch, closing my eyes as she pushed herself up on her toes. She swiftly pressed a kiss to my lips before pulling away.

Opening my eyes, I found her intently looking at me. "I know this is a lot, but we got this," she said with determination.

She was so cute.

I chuckled. "Look at you giving me motivational speeches."

She withdrew her hand from my face and playfully swatted my chest, shaking her head. "Let's go, pretty boy. We have somewhere to be," she said before heading down the alleyway.

With a deep breath, I followed her, trying to ignore the dread slithering down my spine.

Amalia

CHAPTER 25

PRESENT

I was seated in a car with Noah, Nassim, and Jamal, parked onto a side road that led to the Barrera compound while Kai and Valentina were posted on the opposite side of the property to give them a better vantage point to guide us.

Daniela ended up staying behind despite her countless protests after Nassim discovered earlier today that she was pregnant after she'd thrown up for the majority of the morning.

They got into an argument right before we'd left because she insisted she would be fine since it was still early in her pregnancy, but he'd ended up somewhat convincing her to stay put.

Some of Nassim's men were scattered around different corners of the property while the rest of them were packed into an off-road vehicle that was set to run straight through the front barrier in exactly seven minutes to provide us with a distraction so we could infiltrate the *riad* from the back.

Unintelligible mumbles cut through the comms, but I could tell who it was despite the muffled sound of their voices and that I'd just met them a few days ago. They must have forgotten that their line of communication with us hadn't been muted.

"Kai, Valentina, cut the shit. We don't have time for your bickering," I said through gritted teeth as we all got out of the car.

I checked my gun, slamming the clip back before slipping the gun into my waistband, and grabbed my dagger while the others strapped their own weapons.

Kai cleared his throat, offering a brief apology. "Right, so on your way to the back, there are currently four of Barrera's men on what appears to be their breaks. Valentina is now on her way to take care of them, so you'll know when to move in."

The sun was already down and provided us with more coverage as we headed toward the back of the property. We took cover behind vegetation and spotted the four men Kai was referring to.

One moment they were engaged in an animated conversation, cigarettes in hand, and the next, a bullet sliced in the air, taking two of them out. Their bodies slumped to the ground and before the other two could reach for their weapons or even realize what was happening, another bullet brought them down.

Eerie silence hung in the air before a roaring crash reverberated near the entrance, followed by shouting and gunfire cutting through the air.

This is our cue.

"Let's go," my voice roared over the sound of the ensuing chaos.

We ran, closing the distance between us and the pile of corpses splayed on the ground. I crouched down, swiftly rummaging through their pockets until I found the set of keys I was looking for.

I motioned for the others to follow and guided them toward the side where a large metal door stood.

Only the guards used it for their smoking breaks since Barrera didn't like people doing so in the house or anywhere near it since it 'polluted the air.'

Like that's what was polluting the space.

"Clear," Kai informed us. "Everyone is rushing toward the front. I count about twenty men and they're packing."

Using the keys, I quickly unlocked the door and pushed it open. We trickled into the courtyard, the screaming and crackle of gunfire much clearer now.

I whipped around to face them, my voice cutting through the cacophony. "We need to split up," I ordered.

"No," Noah said through gritted teeth. "It's better if we all stay together."

"There are too many men out front and Nassim's guys

will need help," I explained in a hurry. "You and Jamal take the front, Nassim and I will take the house."

"Amalia, no," he protested. "I'm not letting you out of my sight."

I placed a reassuring hand on his arm and met his gaze. "We don't have time to go back and forth. Just trust me, okay?"

He groaned. "Fine, but just know I'm pissed that you're making me do this." He slammed a harsh kiss to my lips. "You better not let anything happen to you."

"I'd like to see them try," I huffed out, attempting to lighten the mood and defuse the apprehension radiating from him.

He managed a small smile, shaking his head before aiming a glare at Nassim. "She can handle herself, but I'll shoot you if anything happens to her."

Nassim gave him a curt nod, but just before we split, Noah grasped my elbow and leaned down to whisper, "My father won't be out there with his men; he'll be hiding inside like the coward that he is."

"I had the same thought."

"When you reach the top floor, push the oil painting with his portrait," he instructed.

My brows furrowed at that.

I knew what he was referring to, but I didn't understand why he was telling me about the large oil painting of Barrera that was at the end of the hallway on the same level where my room and some of the other guards' rooms were located. I always found it quite obnoxious that he had such a large portrait of himself, but not surprising.

"That's the main entrance to the concealed passageways that span the house." Noah clarified, seeing the confusion on my face. "Use them to hide, and you might even find him somewhere in there."

I nodded. "Meet us in the basement cell when you guys are done."

There was a moment of hesitation before I said, "Be safe. I—"

"Listen, we don't have all day," Nassim interrupted, urging us on.

Noah shot him a look above my head before he briefly kissed me. "Save it," he replied. "I love you, too, but you can tell me later because you're not allowed to die. I'll see you soon."

As we parted ways, I headed for the right side of the house with Nassim while Jamal and Noah headed for the front.

Adrenaline coursed through my veins as Kai fired instructions in my ear. I drowned his voice to a low dull at the back of my mind and concentrated on moving faster as I led Nassim into the house.

We moved quietly, our senses on high alert. We made it down the first hallway toward the stairs without difficulty, but as we carefully climbed them, two shadows loomed closer, but their steps weren't in a hurry.

We paused at the edge of the staircase, listening closely.

"It's a disaster out there. Can't we just stay here and pretend we didn't hear anything?" one of them said.

I peered over the corner, just enough not to draw attention, only to see the other guard had paused in his steps. "If you want to get slaughtered by Hamza or even worse Barrera himself, be my guest. I'm not risking their wrath."

The moment he turned back around, I emerged from behind the wall that was hiding me and drove my knife across his neck, blood spattering over my hands.

The dead body dropped at my feet, and I pushed the body down the stairs and out of my way.

Noah had moved behind me while I took care of the man now slung across the steps, just in time to aim two bullets into the other guard in the chest before he shot me, his body slumping to the wall and his gun skidding across the floor.

Nassim mumbled, "You're welcome," as I reached for the dead guy's gun on the floor and headed down the hall with Nassim following right behind.

I checked the chamber to find it full before tucking it under the waistband at my back since both my thigh and shoulder holsters were already full of weapons.

We cleared the floor, room by room, before moving to the floor above and doing the same. We hadn't encountered anyone else as we finally made it to the top floor.

With no one in sight, I beelined for the painting at the end of the hall, Nassim right on my trail.

I sheathed the bloodied knife back into the strap around

my thigh and pushed against the ornate golden frame, my gun drawn up.

A strong musty and damp smell wafted out. I scrunched my nose as we slowly ventured into the dimly lit space, navigating down the narrow hall with caution.

We eventually rounded a corner, only to be met with another long corridor that eventually fed into numerous pathways, each one identical to the last.

Dread swept through me at the sight, knowing we couldn't waste any more time. In my three years here, I'd heard whispers about hidden halls and tunnels but never actually found them to explore them and find out where they led.

I glanced back at Nassim. "We'll need to split up."

"Oh, absolutely not," he countered, shaking his head adamantly.

"We don't have time to check each of them together."

"I don't care. I'm not particularly looking to get shot today," he insisted.

I sighed. "Noah won't actually do it."

"I'd rather not test the theory."

I groaned. "Fine, then you choose, so I can blame you if we get lost."

Nassim began muttering under his breath, pointing his

gun down each corridor as he followed the melody. "*A jrada malha, fine kounti sarha*[1]," he recited softly.

My brows furrowed. "Are you *seriously* basing your choice on a nursery rhyme?"

He ignored me and quickly finished singing. "That one," he announced, gesturing the corridor to the far left with his barrel. He looked at me and shrugged. "I have to start practicing for the little one, and this made the decision faster."

I pinched the bridge of my nose in exasperation. *Por el amor de Dios*[2].

With no better plan and already enough time wasted, I sighed and stepped into the hallway he'd randomly chosen.

But as we made our way down the hall, Nassim spoke again. "Besides, I already knew which one to take," he admitted in a hushed tone.

I halted in my tracks, nearly causing Nassim to collide with me. "Please tell me you're kidding," I groaned. "How and why didn't you say anything earlier?"

"My father used to work here, remember? And besides, it was quite entertaining seeing your face when I started singing," he said, amused.

If only shooting him were an option…

---

1. This is the start of a famous Moroccan nursery rhyme called "A Jrada Malha".
2. For God's sake.

"Just… fucking lead the way," I whisper-shouted gesturing with my gun for him to walk ahead of me.

After a few minutes, he stopped short and faced the wall.

My eyes narrowed on Nassim's back. "What are you doing?" I questioned, frustration licking at my veins if he was stalling us again.

"Just wait," he replied, his fingers brushing against the wall as if he were looking for something.

I was on the verge of leaving him behind to continue searching for where Barrera was hiding when the faint echo of voices sounded behind the concrete wall.

I listened closely, straining my ear to eventually discern that both Barrera and Hamza were on the other side. "We could have saved precious minutes if you'd just told me you knew where he'd be."

He peered at me over his shoulder with a grin on his face. "Where's the fun in that?"

"If your wife wasn't pregnant, I would have shot you myself," I said, the grip on my gun tightening.

He shrugged off my comment. "Ready?" he asked, reaching for something strapped to his thigh. He then stuck it onto the middle of the wall and stepped back, examining it.

My eyes widened. "Is that C-4?" I asked, my voice a mixture of shock and disbelief. "You've been carrying C-4 this whole time?" I whispered-yelled at him.

He faced me. "Yes, now let's move back before we get

blown up with it," he said, guiding toward the end of the hallway where we came from.

Once we were both shielded behind the wall, he retrieved a small remote from his pocket and pressed on a small button, detonating the bomb.

The force of the blast blew the wall, shocking the ground beneath us, and I reached out to steady myself against the wall. A thick haze of smoke billowed out of the wall, shrouding the corridor in a ghostly veil.

Quite poetic for what we were about to do.

We swiftly made our way back, weaving through the debris, their acrid smell stinging my nostrils. As the dust slowly settled, it revealed a clean hole through the wall.

The room inside, one I'd never seen before, bore the scars of the explosion, the surfaces charred and marked with debris. The furniture lay strewn about haphazardly, some of the pieces overturned from the impact.

I could count about ten or so men scattered around on the floor, shielding their faces and disoriented from the sudden explosion.

Nassim and I each took a side, immediately getting to work before the haze from the impact dissipated and they realized we were intruders.

Gunshots and screams rang through the air from my left while I scanned the room on my side and spotted Hamza, cowering in a pressed suit in the far corner of the room. He was hunched with his hands above his head to protect himself.

Jodidamente patético[3].

I headed in his direction, executing every guard on my way to him before they could reach for their guns, leaving a trail of corpses in my wake. I'd almost made it to him when Nassim's voice thundered above the gunfire.

"Watch out."

I looked just in time to duck behind a chair as a bullet came straight at me. It whizzed right past my head, so close to hitting me that it moved my hair from the closeness.

I lay flat on my stomach and shot the bastard in both of his kneecaps. He collapsed to the floor and I aimed my gun at his face, pulling the trigger and shooting him between the eyes.

That'll serve you for trying to fucking shoot me.

I sensed movement in my periphery and turned just in time to fire at Hamza, who had attempted to take me out.

The bullet hit him in his shooting arm, which made him drop his gun. He tried to reach for it, but I quickly got to my feet and rushed to close the distance separating us.

I crushed his hand under my boot and stood above him. "I would say it was nice knowing you, but…" I let my sentence trail as I pointed my gun at his head.

Hamza barely had time to look up, his groans of pain cut short when I shot him, his head evaporating into a crimson void, the collateral painting my clothing.

"Didn't take you for one fond of theatricals," Nassim

---

3. Fucking pathetic.

remarked, his voice calm despite the chaos we'd just created.

I looked over at him to see him standing above a sea of bodies, a proud smile on his face. He was also holding Barrera by the back of his collar with a gun pressed against his temple.

"Sometimes it makes the kill a little sweeter," I replied with a nonchalant shrug. Then I met Barrera's gaze with a smirk. "Nice to see you again, boss. Miss me?"

Noah and I had only left a couple of days ago, but with the state in which Barrera currently was, you'd think he hadn't slept in years.

His skin was even more weathered, the wrinkles around his eyes and on his forehead even more pronounced. Deep dark circles marred beneath his bloodshot and unfocused eyes.

Anger flashed across his face, his jaw twitching with fury. "Fucking traitor," he spat through clenched teeth. "I knew a woman should never be trusted, you fucking b—"

But before he could hurl the insult my way, Nassim swiftly silenced Barrera with a blow to the back of his head using the butt of his gun. As Barrera slumped into Nassim's grip, he let go of him, his body tumbling to the ground.

"Always so charming, isn't he?" Nassim said with a smirk.

I huffed out a laugh and holstered my empty gun into its compartment, then reached for another one. "You're ridiculous. Let's go," I ordered. Pressing a finger to my ear,

I spoke to Kai, "We have him. We'll meet you guys at the rendezvous point."

I heard a grunt as Nassim pulled Barrera's body up. With his body now slung over his shoulder, Nassim said, "All right, let's go before I pull my back carrying him."

I led us to a large oak door and pushed it open, realizing that we were stepping into the far left side of the mansion on the bottom floor.

How many fucking secret doors does this place have and why have I never seen them?

I quickly checked for any other guards, and when the coast was clear, I held the door open for Nassim to come through it.

And as we walked across the courtyard and toward the building at the back where our meeting point with the others was, one thought was at the forefront of my mind.

I might not be the one pulling the trigger in the end, but I was looking forward to this bastard's final breath.

Noah

CHAPTER 26

PRESENT

I FIRED TWO LAST SHOTS, THE BULLETS LODGING themselves straight into the chest of the man running full-speed toward me with a machete in his hands, his body lunging forward and hitting the ground.

A sickening thud from the guy's head smacking on the ground echoed in the air before a loud silence fell upon us. My chest heaved up and down as my eyes scanned the front yard, the aftermath a complete bloodbath.

Piles of corpses littered the ground, including two of ours, their blood forming pools of the filthy gravel.

I'd tried to help one of them, but I'd quickly become a bit preoccupied when one of my father's men tackled me to the ground and tried to strangle me—he was lying somewhere in this carnage with a nicely sized hole right between his brows.

"Not too bad for an old man," Jamal's voice broke through the quiet as he walked over to where I was standing.

"Who are you calling old? Besides, need I remind you that I'm the one who taught you how to shoot a gun?" I countered, raising a brow.

Before Jamal could speak, one of Nassim's men, Ruiz, approached us. "We'll take care of the bodies. Kai just informed us Nassim and Amalia made it out and are waiting for you in the basement."

"Thank you," I replied, giving him a small nod of gratitude. "While we're down there, do you mind doing a sweep of the property?" I asked him. "There might be kids locked somewhere and I want them out, but be careful."

"Of kids?" he questioned, a perplexed expression crossing his features.

My father had a predilection for taking children under his care and shaping them into his most faithful soldiers, exploiting their innocence for his own gain.

He knew that people wouldn't pay attention to kids. They were meant to be naive and harmless, which was why it worked so well for him.

"Some might have been under my father's thumb for a long time. That's where their loyalty will be lying," I explained.

"Prisoners' cells are in that building over there." I pointed to the weathered structure situated on the far right.

He nodded in understanding and turned on his heels, but I called out his name again, remembering something else. "There's this kid called Sabiri. He has a full head of curly red hair. You can't miss him. Can you make sure he's cared for until I get back?"

We'd only crossed paths a few times during my captivity, but every time we did, something about him nagged at my chest, like I could see the pain in my eyes reflected in his. It might be nothing, but I wanted to make sure for myself.

Ruiz gave me another curt nod and left to relay to his crew the information I'd just given him. Nassim would be dealing with the aftermath, but I wanted to make sure his men were at least aware before they received orders from their boss.

Once he was out of earshot, I turned to Jamal. "Let's get this over with." I led Jamal toward the front door from which we'd emerged earlier with my gun ready in case of any stragglers that needed to be taken care of.

We walked through the house that I'd never been able to call home, its walls bearing the scars of bad memories and even worse nightmares.

When we'd left town and I'd learned what my father had done, I knew I'd never come back because all I'd ever known here was loneliness and a person who I'd been supposed to look up to and who couldn't even look at me.

My father, if one could even call him that, had always been a stranger living under the roof, only there to remind me of my shortcomings and how much he'd wished I'd never existed.

I'd be lying if I said a part of me hadn't longed for the father I never had. But all he'd given me was the burden of his name and the scars he'd inflicted me with and tonight, I'd put a final end to it.

Tonight, I'd shatter the shackles he'd drowned me with and free myself from the years of carrying *his* shortcomings as weighted guilt.

"So this is where you grew up," Jamal said from behind me.

"Unfortunately," I responded with a heavy sigh, reaching for the back sliding doors and pulling them open.

We stepped out into the now cool night air, a scent of smoke lingering from afar. It must be from the explosion we heard earlier while we were at the front.

My breath had caught in my throat, my stomach dropping, when I'd heard the sound of whatever it was that went off. I'd been rushing away from the scene at the front when Kai's voice halted me in my steps, assuring me that Amalia wasn't injured and that the blast was Nassim's doing.

We swiftly made it to the intended building. As I reached for the handle of the heavy iron door and wrenched it open since it was already unlocked, memories of the countless times I'd been dragged, pushed, or thrown down those stairs flooded my mind.

I tried to push them away and focus on the task at hand as I descended the narrow staircase, the sound of our footsteps echoing off the stone walls.

But with each step that brought me closer to the cell in the basement, it felt like a path to a defining moment. One that dredged up conflicting emotions within me.

I wanted this chapter of my life to be over with. I *wanted* to break free of my father's chains. But this man, despite how cruel and abusive he'd been toward me, was still my father.

He was still my blood and killing him would be permanent.

There would be no going back after this.

I felt the feathered touches of relief whispering across my ribcage at that thought, but it didn't erase the small ounce of guilt settled deep in my gut.

Not even the sight of my father bound and gagged to a chair in the cell that had plagued my childhood and always appeared in my mind when his name was uttered could ease it.

After a brief moment of hesitation, I took a deep breath and stepped into the cell, leaving only a few feet away between us. I'd schooled my features, making sure none of my emotions flashed across my face because if my father was fueled by one thing, it was fear.

Especially mine. He'd used to thrive on it.

My father's hands were currently restrained behind his back with ropes, his feet tied at the front. His typically polished appearance was now completely disheveled by the earlier explosion.

The light fabric of his suit was torn and tattered in places, blackened by soot and singed from flames. His skin was smudged with ash, streaks of sweat tracking down his cheeks.

Even his once carefully slicked back hair stood at different angles, blood and soot matting it to his forehead.

"Father, glad you could join us," I greeted him in a nonchalant tone. I forced my gaze to meet his and when I did, it was blazing with anger, his features contorted with more resentment than I'd ever seen on him before.

My grip tightened around my gun, but I immediately loosened it, not wanting him to notice. "Take off his gag," I told no one in particular.

Nassim moved toward my father with his gun drawn and yanked the rag out. The moment the fabric passed his lips, he expelled his fury.

"What is this foolish charade?" he gritted out.

His voice caused my gut to clench, the impact of his low and gravelly voice sending a tailspin of flashbacks to swarm my mind.

Noah, no. Focus.

I internally shook myself out of it and listened to the rest of his hate-filled speech.

"I knew I should have killed you myself," my father stated. "I should have forced that bitch of your mother to get rid of you the moment she told me she was pregnant because somehow I knew, I just knew you wouldn't live up to *my* name, even when you were mother's womb." Spittle flew from his mouth as he raised his voice in the end.

Before I could stop myself, I asked, "Why?"

"Why what?"

"Why did you hate me so much?" I said, the words barely getting out from how much my voice shook. My chest heaved up and down, waiting for his response.

A cruel laugh left his lips. "You're just proving my point, dear son. Your emotions were always the reason why I knew you would never amount to anything. You were my worst failure. You were *weak* of mind, so why on earth would I want you to be my heir only for your pitiful, emotional self to take over something that is *mine*?" he explained, his words laced with venom. "You were always your mother's son, always letting your emotions guide your decisions. You were just as useless as she was." He sneered. "Speaking of which, I heard that bitch Camila died years ago. Wish I'd been able to find her and do it myself."

Rage ravaged my veins, incinerating any self-control I was trying to maintain. I didn't want to give him the satisfaction of reacting to his words, but I couldn't stop myself from kicking my foot against the chair he was tied to, sending him plummeting toward the floor.

He cursed at me in Arabic, the last part of his insults cut short when his back slammed against the concrete floor.

I moved closer to where he was lying and stood above

him. "Get her name out of your mouth," I spat out, aiming my gun at his head. "And I am not your son."

"You just keep proving me right." He laughed in between coughs as he tried to catch his breath. "Besides, you don't have it in you to kill me. You were never strong enough to do anything," he mocked, his voice laced with venom.

I didn't respond.

"Go ahead, shoot me," he said, goading me.

I cocked the hammer back into position and placed my finger over the trigger but faltered. I tried to push his words away and just pull the trigger, but my earlier apprehensions slithered back into my brain.

He's still your father.

Why was the abused always the one plagued with guilt? If the roles were reversed and my father was given the opportunity, he wouldn't hesitate in pulling the trigger and finally having his wish of having gone fulfilled.

As if Amalia could see my reluctance, she walked up behind me and wrapped her arm around my own, her fingers resting on my hand that held the gun.

She leaned closer to my ear. "I'm right here," she whispered softly, only for me to hear. "You can do it, Noah. But if you don't want to, I'll do it for you."

I closed my eyes for a fleeting moment before meeting the gaze of the man who'd stripped me of so much.

When I'd seen him for the first time a few days ago, all I could feel was anger and resentment. But now, when I looked at the man who had been supposed to be my father, all I felt was indifference.

Complete and absolute indifference.

I wasn't Noah Barrera anymore. I'd never truly been that person. Not because of what my father believed, but because it was never who I felt I was.

I was Noah Brown, the boy whose mother's love nurtured him until he was strong enough to walk in his own lane instead of in the shadows of the monster who had raised him.

I locked my gaze with his, his eyes filled with a look of victory. Like he'd gotten the upper hand and proven himself right.

"That's what I t—" His sentence died in a muted breath when I swiftly steadied the gun in my hand and pulled the trigger, shattering the last shackle that tethered me to him, keeping me from moving forward.

The bullet had ripped through the air and had lodged itself in between his eyes, the same way he'd done it so many times before to his other victims.

And this time, I'd done it to him.

I stood frozen in the aftermath of what had just happened. What *I'd* just done.

A humorless laugh fell from my lips. "I killed him," I muttered.

The weight of the realization washed over me and suddenly, everything around me seemed to become muted. The space around me seemed so eerily quiet that I could almost make out the faint whispers of my own heartbeat, its thunderous drumming suffocating my hearing.

The air felt thick and oppressive, making it difficult to draw a breath, my lungs struggling against the force of what had just transpired.

My father was dead.

As I watched his lifeless eyes stare back at me, a jagged wound of torn and shredded tissues decorating the space between them, I waited for the waves of guilt or remorse to consume me.

But instead, I was met with an unexpected sense of relief.

I swallowed the unpredicted sob that wracked my chest, but I couldn't stop the tears that followed from streaming down my face. I couldn't contain them no matter how much I tried.

I couldn't quite pinpoint the reason for them, but it strangely felt...

Good, almost... *liberating.*

A cloak still veiled me from my surroundings, but I felt the gentle touch of fingers intertwining with mine, and a familiar warmth pressing against my front as it guided me away from wherever I was.

A hand tenderly brushed my hair back in a soothing motion before it skated down the curve of my face, the pad of a thumb brushing away at tracks falling down my cheeks.

A voice called out my name a few times before I looked

down to see the most beautiful shade of green. Love and reassurance transpired within her eyes as she gently grasped the back of my head, guiding it to rest upon her shoulder.

It was as if she was showing that it was okay to let it out, to feel the way I felt with no shame or inhibition.

The moment my forehead met her skin, I conceded to the floor of emotions that I'd let trapped inside for far too long.

My senses resharpened and the room came back to life. My tears flowed freely now, each one carrying with it a weight that had burdened me for far too long.

I'd thought I'd done the work, that I'd been okay, but perhaps I still had been lying to myself all these years like I'd done so expertly for so long.

Amalia didn't say a word as she held me close, silently offering me solace. She still held my hand, her other one drawing back and forth on my back.

My emotions eventually subsided and my breathing steadied. I lifted my head from her shoulder, meeting her gaze.

She gave me a small smile and mouthed, "It's okay. I love you."

I opened my mouth to tell her the same when a sudden gunshot rang in the air. In an instant, she let go of me, instinctively reaching for her gun, while I swiftly drew mine up and aimed it toward the source of the sound.

My eyes widened when I found Jamal standing above

my father. Tendrils of smoke billowed from the barrel of his gun, dancing into the air.

He glanced up. "Just making sure he's really gone," he explained, with a nonchalant shrug as he casually tucked his gun into the back waistband of his pants.

"You're sick," Nassim chimed in. "But I like your style. Wish I would've thought of it first."

A laugh unexpectedly tore out of my chest, watching me off guard. I brought a hand up, clearing my throat. "I'm sorry. I shouldn't laugh, but…" I began, but it was cut by another burst of laughter.

To my surprise, Jamal joined in, his laughter mingling with mine at how ridiculous the situation was. It was probably quite inappropriate to laugh as my father's corpse lay a few feet away from me.

Our laughter eventually faded into a comfortable silence, except for the occasional dripping of water that had plagued my childhood. The sound used to fill me with dread, but now it felt insignificant.

Before I could ponder on the thought, a stranger's voice echoed in the quiet space.

"Now that that's over, can someone get me out of here?" it said and I quickly realized that it came from the other side of the wall.

Oh shit, Gabriel.

Without saying a word, I briskly exited the cell and marched down the hallway, the others following behind. I rounded the corner I'd watched them take when they'd carried Gabriel's body away last week and walked down another corridor, a cell that was about a quarter of the size of mine appeared at the end.

Gabriel, who was much taller than I'd anticipated, was standing at the door, his arm slung between the iron bars. His gaze lifted to meet mine as I approached. He looked worse than when I'd seen them drag his limp body out, but he somewhat still managed a faint smile.

"At last we met," he greeted me, his voice raspy with exhaustion.

I moved to open his cell door, only to find it locked. *Fuck.*

Before I could ask, Amalia stepped in front of me with a set of keys in hand, solving my problem.

Gabriel diverted his attention to Amalia. "And it's nice to see you again, Ines. Or is it Amalia?" he inquired, his tone laced with curiosity.

"Hey, Gabriel," Amalia replied with a soft smile on her face. "Sorry about last time. I needed a distraction for this guy," she explained, nodding toward me.

He shrugged. "It's fine. I figured after hearing all of that," he said, gesturing toward his right to the wall that separated our cells.

Once Amalia unlocked the door, he stepped aside, allowing her to swing it open. Stepping out of his cell, Gabriel stretched his arms above his head.

"Freedom feels rather nice," he drawled. Then, with a playful smile, he looked at all of us. "Wait, I'm free right?"

he asked, but despite his playful nonchalance, a hint of uncertainty lingered in his voice.

I huffed out a laugh. "You are," I confirmed with a nod. "Nassim over there," I began, pointing toward where Nassim was standing a few steps behind next to Jamal. Nassim lifted his hand as if to identify himself as I continued. "He's the new *Rai's* and will take care of whatever you need," I reassured him.

Gabriel peered over my shoulder, raising a skeptical brow. "So he won't stick me in another cell or use me as a property?"

Nassim answered his question. "The only type of property I like are buildings and I won't stick you in any cell unless you give me a reason to."

"That's fair enough," Gabriel agreed with a nod, seeming to accept his answer.

Amalia interjected as she wrapped an arm around my waist. "All right, I'm exhausted. Let's head out."

I slung an arm over her shoulders, pulling her closer to place a kiss above her head. We all trailed behind Nassim out of this hellhole.

And when we passed my father, I didn't spare him another glance.

Amalia

CHAPTER 27

PRESENT

KAI AND VALENTINA STOOD SIDE BY SIDE, ALREADY waiting for us outside of the building as we all emerged.

Kai wore dark olive pants paired with a black T-shirt that snuggly hugged his upper body like a second skin while Valentina donned a black high-neck, long-sleeved unitard jumpsuit with dust streaks covering it.

Her sniper casually slung over her left shoulder, a large duffel bag on the ground next to her feet as she typed God knows what on the large black tablet in her hands.

"Is he…?" Kai's question trailed off as he watched us trail out of the building one by one, his gaze focusing on Jamal.

"Yeah, Barrera's dead," Jamal confirmed as Noah and I came to stand beside him.

Nassim flanked his other side, while Gabriel lingered a few feet behind us, his hands tucked in the pockets of his worn-out jeans.

With the words officially uttered out loud, it felt as if the tension that had cloaked the compound for decades finally eased following Barerra's demise. As if the nozzle his existence had around everyone's neck loosened and we could all finally breathe easier.

"Thank fucking God," Kai exhaled with relief, and by the amused look on Jamal's face, it was clear Kai wasn't one to regularly curse. "That bastard took ten years of my life with all the stress he put me through."

Jamal huffed out a laugh and shook his head. "Yeah, I think that applies to all of us," he said, glancing over at Noah.

I laced my fingers with Noah's hand, which dangled over my shoulder, and did the same, trying to read him after what had just transpired.

He hadn't seemed fazed after pulling the trigger, but Noah always buried his emotions deep down, afraid to let anyone see them. Barerra's death was all of our end goal, but he'd still been his father.

I hated my parents, but I had no idea what losing them permanently would do to me. Would I feel relief that they were finally gone for good or would I grieve their loss?

Noah met Jamal's gaze, a calmness gracing his features. "Yeah, we can finally move on," Noah added, a hint of relief in his voice. His body relaxed under my fingertips, and solace washed over me at that.

Nassim had a faint smile playing on his lips as his gaze drifted to me. "It's been a long time coming."

I gave him a curt nod of agreement. We'd been working toward this for almost two years and it was finally over.

As the reality sank in, a mix of emotions swirled within me. Relief and uncertainty both battled each other. On one hand, I *was* relieved that our operation had ended with the outcome we'd worked for, but on the other, I felt a little lost.

For the last five years, I'd morphed myself into Ines Bensaid, a ruthless and unwavering hitmen who had reigned terror across the majority of Morocco's regions.

But now that my assignment had concluded, I was faced with the daunting task of leaving this life behind and returning to a moral and structured routine at the Bureau.

I knew they'd offer me time off to adjust after being embedded in this world for so long, but I questioned whether I could rid myself of who I'd become.

Could I simply relentlessly work to erase it, or should I just accept it because, in some way, a part of Ines had become ingrained in me?

On top of that, another question nagged and lingered in the back of my mind even if it had no valid foundation because I knew Noah wouldn't care. Still, I couldn't shake this uncertain feeling about whether or not he'd love this new version of me.

While I'd find a way to move forward if he decided he couldn't, I didn't want to do life without him.

I wanted to do it *with* him.

"We should get going," Valentina interjected as she finished typing whatever she had been, breaking the silence that had ensued and pulling me out of my thoughts.

She crouched down and slid her tablet into the bag. She then grabbed the duffel at her feet, only for Kai to step forward and take it from her. She pulled it back, silently indicating that she had it covered but he persisted, taking it from her regardless of her protests.

She groaned and rolled her eyes, before securing her sniper across her body, the gun on her back.

"We really should," I began, shifting my attention to Nassim. "Do you need any help before we leave?"

He shook his head. "We should be able to manage, but I'll be in touch."

I gave Nassim a curt nod and glanced up at Noah, only to find him already watching me.

There was something special about the way he always looked at me and it made me feel…

Complete.

"I'll be right back," Noah said to me before planting a swift kiss on my forehead and moving his arm from over my shoulder.

It was only as he walked over to Jamal that I remembered Gabriel was still standing behind us. "Shit, I forgot," I cursed, spinning around to face him.

But when I did, I found him frozen in place, his arms hanging limply at his sides, his eyes wide in disbelief as if he'd just seen a ghost.

"Hey, what's wrong?" I asked, hurrying over to him, but he remained unresponsive, his gaze still fixed ahead. I grasped his bicep firmly, shaking him gently. "Gabriel, what's wrong?" I urged, my heart racing with worry.

Still no response from him.

Concerned, I followed where Gabriel's gaze was directed, only to find Valentina standing there with the same stunned expression mirrored on her features.

My brows furrowed in confusion. *What the hell is going on?*

Valentina wasn't known to be expressive, her features typically either locked in a state of boredom or annoyance, especially when Kai was involved.

But the current look on her face left me perplexed.

She blinked a few times, seemingly on the verge of saying something, but when she opened her mouth to do so, she closed it without uttering a word.

Tears welled up in her eyes and that only sent my confusion further whirling because seeing her this emotion was jarring. She opened it again and her next words were spoken in Tagalog. "*Gabi, ikaw ba 'yan[1]?*"

I couldn't understand what she'd just said to him, but by the way Gabriel took a tentative step toward her, my

---

1. Gabi, is that you?

hand falling from his arm from the movement, it dawned on me that they knew each other.

"*Ate²?*" he asked, his expression faltering into realization.

I watched as they slowly approached each other, only a few steps away now separating them. I looked over at where Noah and Jamal had halted their conversation, watching with the same intrigue as I was.

Valentina gave Gabriel an almost imperceptible nod in response to his previous question as she reached out to touch his face like she was confirming he was real, whoever he was to her.

Gabriel briefly leaned into her touch before pulling her into a tight hug. They held each other like they hadn't seen each other in years.

Nassim, Noah, and Jamal had all moved over to where Kai stood, the bag he had been holding long forgotten as he stared at the scene unfolding before us.

"Does anyone know what's going on?" I asked in a hushed tone as I joined them. They all shrugged, each not knowing the answer.

Except Kai.

We briefly turned our attention to him, waiting for a potential explanation. Without sparing us a glance, Kai whispered, "That's her brother."

---

2. Word used as a form of respect to describe to an older female relative or respected friend (especially one's own sister), and means "Sister".

I didn't know how he knew that, but his revelation weighed heavily on my chest because it reminded me of my own siblings whom I hadn't seen in years.

Our circumstances were different, but seeing Valentina and Gabriel's reunion stirred a longing for a similar end result when I'd try to make amends with my own family.

Eventually, they pulled from each other and Gabriel draped an arm over Valentina's shoulders, tenderly wiping the streaks of tears from her cheeks as they approached us.

Kai was the first to speak. "Is this… is this him?" he asked, his tone a mix of hesitation and hope.

Valentina looked at him with another expression I'd never seen on her face before. She didn't speak, simply nodding in response.

The gesture instantly made Kai's body relax, an evident wave of relief washing over him. I didn't know the story between Kai and Valentina or how he knew about her brother since Jamal had seemed just as clueless as us, but the news seemed to bring him solace as much as it did to Valentina.

Gabriel glanced curiously between the two as they stared at each other. "Is this your man?" he asked, snapping them out of whatever unspoken conversation they were having.

Kai blushed and shifted uncomfortably, which was unlike the charismatic men I'd seen over the last couple of days.

Valentina shot her brother a glare, smacking him over

his chest—or at least she'd tried since he was at least a good foot taller than she was.

"*Tumigil ka na*[3]," she scolded, a frown forming between her brows.

Ignoring her, Gabriel extended his hand toward Kai. "I'm Gabriel, her little brother, although I'm not that little anymore," he said in a playful manner, but his tone carried a heavy weight beneath it.

Kai cleared his throat before grasping it in his. "Yeah, she's told me about you. I'm Kai," he replied, offering him a small smile.

Gabriel firmly shook his hand. "Nice to meet you, Kai," he said, returning his smile. "I'll quiz you later when she's not around," he added with a nod toward Valentina.

Valentina pushed Gabriel off with a roll of her eyes, but I could see in her face that she didn't mind her brother's behavior.

"All right, enough. We have to go," she said, her stoic expression back in place as if the last few minutes hadn't happened.

I stifled a laugh at her sudden shift in demeanor and glanced over at Noah, who was doing the same.

"So I guess this means you won't be coming with me?" Nassim inquired, a smile playing on his lips as he looked at Gabriel.

"Yeah," Gabriel replied, nodding. "Finding her was the

---

3. Okay, enough already.

only thing I would have asked your help for, but I guess this saves you the work."

Nassim shook his head, huffing a laugh. "I'm glad it worked out," he said, with a nod of his head. "All right," he began, addressing everyone. "Not that it wasn't a pleasure, but unfortunately, I have some work to do. I also need to call my wife to give her an update before she shows up here, guns blazing, thinking I'm injured."

He quickly said goodbye to each of us, promising me that he'd call in a few days after things settled before he walked toward the front of the house where his men were.

After the rest also said their goodbyes, only Noah and I were left behind, both of us standing in the middle of the courtyard.

Noah draped his arm again over my shoulders, tugging me closer to his side and pressing a kiss to the top of my head. "Let's go home, pretty girl," he mumbled against my hair.

I wrapped my arms around him as he led us to the car we'd parked at the back.

I'd never really had a place to call home, but I knew as we walked to the car that home wasn't a place. It was the person you were building it with.

No matter what happened, I knew Noah would always be that for me.

Home.

Noah

CHAPTER 28

THREE WEEKS LATER

THIS HOUSE WOULD ALWAYS REMAIN A PARADOX TO ME. I loved that my mother found her happiness here, that she'd been able to make this place her own and live her life the way she'd always wanted and deserved to.

While we lived in Colombia, I'd known she had always been looking over her shoulder and making sure I was protected. She'd selflessly prioritized my well-being and happiness over her own.

But here, she'd blossomed back into Camila Montero, the free-spirited artist who loved life and laughed so freely, you couldn't help but join her.

She'd been able to become who she'd always been inside before my father's claws dug so deep, it dimmed her light.

Despite all the love and happiness I'd experienced within these walls whenever I visited her, it would also always be intertwined with the memory of losing one of my favorite people.

It had been the only place I had left that reminded me of her, but one I'd avoided like the plague ever since her funeral.

When I'd been told about her passing, I'd taken the first available flight and had come straight here. For some stupid reason, I'd still held the hope that they'd called the wrong person.

That it hadn't been my mother who had died, that it had been someone else's.

But the moment the door opened and a hospice nurse greeted me with a somber expression, the death of my mother had sunk in.

The townhouse still looked exactly the same as I'd left it, everything that represented my mother encapsulated into a frozen moment in time.

Various of her paintings were hanging over the walls, her last work in progress still mounted on the easel, the last brushes she'd used scattered on the wooden table standing next to her workstation.

Trinkets she'd picked up from *El Rastro* were placed everywhere around the living area and you could see a piece of her everywhere you looked.

As I stood in the front doorway, memories of her flooded back, painting vivid images of her laughing and dancing as she cooked while I sat on the large couch in the living room attached to the kitchen, just watching her and basking in her energy.

After her funeral that had taken place the next day of her passing, I had come back here to gather her things and put the house up for sale, but I hadn't been able to bring myself to do it.

Everywhere I'd looked was just a painful reminder of who I'd just lost. I could barely bring myself to walk inside the house every time I had to, let alone stay over for days to pack up her things, only to uncover more frozen memories that would send my mind spiraling faster than it already had been.

So instead, I'd put off clearing and selling this place for so long because it had always felt like the last remaining tether to my mother.

But I'd realized over the last three weeks that my mother would always be wherever I was.

Grief would always be my silent companion, a constant reminder of my mother's loss, but despite the process not being linear, my father's death had snuffed so many of my inner demons that it felt easier to take this task on.

And I had Amalia with me.

I'd realized that needing someone by your side didn't equate to weakness like my father had reminded me of so many times. It just meant that you didn't have to face life's hardships alone when the person you loved wanted to do it with you, to support you through every step.

Amalia had made so many things more bearable, no matter how hard they'd come to be.

She was my solace, my peace.

After leaving the *riad*, I'd decided to drive all night back to my apartment in Bemes because I hadn't wanted to spend another second in the town where so many of my painful memories coated the air.

I'd known there were many things I'd need to unpack in therapy, but I'd spent the entire drive coming to terms that my father was dead, that I'd ended his life.

But I also realized that breathing had become easier, my thoughts were now freer, and that I didn't have to lie anymore.

We'd gotten there early the next morning and after a much-needed long shower, both Amalia and I had immediately collapsed into bed from the exhaustion.

We'd spent the rest of that week sleeping, eating, being with each other, and getting our story straight for the Bureau since we'd had a meeting with the Director the following Monday.

Amalia and I had decided to keep the details vague and only tell Director Williams what he'd need to know.

We'd informed him that Barrera had been terminated by a rival and assured him that the new *Rai's* wouldn't be an issue, omitting any of our personal ties to Nassim and Barrera from the report.

Although Williams had asked us for more information, we'd told him that we'd both suffered enough and didn't want to relive the details again. Fortunately for us, both of our track records were impeccable so he hadn't pressed further.

Following our post-operation review, we'd been granted the few weeks of leave we'd each requested. We both loved our jobs, but after everything that had happened, our desire for a future at the Bureau wasn't as evident as it used to be.

I'd spent so much of my life working that I hadn't actually lived. And I was tired of doing that. I didn't really know who I was aside from being Agent Brown or Uncle Noah, but I wanted to give myself a chance.

No matter how fucking old I was now.

Amalia was grappling with a similar dilemma and although she hadn't decided yet what her decision would be, I'd support whatever she'd end up choosing.

Instead, she'd been focused on mending the bridge in her relationship with her siblings. Prior to coming to the small town where my mother had lived, we'd driven to Sibaya, where I'd dropped her off at her older sister Antonia's house.

I'd offered to go in with her, but she'd asked if I could wait for her in the car.

Amalia's sister had initially slammed the door in her face when she'd figured out who had been at her doorstep. However, after a few more tries, Antonia had relented and let Amalia in.

Nearly an hour later, another car had pulled up into

Antonia's driveaway. A man around Jamal's age who looked like a carbon copy of Amalia, whom I'd assumed was her little brother Ángel, walked out and headed inside the house.

I'd anxiously waited for what felt like hours, praying to whoever was out there that she'd come out with anything other than the scared look she'd gone in with.

And she had. She hadn't necessarily had a smile on her face, but when she'd approached where I'd been parked on the other side of the street, I'd sensed that the weight she'd carried going in had been lifted off her shoulders.

Once she'd settled into her seat, she'd begun recounting everything that had transpired while I'd started our drive here.

Her siblings were still furious with her, but they'd been willing to hear her out and to give her a chance because I'd learned through all of this that that's what a real family was about.

I might not have grown with much of one, but I'd found one along the way within Jamal and Amalia.

I looked over at Amalia who was standing next to me, finding her quietly watching over me. She gave me a small encouraging smile and laced her fingers with mine.

"You ready to do this?" she asked, giving my hand a small squeeze of support.

The usual anxiety whenever I'd been here and that made me want to turn around and delay clearing this place out started creeping up my chest, but I pushed it back, grounding myself in Amalia's touch on my skin as I let out a deep breath.

"Yeah," I finally said, stepping inside with her by my side. "I am."

We had spent hours and hours going through all of my mother's things with Amalia, putting anything I'd wanted to keep in a separate box.

Once we'd been done, I'd said a final goodbye to the place and, with Amalia's hand in mine, walked to the car and had driven to our final stop before we'd head home.

I crouched down in front of the grave and stared at my mother's name engraved on the granite tombstone. I hesitantly ran my fingers over her name, each embossed letter a painful reminder of her absence.

This was my first time seeing it again after her funeral and grief squeezed around my ribcage, unsure of what to say.

"Hey, *mamá*," I began, my voice cracking at the end with emotion. I paused, struggling to find the words. I took a deep breath and continued, "I'm sorry for not coming sooner. I wanted to, but…"

My voice faltered because there weren't any excuses that could justify my absence. I'd wanted to come so many times, but every time I'd tried, I couldn't bring myself to.

Being here always felt like too much to brave on my own.

The ache around my chest tightened as I said the next words. "*Te echo de menos*[1]. Every day. I won't hide the fact that I'm still a little mad at you for not telling me about what was happening. I can't blame you for wanting to pass on your own terms, but I wish you'd given me the chance to say goodbye."

I swallowed against the lump in my throat.

"It's finally over, *mamá*. He's gone and I guess we can both be free now, wherever you are. I know I am."

Tears welled in my eyes, but I pushed them back down.

"Remember when you told me about finding someone. Well, I actually had at the time. Let's just say I'd been a little stubborn to realize it, but she's the best thing that has ever happened to me. Well, after you of course."

That last part garnered me a small laugh from Amalia. She'd been standing at the gate of the small enclosure I was inside, close enough to hear me this whole time, but she hadn't said or moved to give me space with my mother, but still there if I needed.

"The way I'd originally planned this was a lot different than this, but I'd really like for you to meet the love of my life." I glanced over my shoulder. "Would you like to meet her, baby?"

---

1. I miss you.

She nodded. "I'd love to," she said, approaching where I was.

I'd always wanted them to meet, but life just had other plans. Despite not this being the way I'd imagined their first encounter to be, my heart still soared at the sight of Amalia sitting next to me.

And I joined her.

"Hi, I'm Amalia, the love of your son's life apparently," she teased, briefly glancing at me before bringing her gaze to my mother's headstone. "You raised a good man, and despite his occasional flaws, he's all right," she said, nudging me with her shoulder.

I raised a brow. "Oh yeah, I'm just all right?"

"Most times," she said, letting out a small laugh.

I leaned closer to whisper in her ear, "I'll teach you what 'all right' is later."

Amalia cleared her throat. "In all seriousness, he's also the love of my life. I wish I could have met you so I could have told you this in person, well, I guess I am, but thank you for protecting and taking care of him the way you did."

If I wasn't already madly in love with this woman, I'd fall in love with her all over again. I didn't know what I'd done to deserve Amalia, but I'd cherish every second of it.

She made me feel loved and valued, and there was no greater gift

Knowing the cemetery was about to close, I stood and brushed the dust off my pants. I offered my hand to Amalia to help her stand. She took it and as she got up, I used my palms to brush the dust off her backside selfishly.

Amalia took her hand from mine and pushed against the one, slowly brushing the curvature of her ass. "Stop it. Your mom's right here."

My shoulder shook with laughter. "Oh, she doesn't mind," I started, looking back at my mother's grave. "Right, Mom?"

Amalia smacked my shoulder. "Noah."

With a smile playing on my lips, I brought a hand to rest over her headstone. "I love you. I'll be back, I promise."

I grabbed Amalia's hand and pressed a quick kiss to her forehead. I then moved to walk away, but she stopped me.

Before I could ask her why, she looked at my mother's grave and said, "I promise to take care of him, Camila."

A bright smile pulled at the corners of her lips as she looked back at me.

Did I already say I loved this woman?

I mirrored her smile and moved my free hand to cup her cheek. "I love you," I whispered as I brought her closer to press a chaste kiss on her lips.

Goose bumps scattered across my skin and suddenly, the sun peeked over the clouds, shining brighter as if my mother was smiling down at us.

I know, mamá.

Pulling away, I draped my arm over her shoulders, still

holding her hand, and guided us down the path where my car was parked.

Once we were both settled in our seats, I drove us back to our hotel where we'd spend the night before heading home tomorrow morning.

We'd been back at our hotel for the last two hours and were lying in bed after showering, just basking in each other's presence.

I brushed my hand through her hair, her head resting against my chest, while my other arm was wrapped around her, skating circles over her bare lower back.

This was where I felt the happiest. Amalia made me feel the happiest.

I knew things between us weren't perfect, but there was no such thing as a perfect relationship. Amalia made me feel safe and loved. She felt like home and I didn't want to waste more time than I'd already had.

"Marry me, pretty girl," I breathed out, nervousness creeping up my chest.

She looked up at me, her eyes widening. "What?"

"Marry me," I repeated. "I shouldn't be greedy after you just gave me a second chance and you can say no I'd understand, but I want to marry you. I don't want to keep waiting and delaying what I've known for a very long time even when we were apart. I love you. So much sometimes it hurts. I want to do life with you. I want to spend the rest of my life waking up next to you, and keep annoying you until you challenge me to a fight. I want you, Amalia Abara. So marry me."

For a few moments, Amalia just looked at me and couldn't help the dread plummeting in my gut. Not that it wouldn't break my heart a little, but I'd understand if she said no.

I was just tired of waiting for the inevitable. I'd wasted so long trying to do the right thing and not feel my emotions to the fullest. But when I looked at Amalia in my arms, I wanted this to be forever.

"Yes."

A single word had never sounded better.

Noah

EPILOGUE

FOUR YEARS LATER

Holy fucking shit.

I was on the verge of becoming a father.

Me. A father.

I was elated and terrified all at the same time.

My father's cruelty had left scars that had always made me scared at the idea of having kids of my own.

Although I'd cared for Jamal for many years and he was family, being a father felt like stepping into uncharted territory that I didn't know if I could live up to.

Our experiences, good and bad, shaped us whether we wanted them to or not. But over the last four years and particularly these past nine months, my perspective had shifted and I'd come to realize that I could do it. That I could be the father I'd always longed for.

I was aware that I'd inevitably make mistakes along the way, but I knew I'd never be my father. The scars from my childhood hadn't magically disappeared, but I'd made a vow to myself that I'd fight every day.

To show up on both good and bad days because I wanted to keep fighting. My wife and soon-to-be-born daughter made me want to keep fighting.

Watching Amalia's pregnancy evolve had been one of the most beautiful and humbling experiences. My love for my wife already had no bounds, but every day, I kept falling more and more in love with her.

Her strength. Her resilience.

The encompassing peace having her in my life gave me.

She made me a better person. She made me *want* to be a better person.

Now, she never shied away from putting me in my place when I was wrong or when I was self-sabotaging but she gave me the space to heal at my own pace.

Despite all of my demons, she loved me *because* of who I was, not in spite of it.

I'd known the moment I'd laid eyes on her that I was in trouble and I wouldn't change it.

She was the best kind of trouble and no matter how cheesy it sounded, I was truly the luckiest man on earth that I got to experience her love and have her by my side.

And I couldn't wait for our daughter to experience it too.

Nurses had been bustling around and doing an amazing

job, but my attention had been solely focused on Amalia this whole time.

She'd been in labor for the last sixteen hours and pushing for the last two. I hated how much pain she was going through. Every strangled cry and twist of pain crossing her face tightened the knot in my chest even further.

I wanted to do something, anything, but there was nothing I could do but stand next to her and support my wife with whatever she needed me.

Especially after she threatened to kill me if I left or passed out on her. And I knew her promises weren't empty because I'd seen her literally end people before.

I'd rather not be another one of her victims.

Amalia let out another loud scream, squeezing my hand even more tightly than the other times, and in the next moment, Dr. Alonso announced, "You have a beautiful and healthy baby girl."

The first cries of our baby filled the air and turned my attention to where they lifted her up and nothing could have prepared me for this moment.

Nothing.

A well of emotions washed over me as I watched the team place our baby skin-to-skin on Amalia's chest as they cleaned her from the other side of where I stood.

My breathtaking wife had tears falling down her cheeks and I quickly brushed them away as I placed my forehead against her.

"You're fucking incredible," I said, kissing her temple and letting my lips linger for a moment before I pulled back.

I pushed her hair out of her face, brushing the strands behind her ear, as I watched her mesmerized by our daughter.

"I really am," Amalia said between sobs, brushing her thumb back and forth over our daughter's chubby cheek. She looked down at her with the most beautiful smile on her face. "You've been in my vagina forever, but I love you so much."

She dropped her head back on her pillow in relief. "Holy shit, fuck sorry. I don't know, can she understand me already," she continued, laughing and crying at the same time.

"I think you're safe," I replied with a laugh before pressing a chaste kiss to her lips.

The staff kept working, briefly taking our daughter away to assess her and do everything they needed to, while the doctor finished helping Amalia.

I stood watching the bustle as I replayed in my mind everything that had just happened.

I was a dad. To a beautiful girl. Both she and my wife were okay, healthy.

Safe.

I hadn't realized I'd been standing frozen in place, tears freely falling down my cheeks, until Amalia's voice broke through whatever fog had kept me under.

"Baby, come here," she said softly.

When my gaze met hers, she was gesturing for me to join her on the bed.

"Oh, I don't want to hurt you or her," I replied, looking between her and our daughter that she was holding in her arms, wrapped in a blanket with a hat covering her head.

Amalia raised a brow. "I just gave birth, so anything I say goes," she said, reaching for my hand and pulling me closer.

I laughed. "That's not a rule, and I already do anything you tell me to, pretty girl," I noted, gently joining them on the bed and draping one arm around Amalia's shoulders.

"She's perfect," I breathed as I stared at her in awe, an overwhelming love washing over me. She was so small, so delicate and just so beautiful. And she was mine. Just like the woman lying next to me.

I turned my attention to my wife, finding her gaze already on me with that beautifully soft smile of hers. Her green eyes shone with tears as I brought my face closer to hers.

"*You're* perfect," I murmured against her lips before giving her a tender kiss.

When I pulled away, Amalia asked, "Have you thought of any names?"

We'd been debating between two names but wanted to wait until she was born before settling on one. The moment I'd laid eyes on our daughter, I instantly knew which one was meant for her, but I wanted to see what Amalia thought first.

"What do you think?" I brushed a finger over our precious daughter's face, memorizing her features, while I waited for her response.

"Ameena," she began, reaching with her free hand to brush my hair back as I looked at her. Her smile warmed as she said her next words. "Ameena Camila Brown."

My brain could barely register that we'd settled on the same name when I'd heard her say my mother's name.

My heart swelled with even more emotion and a tear escaped my eye. Amalia tenderly wiped it away.

"I love it and I love you," I rasped before leaning in to kiss her once more.

"I love you too," she replied softly when we pulled away to direct our attention to Ameena.

A quiet hum cloaked the room as we just held each other.

All my life, I'd felt as though I'd been navigating through the dark, too broken to ever dream about a life where happiness was possible because it always seemed so out of reach.

But despite all of the burdens I'd carried in my life, it led me right here.

Exactly where I'd always been meant to be.

Amalia

EXTENDED EPILOGUE

FIVE WEEKS LATER

"WOULD IT BE RUDE IF WE DITCHED THEM?" I ASKED AS I stepped out of our house and into the backyard, where my husband was leaning against one of the pillars a few feet away from everyone else.

Noah glanced at me, a soft smile playing on his lips, and lifted his right arm. I nestled into his side, wrapping my arms around his waist as he draped his arm over my shoulder.

He then tugged me closer and planted a kiss on the top of my head. "I mean they are here to celebrate our daughter," he replied with a chuckle.

Our daughter.

It still felt surreal that just five weeks ago I'd given birth to Ameena. I still was wrapping my head around the fact that I was a mother.

I'd always wanted kids, but with how my life had turned out, I'd never thought it would be possible.

But life always had ways of surprising you when you least expected it.

Noah and I had just bought our house here in Sardenya and been married for almost two years when two pink lines had changed my life.

I'd stood there in the small bathroom of a gas station because I'd thrown up for the third time that day. I'd decided to take a test, thinking nothing of it, until it had come back positive.

I'd shaken the test a few times, thinking the lines would fade away or my imagination would stop playing tricks on me. But the reality had remained unchanged—I had still been pregnant.

I'd always envisioned that I'd plan this elaborate reveal and surprise Noah if that had ever happened. Yet in that moment, all I'd wanted was to have him by my side.

So I'd immediately called him and waited anxiously for him in my car.

He'd dropped everything at work and had shown up less than ten minutes later, since I had just left the office when I had to pull over and use the bathroom.

The moment he'd thrown my car door open, I'd brandished the test in his face, unable to say the words because I had still been overcome with so many emotions.

I *had* been happy, but I'd also been so fucking scared.

My mind had kept reeling around my fear that I wouldn't be good enough for our child.

My parents had left us when I was barely a kid myself and I didn't know what it was like to have good parents.

But all of my nerves had dimmed when Noah's hands cupped my cheeks and he'd assured me that we could do this.

That together we'd raise our baby with every ounce of love we had in us. Because if two people could love each other the way we did, then we would always do our best to make sure our baby would be a part of it.

And every day since then, he'd shown me exactly that.

A few days after I'd given birth, we'd come home and spent the last few weeks on our own getting adjusted to our new routine of three.

My sister had flown to Sardenya, where we now lived, the week following Ameena's birth to stay and help Noah and me around the house and anything I'd needed. But she'd only been able to stay for a week since she had her own little family to take care of.

Although the past five weeks had been the best weeks of my life, I was *exhausted*.

I sighed. "But we've barely slept over the last month, and Ameena is *finally* asleep. This would be a great time to catch up on some hours of our own," I countered.

"I would love to take you up on that offer, but I think they'd notice if we were both gone. Besides, we haven't seen any of them since they left the hospital after you gave birth."

I hated when he was right. We hadn't seen our friends in over a month and they *were* here to celebrate Ameena.

Theo, Sofia, Jamal, and Sienna were all seated around the large half-moon sofa set at the back end of the courtyard, with food scattered on the wooden round table in front of them.

Theo and Jamal were engaged in a deep argument over god knows what, while Sienna held a phone between her and Sofia, most likely watching those strangely shaped cars she loved to watch race.

Sofia seemed lost to whatever Sienna was explaining to her every once in a while, but an amused smile played on her lips whenever Sienna jolted from her seat.

Meanwhile, Gabriel lay on a large blanket splayed on the grass a few feet away from them, playing with Theo and Sofia's three-month-old daughter, Nesrine, and Jamal and Sienna's four-year-old daughter, Selena.

On the other side of the garden, Kai and Valentina sat together at a small table. They'd just celebrated their first year of marriage a few months ago but were still exactly the same as when I'd met them that night a little over four years ago.

Although their relationship had come as no surprise to any of us, we'd pretended we had no idea when Kai had told us they were together.

They were playing chess, their favorite thing to do aside

from bickering, and if the small smile playing on Valentina's lips was any indication, she was about to win.

I was about to suggest to Noah we join the rest of the group when Selena left Gabriel's side and barreled toward us.

"Tonton Noah," she shouted before crashing into Noah's legs. She circled her arms—or at least as much as she could—around his legs, squeezing.

Noah placed a hand on her hair before crouching down to her level to take her in his arms.

"Hey there, *zwina diali*[1]," he murmured against her hair before picking her up. "Did you need something?" he asked her, but she was too busy roaming her hands over his face.

Selena placed her small hands over his cheeks and squished them together. "You've got a funny face, Tonton Noah," she noted with a small laugh.

God, she's adorable.

"Oh yeah," Noah managed to get out, but the words were distorted by the way she was pushing his cheeks together. "*Ghadi naklook*[2]," he whispered before surprising her by playfully nibbling on her hands when they got close enough to his mouth and blowing raspberries on her face and neck.

Her infectious laughter rang out in the air and the sight of them together warmed my heart.

---

1. My beautiful girl.
2. I'm gonna eat you up.

Is it too early to want another baby?

Suddenly, our daughter's cries echoed through the baby monitor that was clipped to the back pocket of my pants.

"You want me to go get her?" Noah asked over his shoulder.

I shook my head. "No, it's okay. I got her." I lifted on my tiptoes and kissed his cheek. "I'll be right back," I said before I headed for the back door.

"All right, let's go see *mamak ou babak*[3] while Tata Amalia gets baby Ameena," Noah said to Selena before they walked away, and I headed for our daughter's nursery.

Once I made it into Ameena's nursery, I marched to her crib, her cries gradually subsiding when she sensed my presence.

Gently lifting her into my arms, I cradled her close, whispering soothing words and tenderly stroking her cheek until her cries softened into small whimpers.

She nestled against me as I grabbed a pacifier and draped a blanket over my shoulder before heading back outside. And as I made my way toward our friends and family, a sense of tranquility washed over me.

I'd always secretly longed for a bigger family. Antonia, Ángel, and I only had each other growing up, and it had been us against the world.

But we'd hidden our pains from each other for so long that we didn't get to enjoy our childhood as much as we

---

3. Your mom and dad.

would have liked because we had to help each other to survive.

This little family Noah and I had created and all of our friends together felt like the perfect extra piece to our story.

This felt right and I couldn't imagine being anywhere else.

Thank You!

Hey lovely,

Thank you so much for reading *Burdens*! If you enjoyed this book, I would be grateful if you could leave a review on the platform(s) of your choice.

One review can make all the difference !

Love, Seraya x

Also by SeRaya

THE VENDETTA SERIES
A series of interconnected standalones
Nemesis
Ashes
Burdens

A BRAND NEW SERIES
A secret is coming early 2025…
Stay tuned!

Keep in touch with Seraya

To stay up to date on SeRaya's upcoming projects, connect with her on social media, sign up for her newsletter, or go to her website.

Reader Group: facebook.com/groups/serayaswarriors
Website: authorseraya.com
Instagram: www.instagram.com/authorseraya/
Tiktok: www.tiktok.com/@serayawrites
Goodreads: goodreads.com/authorseraya

Acknowledgments

It's quite surreal to write these words, but The Vendetta series has finally come to an end, and I don't know how to wrap my brain around it.

Noah's story planted itself in my brain a few years ago and blossomed into something beyond what I had ever imagined.

I got to fulfill my dream of becoming an author, of being able to put my creativity onto paper and do something for *me*. Something I'd never really had the chance to do before.

So to the younger version of me who didn't think we'd make it—You did it, baby.

This book was the most challenging yet most rewarding book to write because Noah's story draws a lot from my own. It was quite hard to dig into wounds that never were able to heal and bleed them onto paper, but in a silver lining way, it helped me realize that I was never the problem. That being loved should never come with conditions.

That I was and will always be enough.

There are so many people to thank, and a few words will never be enough, but let's give it a try.

To my girls, you know who you are—I am eternally grateful for every single one of you. You have supported me and become the family I never thought I'd have. The love and encouragement you have given me is something that I will never forget. Thank you for being there every step of the way, for being my ride-or-die, and for being some of the best people I've ever known.

To my brain twin, whom I could have never done this without—There is so much to say, so I'll keep it short and start by saying thank you. Thank you for being there for me, for showing up for me every day, and for literally sharing brain cells. Without you, none of this journey would be possible, and I hope we get to do more of it together.

To Jess, Kylie, Salma, Emily, and Esther —I'm *so* lucky to have people on my team who care about my characters and my stories as much as I do. I am so grateful for your input, and your feedback helped make Amalia & Noah shine the way they deserved <3

To Cat—My genius fairy! You always create magic, and I'm so happy to have you bring my stories to life. I'm obsessed with you and love you!

To Emily—Thank you for making my words shine and making this story the best it could be. I couldn't do this without you!

To Shaye & Lindsey—You've become such an integral part of this journey, and I couldn't do it without you. Your support and help have been one of the biggest blessings in my life, and I'm so grateful to have you both by my side.

And last but not least, to you the reader—Thank you for taking a chance on me and my stories. This story was very special to me, and I hope you fell in love with these two just as I did writing them. None of this journey would be possible without you lovelies and I cannot wait to see where we go next!

Love, Seraya x

About the Author

SeRaya is a hopeless romantic twenty-something living in one of her favorite places in the world. She loves writing swoony and steamy love stories about fierce and imperfect characters who find their happily ever afters. Her stories may be emotional rollercoasters and she does have a weakness for slowburns, but that never tempers the heat that comes when it ignites.

She's always had a love for writing and is so happy that she gets to share her characters with you!

When she's not frantically trying to make her deadline, she loves being cozied up with a good romance book, rewatching her favorite shows, and discovering new food places.

Printed in Great Britain
by Amazon

56281962R00233